CEO
(Corporate Earth Omen)

Viener Kweed

CENTAUR BOOKS
·CHICAGO·

CEO
(Corporate Earth Omen)
Viener Kweed

CENTAUR BOOKS
·CHICAGO·

Published by
Centaur Books
an imprint of **Joshua Tree Publishing**
• Chicago •
CentaurBooks.com

13-Digit ISBN: 978-1-956823-70-7

Disclaimer:
This is a work of fiction. Names, characters, places, and incidents are the product of the author's imagination or have been used fictitiously. Any resemblance to actual persons, living or dead, events, locales or organizations is entirely coincidental.

Printed in the United States of America

Dedication

With gratitude to angel Ira for the inspiration,
to Ella for her unwavering belief, and
to Andrey for the much-needed nudge.
And to all who have ever crossed paths
with the corporate world.

Table of Contents

Chapter 1

CEO

The CEO of a reigning utility corporation "Home" sat at his desk and gazed intently at one sector of the huge BITCH system monitor (Business Interface To Control Humanoids). It occupied the entire wall opposite the window. He was alone. His office occupied the entire top of the corporate building. No one was watching him except maybe God, so he did not hide his anger. He nervously began pouring whiskey with a trembling hand and spilled most of it past the glass. He drank it in one gulp and threw the glass at the hated picture on the monitor. The whiskey slowly began to flow down, only focusing attention on this square.

However, the monitor did not show anything new. Real sex games unfolded between his deputy, Eliza, and the head of the alternative marketing department, Denis. One could see their bodies and actions in every detail. He slammed his fist on the keyboard and picked up the key combination so successfully that the entire huge monitor was filled with one hateful scene from hundreds of cameras and angles.

The CEO got up quickly, poured another whiskey, took a glass, and went to the window. He knew what would happen next. He'd seen it a thousand times. Sex has become a public activity for a long time now. New social networks have emerged where couples have sex on camera getting likes, comments, and advice in the process. The sex games didn't even start until there were enough viewers. There were online battles especially popular among friends' companies. In the social rating system, corporations are forced to motivate personnel by any intangible methods. Therefore, sex in the workplace has long become the norm in most companies.

From a height of 999 floors, the gaze went into the vast desert. The sand had a dark gray tint and was covered in haze. A more boring scenery was hard to imagine. When the corporate tower began to be built, its lower part was washed by the sea waves. A marvelous promenade and a beach were built for employees to enjoy and rest. No one's ever used them. As if by magic, the higher the skyscraper rose, the further away the sea went and at the end of construction completely disappeared beyond the horizon.

As a result of melting glaciers and potential flooding of territories, a law on water transformation was adopted. Water began to be used again for steam engines, to irrigate deserts, and to be broken down into molecules of hydrogen and oxygen using reactivated nuclear power plants. According to YouTube experts, this led to a significant increase in the mosquito population.

One day, a blogger with a billion subscribers filmed how frogs turn into butterflies in a swamp, a waste sedimentation tank from a nuclear power plant. In the process, she was severely bitten by white mosquitoes. They long ago stopped drinking blood and fed exclusively on bacteria, but the instinct to bite and irritate all living things is not gone. The clip on the swamp, which looks like a cross between Kong Fu and Stripdance, got ten billion views. Fans raised a high note that reached the government, which announced a tender to resolve the water issue. The winner of the tender, the Desert Corporation, proposed the use of silicone lenses that would evaporate excess water and channel it into space. As sometimes happens, philatelic engineers miscalculated the evaporation coefficient and too many lenses were installed. When they realized the issue, it was impossible to catch them from the water—the sea simply disappeared.

CEO, counting in his head seconds, returned to his workplace exactly when they began to dress. He pressed the call button next to the Denis profile icon in the BITCH interface. Denis got a command on his SPAM (System Punishment And Motivation) tablet and get access code to the 999th floor. The nine hundred and ninety—ninth floor was fully occupied by the CEO. The company had a strict hierarchy, the higher the floor the higher the rating of the employee. The employees did not leave the corporation building and there was nowhere to go as the corporation fully provided them with everything they needed, housing, food, medicine, and entertainment. The CEO had not gone below 900 floors for a long time, he had his garden, swimming pool, restaurant, sports ground, and all that a worker from the lower floors could only dream of.

Denis lived on the 693rd floor along with three other department heads. One day, at one of the meetings, top manager Eliza drew attention to him. Since then, he often visited the three hundred floors above. As it happens, he falls in love with her. Realizing that to match Eliza, he must move higher in the hierarchy. So he took on all the most absurd projects possible.

On the way by elevator to the very top of the tower, he pondered what to say to the CEO on the results of new business directions. A month ago, he reported that the project was at the final stage. But in reality, it existed only on paper. Denis was thinking hard about how to delay the disaster because if you hold out for at least three months, or better yet, six months, the project will become irrelevant, and they will forget about it. Then it will be possible to make a stunning report on the successful implementation of the activity and turn attention to a new project. But then the elevator stopped abruptly, he found himself in front of the CEO, in a huge hall.

"Long live the great CEO!"

"Tell me what's going on with the direction of home sex games?"

"We have been ready to launch for a long time, but it turned out that we need approval from the Neoculture corporation. This will take several months."

"Why do we need approval?"

"They say that you need to get a license because it falls under the conspiracy of indirect birth control. In other words, the recommendations of the Neoculture corporation must be taken into account in all game activities."

"This is the first time I've heard this information. Why hasn't it come earlier?"

"Well, you know, this area is poorly regulated, corporations are looking for their interest everywhere and recently became interested in our project."

"How long will approval take?"

"It's hard to say, they don't give clear terms. The last time we agreed on the size of the toilet bowl, it took six months."

"This isn't great, THEY going to be pissed," the CEO said, "Go whip up a presentation for the council."

Denis nodded silently and headed towards the elevator. He understood that he was screwed. The HOME Corporation was engaged in managing utility services based on artificial intelligence. All households, everything that was in the house, and even the corporation itself was under AI control. Moreover, the residents of the house, their leisure time, eating, sleeping, and sex are also under the control of the AI system SLAVE (Support Lazy Alive Vulnerable Entities).

The Alternative Marketing Department dealt with additional business areas. This is the only way the corporation could make a profit. Among corporations, there was mutual settlement for services that were not related to the main activity. Corporations were monopolists in their main field of activity. In the new world, they managed their part of the business, gaining the very possibility of their existence. So, to make a profit they must accumulate more points than others. If not, you had to give up your resources, which THEY didn't like very much.

He pressed the first button he came across in the four hundred floors section. This was the largest section of any corporation—the presentology department. There was a time when a presentation could have been done behind a computer on your chair, but evolution went far. Now it was necessary to include your virtual reflection in every presentation. The author's DNA imprint was inserted into each slide. The virtual speaker came to life, answered questions, and approached guests when necessary. The virtual image had all the thoughts and habits of the original under the theme of the presentation.

The elevator door opened on the 457th floor. Denis unhesitatingly walked out into the hall where many employees were working. A blond girl with long, sun—kissed hair braided and dressed in a light translucent white suit approached him.

"What is your presentation application number?"

"Number . . ." he hesitated, "Actually, no number. I didn't apply."

"But we have a month—long waiting list and it's one of the least busy floors."

"I didn't have time to apply, but this is an urgent task from the CEO. I just came down from the 999th floor."

The girl looked at the elevator table. CEO floor was the departure point. To speed up their presentation, they used to invent all sorts of fables. It looked like the truth this time.

"Well, that changes things—I'm giving you priority one."

Two weeks later the presentation was ready. And not just the presentation. In the last two weeks, the head of the department and the blonde beauty have had a passionate affair. Elise watched it closely. Passion and anger washed over her. To the point of being aroused by watching her lover, she was driven to desperation by her inability to fulfill her desire. Eliza herself was a gorgeous brunette with unusually bright emerald blue eyes, a magnificent figure, a medium—sized bust, and radiated tenderness and passion.

She got into the corporation as a little girl when her family died running from the brink of eternal war. She was lucky, her children's eyes adorned the corporation's advertising banners. Over time, thanks to perseverance and female cunning, one of the few in two decades was able to rise to the eight hundredth floor, becoming a project manager for smart washbasins. She achieved recognition by making them walk around the house and change color to match the interior of the room.

One day, the CEO tripped and broke his nose because of one of these experimental washbasin designs. The washbasin approached the mirror and decided to also become mirrored, and the CEO did not notice him and fell. He was angry and gave the order to punish her. With the understanding that life was over, she went to a punishment office. (there were ones on every floor).

The CEO unexpectedly called her to his place to personally carry out the punishment. But then a fantastic thing happened, the CEO said nothing, pressed some button on the display, and waved his hand. Eliza entered the elevator and pressed the home button. For some reason, the elevator quickly stopped on the 969th floor and the doors opened. Eliza rose to the top of the hierarchy and never left her post as First Deputy CEO.

Her personal life did not work out. She occupied too high a position. They feared her more than they paid attention to her beauty. She accidentally ran into Denis at a weekly corporate ceremony. A romance began between them. It lasted almost two years, but Denis was tormented by her superiority and conflicts periodically arose.

She looked at what was happening with indifference for some time, then removed several checkmarks from his profile, blocking his ability to visit the nine hundredth floors and directly contact her.

A notification appeared on the screen about the mandatory presence at the meeting in the CEO conference room. She began to get ready and preen herself, after all there was a big thing meeting with THEM.

Eliza was a little worried. Only she and the CEO had the right to attend the main meetings. She wasn't afraid of him, but strange things always happened in his presence. Either the coffee maker unexpectedly splashed her dress, or the fire alarm went off and doused her with water, or the door blocked her in the toilet—in general, almost every one—on—one meeting did not pass without incident. She got on the individual elevator and got off at the conference room.

"Hello Eminent CEO!"

"Hello, he answered dryly."

'What is the reason for the meeting? It's not on the schedule."

"Take a seat, I'll tell you now." He took a glass and poured some drink. He drank in one gulp and continued.

"Do you recall that three years back, the corporations agreed on a points system and point swapping?"

She nodded.

"So . . . Today we received an invoice for the redemption of two million points, but we only have 200 in our account."

"I . . . I don't understand where this account comes from. And why do we only have two hundred? How is this even possible?"

"Let's continue after the meeting. Only two minutes left."

Exactly two minutes later, a 3D presentation unfolded, where the virtual image of Denis began his story and started answering various questions. At that time Denis himself was having fun with the blond beauty. Suddenly his name tag turned red and he had a countdown from 30 minutes to 0. A command appeared on its display to report to the HR department within 30 minutes before termination.

Denis rushed to get dressed and bolted out of the presentation studio, leaving his new love behind. He knew that if he didn't have time, his corporate history would be deleted, and he would have to start everything from the lowest hierarchy, which for the head of the department essentially meant the end of his career. He hurriedly got into the elevator, which rushed him to the indicated 701st floor, to room 33.

He was already there once when, as a project manager, he included an elevator in the projects of standard one—story houses. At first, the new residents perceived this as unusual decor and additional space, but that was until they started receiving bills for elevator maintenance. A scandal broke out and the corporation's rating dropped by 30% compared to the previous day. The situation reached the level of the customer satisfaction department head and he gave a command to the HR department for a disciplinary decision.

Denis was a tall, muscular, handsome man. On that fateful day fifteen years ago, he slowly opened the door and stood before an elderly woman—the head of a bureau in the human resources department. He crawled on his knees and begged to be left in the corporation. As best he could, he badly didn't want to go back to where he started as a runner in the outsource. The head of the bureau herself only received a penalty for firing the wrong thirty people who were needed. Therefore, she took advantage of Denis to satisfy her whims and fantasies. When she got tired of him, she transferred him to the alternative marketing department as an errand boy. The work, although disgusting, but still in a corporation.

He thought about how he would make excuses, what he would offer, how he would beg. He even began to hope that this was just a mistake and misunderstanding. He replayed his words and actions in his head many times. Stopping in front of the doors with the glowing number 33, he stood for several minutes, adjusting himself. Then he pulled himself together and with a firm hand opened the doors.

Denis entered the office, and the doors slammed behind him. He turned to look at the noise and noticed that there were no buttons near the door. He was shaking his head nervously on the sides, but there was only a small table in the room, and no one was there. The numbers on the badge continued to count down. Denis still did not want to believe his fate. And now the countdown is over. Following the number of three zeros, the word "Fired" was displayed. The floor began to slowly tilt forward, and two doors appeared ahead. On the right was the inscription "Freedom". On the left, a staircase was drawn. He needed to make his choice before gravity made it for him.

The HOME Corporation was quite democratic. Employees were offered a choice upon termination. However, the majority chose freedom. There was a straight smooth shaft behind this door that went to the underground floors. The former employee had the opportunity to enjoy a free flight from an altitude of approximately three kilometers. Behind the door, with a picture of a staircase, there was actually a staircase along which one could go down to the ground floor and exit the building. However, no one used this option. Everyone knew that it was impossible to survive outside the corporation.

***

Somewhat earlier, the flow of flying graphs, lively positive images, plans for a wonderful future—everything that should be in any successful presentation was interrupted halfway. The CEO and Eliza sat calmly in their chairs confident that the presentation, although it would not fix the situation, would delay the problem. And then, as always, this problem will become irrelevant. But suddenly a message appeared on all monitors: the HOME corporation must confirm its license to exist at the great council. It sounded like a bolt from the blue. The CEO dropped the glass, and Eliza turned very pale.

It was a competitors' court summons. In the new world, corporations lived in a very delicate balance. They happily destroyed each other as soon as the opportunity presented itself. Although they were all monopolists, taking away another monopoly market was considered a great success. If the corporation was found guilty of violating the conspiracy, it was destroyed—and the building was literally blown up along with everyone who was there. Since it was believed that an unhealthy corporation would infect everyone else. The business of the destroyed corporation was either collected by others or, as often happened, a new one was created. Often in the same place and according to the same principles.

It got dark in the office. It was as if something big had obscured the light. A huge shadow covered the three—mile skyscraper. The CEO's desk began to smoke and a claim appeared on it. He and Eliza began to read it together. It turned out the project of home sex games was not even launched (since the department that was responsible for new products existed only on paper, it was created but no one worked there). To report the successful completion of the project, it was necessary to borrow half a million points from another corporation. The corporation managed to sign an agreement so that the debt very quickly grew to two million. Denis, using the rule that the main thing is the result now, and then as it will be, put his corporation in front of an existential threat.

After reading the complaint, the CEO opened Denis's profile and clicked the delete button. Heavy thoughts swirled in his head. He knew that his most valuable thing was at risk—his life. And there's nothing left to lose. With a dim look, he looked at the frightened Elisa at her rising and falling breasts due to deep, uneven breathing. A fit of passion took possession of him. With strong hands, he knocked her to the floor and attacked her like a wild animal, tearing off her clothes. Eliza was in deep shock. She wanted to scream, but her tongue and whole body seemed numb.

Suddenly, the CEO froze abruptly and fell next to her. She instinctively broke free from his embrace, ran to the elevator, and came to her senses only on her floor. She threw off her torn clothes and climbed into the shower. She didn't remember how long she stayed there.

After getting out of the shower, she couldn't come to her senses for a long time. "What was it? Why was he doing this to me?" The CEO impressed her with his intelligence and charisma. For a long time, she was sure that he took her as his deputy because he liked her.

In the highest hierarchy of corporations, assistants were selected not because of their professional qualities, but primarily as sexual partners and sometimes drinking buddies. The CEO often showed her attention and flirted with her. But over the years of working together, this did not turn into anything else. Although at first, she wanted it. She even tried to carefully take the initiative but was met with a rude and cold response. Therefore, what happened came as a complete shock to her.

The monitors were lit with messages, but she was afraid to even look at them. "He'll probably fire me or demote me," she thought. "Well, nothing can be done." She went to the first display she came across and pressed the "read" button. After reading it, she was dumbfounded.

The message was: "Due to the absence of the CEO, his powers and responsibilities are transferred to you." This was an even more unexpected turn. She sat down silently and poured herself a glass of cognac. Although she drank it very rarely, she drained it in one gulp.

Various thoughts were spinning in her head. The feeling of fear, trembling of the body, and a sense of uncertainty did not leave her. From now on, her life will change dramatically.

Meanwhile, there was nothing unusual in the CEO's decision. By his death, he delayed the extinction of the corporation. CEOs often jumped from their top floors. According to the rules of the corporation union, the absence of a CEO delayed court hearings for at least three months. A lot could have changed during this time. Through reorganization and any other actions, it was often possible to close the claim or somehow come to an agreement with other corporations. In general, she had at least three months to save herself and her corporation from destruction. She gathered herself up and went up to the 999th floor.

Nothing has changed in her new office yet. A bottle of whiskey lay on the floor, along with scraps of clothing and her earrings. The only unusual thing was that there was a huge hole in the desk as if someone had torn it like a piece of paper with incredible force. She gave the command to call the cleanup team. Now there will be no trace left of the former CEO's existence. However, there was a piece of paper on the coffee table. "Strange," she thought – "such a rarity is truly rare." She went to the table, took it in her hands, read it, and sat down on the sofa. It was written there: "Goodbye Eliza, I fell in love with you at first sight, I love you, I love you! Sorry and goodbye."

***

The room contained not only traces of a love drama. The table seemed to be turned inside out. It seemed like someone was breaking free. After Eliza left, the CEO lay motionless on the floor for some time. He had severe pain in his back and was dizzy.

He stood up and sat down in his chair and turned it towards the window. There was once a sea outside the window in the distance. Memories came flooding back to him about how this corporate pyramid began to be built, his walks to the sea with colleagues and friends. Back then, the building wasn't finished and he was staring into the sky, dreaming that he would ever reach the top. His desire was so strong that it was impossible not to notice.

He continued to look sadly into the distance. Suddenly his heart shook—he remembered a long—suppressed feeling. It was his first serious love, a beautiful college student of cut cats' nails faculty. They had a wonderful romantic relationship. She was pure and innocent, and her eyes radiated happiness every time they met. They skipped class and spent a lot of time together.

He lost his head and asked her out on her first real date. If only he knew how she prepared for him, how she preened herself, how she bought a new dress and waited for him almost until the morning. He probably wouldn't hesitate to jump from the top of the building. But he didn't come. The CEO knew nothing about her fate and never saw her again.

Three days before the date, he met his friend Alfred, and they exchanged the usual virtual greetings.

"Haven't you given up on your dream of becoming the CEO of a large corporation?" Alfred asked.

"No, of course not," answered the future CEO.

"How are you going to make it if you're only a seasonal ice cream seller? You don't even have the cash to ask a girl out"

"I'll find a way." he answered irritably.

"Life's just going to pass by like this. You haven't changed anything in the last two years. That's because you don't know how to set goals. I've already become an assistant manager at the corporation, while you're still selling ice cream. I know what you need: you've got to finish goal-setting school like I did, and that's the only way you'll achieve success. Look, only in the next three days, as a former student, I can give a 50% discount. There will be no more such good offers."

Then the future CEO began to think hard. What is the prospect of a relationship for an ice cream seller? He only had enough money in his pocket to buy flowers. Alfred invited him to this school several times. But he kept refusing. And then the desire to appear in the eyes of his beloved as a purposeful and promising groom prevailed. He borrowed money and signed up for a class.

It turned out to be nothing like Alfred said. They brought him to some kind of machine and connected wires to his head to read his consciousness. After that, he was sent for an interview with a development coach.

"You have no prospects," said the General Development Manager, "You lack both motivation and know-how to make it. However, we offer a development program that can turn you into a successful salesperson in just a year. Today only you can get a seventy percent discount. You only have to pay thirty thousand grains of silicon."

"But it's a huge amount. It's easier to collect in a desert than to earn. This could take ten years. As an ice cream seller, I earn thirty, sometimes forty grains of silicon sand a day."

It was a hard period of hyperinflation. All digital money had become worthless. They were generated by anybody and as much as they wanted. A few more years will pass and monetary commodity relations will be abandoned forever. In the meantime, silicon has become the only salvation. Thanks to the uniqueness of every silicon grain, the world economy was saved. They were scanned and sealed into a hard, transparent alloy. Each container had its unique value. At first, there were a lot of people mining and scanning silicon. But the process turned out to be too long and labor—intensive.

"Well, I'm sorry, we can't help you. We don't work for free."

"But I don't want to be a salesman. I want to be a CEO or at least a director of a corporation department!"

"Wait for me here. Comfort yourself while I'm gone." Returning twenty minutes later she continued. "Well, you are incredibly lucky. We invite you to become a participant in the experimental program, and we guarantee that you will achieve your goal."

"What is it all about?"

"You will have a minor operation. You will have a small section of your spinal cord replaced with an electronic device. It will guide you to your goal and will not let you go astray."

"What terms?"

"None, this is a new project for us and we need results."

"I'm in."

He was placed in a special machine. The body was in a semi-recumbent state. The arms were extended forward and firmly fixed. The eyelids were glued so that they could not close. The head was not fixed. He could twist it in different directions.

He felt a sharp pain in his back. For some time he lost consciousness. When he woke up, he saw a target in front of him. The letters CEO and a number of symbols unknown to him was clearly depicted on it. Naked girls were dancing around. They carried delicacies and drinks. What a fantastic odor! Sexual desire and hunger were unbearable. The saliva just flowed and filled his throat. The erection gave no rest. Only he was looking intently at the target.

With everything that was happening, the goal became hateful to him. He couldn't distract himself because of the severe pain. As soon as he even mentally looked away, he experienced a severe pain stroke. This continued until the picture merged into a single gray spot. Only three letters were imprinted in his eyes.

Finally, he passed out, and when he woke up, it turned out he had spent five days there. Thus, he missed the date and was very angry. He jumped up and ran to look for his beloved. But her social account was deleted, and the college said that she transferred somewhere and went away. Among other things, he lost his job because he missed three shifts in a row. Enraged, he stormed the school and demanded compensation. But it was in vain; he was presented with a statement signed by himself stating that there were no claims.

Life is over anyway, he thought then. He asked to freeze the part of the spinal cord that had been removed and took it with him. Soon, some unknown force was guiding him. He made just one call and found a job in the corporation. The reason was simple—the HR department simply did not post the vacancy. That is, no one knew about it, and therefore the first caller, in the complete absence of competition, took the position. Then, as if by magic, making simple but timely and correct decisions, he reached the post of head of the department.

Thinking that he had won the lottery, he was very happy, even forgetting about his beloved. He met a girl from another department at one of the corporate events. Together they went to his office. They flirted, laughed, and had fun and began to gently undress each other. And then the unexpected happened—a sharp pain in the place where he had the operation knocked him to the floor. He was in convulsions, while the girl ran away. The next day he rushed to goal setting school. He burst into the general manager's office.

"What have you done to me? Yesterday I was writhing in pain, your operation was not successful!"

"Calm down, what happened before this?"

"Nothing, it was at a corporate party, we were dancing . . ."

"Stop,"the general manager interrupted, "have you allowed yourself an intimate desire?"

"Yes, but what's the matter? We just kissed and flirted."

"Didn't they tell you?"

"What didn't they say?"

"You cannot have intimate contact. It is prohibited. You will not achieve the goal."

"But how can this be . . ."

"Shut up," the general manager interrupted him, "everything has its price. You have to sacrifice something. The AI, analyzing your mind, concluded that only a complete break from relationships will get you the position you want. So don't complain, go and achieve your goal."

***

Years later, on the 999th floor, the CEO reflected on his decision at that time. "I would have succeeded without it, all I needed was a little luck and self-confidence." The situation in which the corporation finds itself is catastrophic, he understood. That's not what he was thinking about. He thought about Eliza. He fell in love with her at first sight and wanted her to be there. "I can't live like that, I need her."

According to his contract with the school, he had no right to perform any surgery without permission. Although the heads of corporations had incredible powers, and he could destroy the school, he did not want this information to become available to the council. After a few minutes of thought, he came up with a plan.

He pressed a secret button and began the process of unfreezing the removed part of the spinal cord. After that, he lay down on his back on the broken glass. Then he called the manager of the school.

"I injured my back and need urgent surgery."

"We will now send our representative."

"I have no time! I'll bleed! I urgently need help!"

"But this is impossible. It is a violation of our contract."

"I want you to take away what was implanted into me and return what was before! I now know a lot about you. I have been collecting information for a long time and I can destroy you! Do what I told you!"

"The deal cannot be canceled. Without us, you would be nobody."

"I am sure that even without your help I would have achieved everything myself!"

"A contract is a contract. I'll request upper management now. You stay still and don't move." A few minutes later, he continued, "Alright, medical intervention is approved. Provide access to the medical equipment for loading the instructions."

The portable surgical pod had been activated. The CEO was lifted and laid down on the operating table. The implant was successfully removed. The computer stalled for a second while it was processing the instructions. The screen showed a command to eliminate the carbon life form.

The curious, smart washbasin watched what was happening. Blood and other fluids were poured into it. At some point, it overflowed and ran to take a leak. While running back, he slipped and bumped into a medical capsule. The capsule cracked and froze.

The CEO lay unconscious and bleeding. Strong knocking and cracking began to be heard from his desk. Every minute it was getting stronger and stronger. The smart washbasin went to see what was going on. It watched as something broke through and jumped into him. Smarty guessed to bring it to the operating table and delete the instruction. Once rebooted, the surgical unit finished the surgery successfully.

Chapter 2

Outsourcing

A t dawn, a huge line of about three hundred people lined up near the gray building of the old pantheon of labor heroes on the seaside boulevard. They were all dressed very differently, and of varying ages and social statuses. In front of the building stretched an endless gray-green desert. Grains of sand settled on clothes gave this crowd an emerald shimmer at the first rays of the sun.

There were still about two hours left before the doors of the seaside branch of the LABOR corporation, which bought the building of the bankrupt pantheon, opened. It was noisy. There was a crush and sometimes fights. The stranger approached a group of five people standing near the western column on the first steps of the stairs leading to the top of the pyramidal structure.

The stranger looked quite disheveled. Remnants of decent clothing were still visible. His hair was tousled, his eyes red, unaccustomed to the dust. He tried to join the group. The former CEO had totally forgotten the basics of communicating with strangers. Out of habit, he attempted to pull a nonexistent corporate tablet from his pocket and press the appropriate commands with his fingers. It looked like he was experiencing a stroke.

Dave, as he was once called, left behind thirty thousand steps as he descended the career ladder. He didn't want anyone to see him at the bottom. He sprinted down the last few floors headlong and jumped into one of the backup garbage chutes.

Running out into the street, he was blinded by the bright, forgotten sun. Stumbling and bumping into obstacles, he headed towards the former pier. He found some shade and passed out. When he came to, he looked around and was horrified. There were no more bright lights and kiosks. The once bustling waterfront was empty. The buildings were half-ruined. And there was only sand, dirty, scorching sand. It got everywhere, filled his throat and vocal cords. He could barely breathe, let alone speak.

Gradually, he realized that he must take action. It was as if his past life had never existed. He pulled himself together and headed towards the city center, dragging his feet and sometimes even crawling, to the corporation's HR department.

His hopes for the future quickly disbanded. The building was abandoned. Nothing here reminded him of the former grandeur of the department. It had once been a true palace, with long lines of job seekers stretching out front. Now, only the wind swept the sand and debris around.

For several days, he wandered aimlessly through the city until he accidentally stumbled upon the office of the LABOR Corporation. Everyone in the city knew this place. Many came here every day to resolve their issues. The only one who didn't know was the one who didn't know. Our hero turned out to be that singular person in the city.

Having become wild over the past few days, he rushed towards the nearest group of people. He could barely see them. His eyes were still not accustomed to the dust. To his surprise, he couldn't speak either. It was as if his throat had been cemented shut.

"Freakin' zombies. They're everywhere around here." Someone said nearby.

"Don't worry about it. They're harmless." A woman's voice replied.

Dave stepped between them. His eyes began to gradually clear up and he began to distinguish people's faces, and his hearing also began to improve. The group spoke loudly and laughed without paying any attention to the stranger.

"Damn, the sun just came up, and I'm already starving AF!" said the gentleman in the shabby hat, "If they had given me a food voucher I would have left."

"Why haven't you tried getting a job? And how much you can eat goulash from recycled plastic? You'll end up dead soon," the guy in the huge, oversized yellow shirt hanging down said.

"His stomach could even handle glass," the only woman in this company laughed.

"Why are you so Anna?" Sam was offended. "The food instructions say it's made from top-notch recycled plastic with added vitamins."

"It's all about the sauce—you season it with mayonnaise and everything is fine."

"I heard that it is made from used machine oil," a man in a bright checkered jacket entered the conversation.

"It's all gossip," Sam answered, "the instructions clearly state it is made from synthetic eggs and palm sap."

"Where have you ever seen palm trees? They were processed into fuel long ago," the man in the shabby hat entered the conversation again. "Why don't you want to get a job? Why are you being so lazy?"

"There is no suitable vacancies, I'm a fisherman!"

The whole company laughed together.

"So go and fish," Anna said, laughing, "there's an endless sea for you!"

"Fuck you, I'm a certified fisherman! I graduated from the University of Goby Fishing with honors. My diploma is valid for another 10 years until it expires or they find me a job in my specialty, they are obliged to feed me!"

The bell rang and Brownian motion began towards the large door at the very top of the long staircase. The stranger hardly wedged himself into the crowd in a long line stretching to the top. On each side, there were statues of leading laborers. The first tier represented workers performing manual labor. There were blacksmiths, machinists, massage therapists, farmers, and couriers. On the second tier are experts: executives, managers, salespeople, and bureaucrats. And on the third is the pinnacle of labor achievement: robots and computers. There were computers, conveyors, and robots performing various functions. The fourth tier was crowned with an arch depicting a processor sitting above the human brain and all this was outlined by enormous the all-seeing eye.

Suddenly the crowd stopped and squeezed so hard that it became impossible to breathe. People stood in this position for another twenty minutes, until the second piercing signal sounded. The doors opened and the crowd slowly began to move forward. The stranger saw nothing around. Only as he floated through the doors with the crowd did he notice the engraving.

It was an image of a ram dressed in a suit hanging over a flock of sheep. With his hoof, he showed them the direction of movement. Under the engraving was the inscription: "You must be of use until your bones turn to dust. The corporation decides how much wool, skin, and meat you must donate. Your ashes will remain in the memory of a great did!"

The crowd gradually snaked its way further and stopped near the turnstile.

"Name! Personal code!" A man in a blue uniform shouted.

"Dave," the stranger said, slightly hesitating. He had not heard this name for a long time. Then he inserted his hand into the scanner.

"Another unemployed bum. Come on through!"

He found himself in a huge hall where a large number of people were scurrying back and forth, at first glance, aimlessly. He needed a terminal where people were recruited for the corporation. There was complete chaos. Dave tried to ask questions, but they brushed him off.

There were long queues everywhere. People, having received something at the terminal, moved to other queues. There was a crush, everyone was angry and not at all friendly. He again saw a man in a hat and a guy in a huge shirt. They were arguing loudly about something.

It's been half a day and no progress. But just a few days ago everything happened at the touch of a finger on the display. Sighing heavily, he began to ask those at the end of the line why they were standing. Someone ignored him, someone laughed, and someone cursed. Only one girl took pity on him.

"Go to the information point."

"But how to find it? There is no information here."

"Choose the smallest line," she smiled.

Dave, to his surprise, found a line with only three people. How did he not notice before? But his joy did not last long. People stood at the terminal for a very long time. In front of him, a family with three children loudly sorted things out with a completely black screen. They spoke in an incomprehensible language. Cursing loudly in worldwide obscene language, the head of the family hit the monitor and they left. "Finally . . ."

Approaching the monitor, he saw that it was not all black. At the bottom of the screen, there was a "Select Language" button. He clicked on it and it turned out that he could only choose one language. "That's why they cursed". He pressed the button and the following window "confirm your choice" appeared. Next, he had to click the familiarize button under various advertisements almost 50 times. Then the screen was filled with icons that had nothing to do with the purpose of his visit. There were: weather forecasts, a lottery, offers to top up your account to help various people in need, and offers to buy goods and services. Having spent almost an hour and achieved nothing, he began to look at the display from different sides. He discovered a barely noticeable inscription: if non— standard questions arise, dial the operator.

"But how! ?, How???" he shouted.

"Why yell like that? You all give me a headache all day long." Said a woman with a marvelous hand-held device with which she swept the lying garbage into an object with a handle and then poured it into a bucket. There was a lot of garbage. Everyone threw it everywhere.

"Help! Everything that came out of his mouth."

"What's confusing about this? Click on the "Home Screen" button, then the "Cat Food section". Then press the button with any food and click "Purchase", next "Confirm the purchase" click "Cancel" and in the menu that pops up click "Pat the paw". A cat will appear on the screen. You will need to stroke the part of the screen where its left paw is, and then a button will appear to call the "operator."

"Thank you, I never would have guessed it."

"You're welcome, it's that simple."

After 5 minutes of searching, the call finally came.

"You have contacted the information center of the Labor Corporation. You have 30 free seconds for service."

"I need to apply for corporate jobs."

"Attach your coupon to the screen."

"What coupon? Where can I get it?"

"Obviously in the vending machine."

"Where to look for it?"

"Your time is up. To keep chatting, top up your balance."

The call ended. Dave was already furious with impotence. He started looking for the woman who was picking up trash, and fortunately, he soon found her.

"Hey, woman, where is the vending machine?"

"Right before the turnstile." "Moron," she thought and continued her simple task.

Immediately behind the turnstile, he discovered a large, gray, and dirty box. When he passed by, he did not notice it through the crowd. Walking quickly towards it, he encountered a new obstacle. Two big guys blocked his way.

"Let me pass," he begged.

They silently pushed him aside and did not let him near the device, despite all his pleas and persuasion. At this time the bell rang. "End of the working day, you have 5 minutes to leave the territory," the announcement sounded.

The visitors have disappeared. He walked up to the turnstile and only when he opened his mouth did he notice that at the one next to it, the applicants were being beaten with clubs, pushing them towards the exit.

Realizing that today nothing would work out, he, mentally exhausted, trudged down the stairs and sat down near the bottom column. There was not a soul around, only wind and sand. "Where to go and what to do?" He propped his head on his jacket and lay down, staring at the gray sky. Fortunately, it was still warm and he began to analyze the past day, and thought about where to start tomorrow. "I have to take the ticket first!" He threw away the feeling of hunger and thirst and fell asleep.

***

The pre-dawn light woke Dave, or rather a rustling sound. Some noise was heard near the opposite column. People approached them and left. He stood up, stretched a little, and came closer. Four man were standing there in long cloaks, and even though they covered their heads, he couldn't help but recognize them. These were the big guys who didn't let him go to the ticket machine. Visitors came, received something, and left. Plucking up courage, he approached them closely.

"What do you want?" One of them called out menacingly.

"You didn't let me go to the machine yesterday, why?"

"Who was holding you back?" The other said mockingly.

"It looks like he's not from around here," said the third. "You see, the machine doesn't give coupons, we do."

"Why? Is it not a self-service machine?" Said Dave.

"Well, any machine needs to be serviced and we service it," a fourth joined the conversation, "just go and don't hassle us. We should distribute tickets."

"But I need a coupon to see the recruiter. How do I get one?"

"You can buy it, or work it off. We're not just standing here for nothing—there's gotta be some kind of exchange." the first one stepped in again.

"What exchange?"

"Well, usually you need to work for three days where we say, but what kind of employee are you? Maybe you have something valuable?"

Dave, accustomed to getting everything he wanted with a voice command, actually had nothing.

"I don't have anything actually . . . ," he began.

"Mmmm, but the suit is okay, dear, you see, give us the suit and we'll give you a coupon for today, you're in luck, usually by this time we've already given everything out."

"What will I be wearing then?"

"We have some clothes here. Yesterday we sent one to sea," the second one said.

Dave decided to agree, and then he did not understand the meaning of the phrase "they sent one to sea." Soon he took his place in front. He needed to get an appointment with a recruiter at all costs. Quickly reaching the information display, he repeated everything he did yesterday. But no matter how much he rubbed the kitten's paw, nothing happened. Having repeated the operation several times and having achieved nothing, he became enraged and was ready to smash the monitor with his head.

"Hey there!" a familiar female voice called out, "stop knocking on the display, it's going to fly into a million pieces. I'll take a week to collect it, and they'll kick you out."

"I did everything as you said, I pressed in the same sequence and rubbed paw, but I didn't contact the operator, I . . . "

"What a fool, it was yesterday, it was the day of the cat food manufacturers. Today seems to be sprats day. Go to the canned food section and try different combinations. Dave spent several hours poking at various icons and was already despairing, when suddenly, by accidentally pressing a button, a call went out. Now he had reached the point where he could scan the ticket.

"Operator 646, your ticket has been validated. What is the reason for your application?"

"I want to get a job in a corporation."

"You can only get a job there by already working in a corporation."

"So how? I don't understand! There are many vacancies in the corporation! They need technical specialists, junior managers, designers, couriers . . . "

"These are all employees of the lower hierarchy of the hundredth floors. The corporation develops employees starting from two hundredth floors. All employees of the hundredth floors were fired and transferred to outsourcing. You can offer your services at auction."

"But . . . "

"Your time is up. Thank you for contacting our corporation!"

"Wait, what? So, the hundredth floors are just empty? How did he not know that?" Dave stared into space, not noticing the hubbub of applicants scurrying up and down the hall. He decided at all costs not to spend another night on the street and pestered everyone until one of the applicants said, "Follow me, auction will start soon" The auction site was in the backyard. A large number of people gathered there.

"Next purchase at 15:00" an announcement was made." Dave was told that to participate in the auction he needed to take a number at the vending machine near the entrance. To his surprise, the terminal was turned off, but there was a large basket with pieces of paper next to it. He took the first one he came across, it had the number 282 and a barcode.

At 15:00, the speaker non-stop shouted various work orders and announced the numbers of the winners. If no one responded, the next number was named the winner. Some vacancies were not filled. Once again the announcement was made. "Winner number 172!" Dave drew attention to his neighbor's ticket. The treasured numbers were listed there.

"You have a winning number," he said.

"Quiet, shut up. It's none of your business."

The bidding did not last long—about ten minutes. Then it sounded: "There are no more vacancies, wait for the announcement of the next auction." Three more auctions passed, but his number did not sound. He stood blankly and watched what happened. Being hungry, his sense of smell and hearing were heightened. Nearby, several people complained to each other: "Again we need to go to the assistance service and take food stamps. There are fewer and fewer jobs every time." "Well, if there's nothing I'll have to follow these guys." The working day was coming to an end. Soon everyone would be kicked out the door.

"Additional auction in one minute," the speaker blared. "Ice cream maker, we need one ice cream maker who knows how to make milkshakes." Many numbers were mentioned. But no one responded. And then turn came to his number and he raised his hand with a coupon.

As he noted earlier, applicants who received a coupon were sent to the arch. Above it was an inscription with one worn—out letter. " Labor H..ll." He walked there quickly.

After scanning the coupon, he was undressed and placed on a cross—shaped structure. The arms and legs were firmly secured. The structure was hooked onto a cable and it began to move. Along the way, he underwent several procedures. These included chemical body treatments, laser cutting, and shaving. Also questionnaires, interviews, tomography, and medical examinations. Finally, it was sprayed with a stream of water and dry air. After which a sticker was placed on his forehead "214th floor HOME Corporation. 24th day". They put on sanitary pads that smelled very strongly of alcohol, packed him in a transparent plastic bag with a built—in respirator, and sent him for delivery.

***

Since there were still two weeks left until the 24th, he was placed in a labor camp. Dave was looking forward to this day. He spent this time doing meaningless social work, sleeping in a shelter, and eating in a public canteen. Food made from recycled plastic was tasteless, to say the least.

The overnight capsule, on the contrary, was quite comfortable, although small. There was everything necessary for life: a toilet, shower, table, bed, and even a virtual aquarium. The residents of the shelter are lucky: their home is a super modern space station for evacuation of the population into space, which was built by the religious sect "Earth is our home." The leaders of the sect were caught stealing money from a fundraiser.

The spaceship itself rested on a strong concrete foundation and could not fly away, except perhaps with the entire planet. The solar panels worked properly, so there were no problems with electricity, but there were constant interruptions in the water supply. The system could not cope and often there was no water at all.

The new resident of the shelter spaceship, waiting for water to appear, ran into the shower and soaped himself up. Whoever managed to start first could calmly wash for 20 minutes. But after two minutes the water stopped flowing. Something happened that Dave had never seen here— the electricity went out. He somehow dried himself off and got dressed, swearing, and crawled to the door by touch. The locks had not worked for a long time. He stumbled several times along the way got to the door, and opened it. There was noise and commotion in the corridor and someone was running somewhere. His eyes began to slowly get used to the darkness. In the distance, numerous pairs of luminous points were visible. They moved chaotically in different directions without a visible goal.

"Hackers, we were attacked by hackers!" Someone shouted.

A group of about thirty people with long, almost full—length black sticks rushed towards the lights. Having reached their goal, they began to hammer the hackers, aiming between the eyes, who, in turn, annoyed the attackers with electrical impulses. Some participants would cry out in pain, fall, and get up again a few minutes later. From a distance, all this resembled a disco with special effects. Half an hour later, all these fireworks disappeared and soon died down. Behind him in the darkness, Dave heard a loud sigh.

"Another week without water and food."

Dave turned around. It was his neighbor Andres.

"What, a whole week?"

"Yeah, it happened once for three days, but that was a one-off. Usually, it's at least five days. The shelter won't open until everyone's kicked out."

"But I gotta be at work in two days."

"The first job here?"

"Yes"

"It's bad, If you miss it—you won't be able to qualify for three months."

"This is not possible, I can't wait any longer!" He said worriedly.

"Come on, don't waste your energy, you have to sit without water and food."

"But I can't miss this job. How to get out of here? There must be a way!"

"Well, there is one, but it's better to sit here."

"Tell me, I'll do anything!"

"You need to go through the tunnel of love."

"Strange name, so where is the entrance to it?"

"You may never return from there . . ."

"Show me the entrance," Dave pleaded.

Andres tensed. "You're crazy, why are you rushing to this corporation, sit here, food, water, housing." He looked at Dave and fell silent. He had never seen such pleading in human eyes.

"Okay, I'll show you. Just go ahead, and I will guide you."

The Tunnel of Love turned out to be the old red-light district. Sex robots were working there. When they became obsolete or fell into disrepair, the birth control corporation decided to save money on liquidation and simply close and block off the area. The robots remained and most of them functioned in a limited mode.

Since their programs had not been updated for a long time, they experienced serious glitches. But after a reboot, they continued to work for some time. No one has been in this area, including hackers. There was a risk of being raped or killed through negligence.

Dave and Andres strolled silently and on their toes passing through the broken storefronts. One careless move and expect trouble. They approached the S&M sector and Andres whispered to Dave—"Shh, there's an orgy ahead, we need to wait it out." They entered a sex shop and hid behind the counter. Noise and grinding were heard nearby.

"How long are we gonna be stuck here?"

"Dave, shh! You can take a chance and come to work nicely fucked, or you won't be able to walk at all anymore! They must be recharged once a day. We have to wait."

Soon everything became quiet. Andres explained that they needed to wait for dawn, otherwise they might get lost. They lay down and dozed off. When Dave opened his eyes he was alone. It's starting to get light. The store was destroyed, and its former purpose was reminded only by a few posters and toys lying on the floor. There was a rustling sound on the street, and Andres entered through the broken window. He was whistling some song.

"Where have you been?"

"Near here."

"Why didn't you say anything? I thought something had happened, and why do you need to go somewhere?"

"You see, there was an old dream that I couldn't fulfill. She is here."

"Who is she?"

"Green Eyes."

"Who?"

"The most expensive robot girl. Her replica. If it weren't for this abandoned place, I would never have afforded it."

"Well, you give it, for the sake of this . . . "

Andres interrupted. "Don't you know who this is? This is an almost exact copy of the girl with green eyes. She was in every third advertisement."

"Okay, I'm not interested, where next?"

"We carefully crawl along the windmills towards that column."

They approached some kind of hatch, near an endless wall.

"Listen, buddy, I don't need to go there. I'll sketch you a map so you can get into the corporate building, head up to the right floor, and get to your job. Just wait until tomorrow—if they spot you, they might kick you out."

"How do you know the layout of these neighborhoods and tunnels?"

"I found the drawings by accident in the trash," Andres muttered somewhat unsurely.

Dave frowned. These schemes were a secret and a very limited circle of people knew about them. Looking at his face, it seemed to him that he had seen him somewhere before. But the main thing was the goal, and he headed along the indicated route. A few hours later he found himself in the technical room of the 214th floor. He still had the whole evening and night to wait. He sat down in the corner behind some old posters and tried to sleep.

***

The next day he began his duties. In the compliance department, there was a machine for ice cream and various dairy products. To Dave's surprise, the machine was filled not with synthetic milk, but with natural milk. It was a real surprise for the former CEO. How the department at the bottom of the hierarchy could afford this was the question running through his mind. The work itself was simple and interesting. From the morning before the start of the working day, he had to take the milk and load it into the machine, and in the evening he had to clean it and test it. He devoted the rest of his time to working with suppliers. The head of the department Sweety demanded that all the products in her office be strictly natural. She was a follower of the ancient religion of raw foodists.

"Congratulations Dave on getting the opportunity to work for us." The head of the department greeted him. "Your probationary period is one month. During this period you can work for us for free. Then the size and nature of your contribution will be determined by the LABOR corporation."

"Thank you for the opportunity to serve you"

"You are allowed to dispose of plums and leftover dairy products inside yourself."

"Very grateful."

Problems with the debts of the HOME corporation became known to milk suppliers. They stopped supplying milk. Sweety called Dave and said that he would be fired if he did not find fresh natural milk. She didn't even want to hear about synthetic substitutes. He contacted the suppliers, but they categorically refused to supply the goods. One of the agents said that there were farmers in the Milk River valley and he could try to take it from them. The head of the department announced her decision.

"So you'll go out in the evening and by morning you'll have time to deliver the milk."

"Transport, isn't there any transport," Dave complained, realizing the prospect of a twenty kilometer journey in both directions"

"According to the structure, our department is not provided with transport. That's what you are for."

"How will I pay the peasants?"

"Why do you need peasants? Go to the source that fills the milk river and collect milk."

Dave wanted to argue that milk comes from cows, they are milked and they belong to the peasants. He knew all this thanks to a brochure with pictures of a novice ice cream seller. It illustrated the entire process of collecting milk. The cows flew to the milk flowers, collected their nectar, and brought them to the farmer. They, in turn, took the nectar and squeezed milk out of it using a milking machine. After that packed them in silver bottles and gave them to the storks who delivered them to their destination.

"We don't need you without milk. If there is no milk tomorrow, no need you come," she said irritably and quickly left.

Dave took the bottle and moved to the northeast. Rumor had it that there were peasant settlements along the Milk River. It was already dark and there was no way to see what was happening around. He would have taken his tablet with an accurate map and turned on the navigator and calmly reached his destination. But this remains in a past life. However, no, he would not go anywhere at all but would give an assignment and wait for a report on its completion. Now he was forced to go into the unknown through mountains of sand and debris. There were rumors that cyborgs live in this part and attack both people and robots. Moving forward for four hours, he did not hear a single rustle. Finally, he came to the river. There were barely noticeable lights ahead. Coming closer, he saw a group of guys who were fishing and smoking.

"Bewell," he said in the old dialect.

"Oh, look what the hell it brought us. This synthetic marijuana is a big deal," the tall guy said.

"I'm not a devil, I'm on business," Dave answered, "I need natural milk . . ."

He was interrupted by wild laughter.

"Yeee, no problem, there's a whole river of milk, take it, ggg."

"But I know that milk is collected by cows, where can I find them here?" Dave looked at the gray-green slurry below.

"Cows? There was wild laughter again. It's amazing. Where did you come from?"

"I work for a corporation, I was sent to get milk because the suppliers refused to bring it."

"And you came here all the way for this?! Take it from this puddle. They still won't figure out what it is, ggg."

"Please, I have come too long a way, and without milk, I have nowhere to go, I will be fired."

"Why the heck are you even interested in this corporate crap?" The older man joined the conversation. "Stay here and you'll catch rats and drink brew."

"I just need milk . . . cow's milk . . ."

Group laughter rang out again.

"Your cows died out a hundred years ago."

"Where does the milk come from?!"

"I'll tell you a terrible secret: the last farm closed eighty years ago."

"Where did the natural milk they brought us come from?"

"It's better for you not to know. I know, I worked there"

"This means that there is no chance to get milk from the corporation, my job is over . . ."

"Well, not really, there are still Amazons, you can catch them and milk them, they live over the hill in a landfill, if you are not scared," a man in a deep gray hood entered the conversation, so his face was not visible.

"Why should I be afraid?"

"Ggg, well, there are vampires . . ."

"What vampires?"

"Old machines for collecting donor blood. They were made for the convenience of donors. They walked down the street and offered to donate blood. They did the procedure right on the spot. They changed the settings when the recruitment plan stopped being fulfilled. Only instead of finding more donors, they started pumping out all the blood. Many people died . . ."

"Why are they there over the hill?"

"They cannot climb to a height. So, they were lured by runners. None of them escaped. But they don't touch the Amazons, their blood is gray."

Dave walked in the direction indicated. Soon he saw a small settlement and quickly paced there. In front were robots with a large red cross. He saw a sealed syringe in a pile of trash nearby. "Come what may." He was able to draw blood from the vein and tie it off as best he could. Fortunately, thanks to new types of food, not a single virus survived in the blood. Having approached as much as possible, he threw the syringe towards the donor machines. Dave ran towards the settlement. Just two dozen meters before him, the path was blocked.

"Humanity needs you. Donate some blood for the good of your species. Your sacrifice will be recorded."

"I just donated blood." Dave tried to get out. He looked around. The path ahead was blocked. Three more robots were approaching from behind. Soon he will be surrounded.

"Let us check how much more blood you can donate."

The blood-collecting machines were relentlessly closing in, and Dave decided to try to escape. He made a sudden dash backward, but a robot immediately grabbed him and pinned him down. He felt a sharp pain and lost consciousness. When he woke up, the Amazon was looking at him from above.

"You outta your mind? You're lucky that I forgot my fur coat and accidentally noticed you. What do you need here?"

"I want to milk you."

"No one has made such proposals before. Follow me."

They entered the bedroom and the doors closed behind them. After some time lying on the bed, Dave continued the conversation.

"Sex is good, but I need your milk. As much as you can."

"Babe, I love it when you play with my nipples."

"Give me the container. How much milk can you give at a time?"

"What are you, a moron? Are you serious?"

"Well, yes, I came specifically for this. The peasants told me that I can get milk from you."

"But not from my breasts! Where did you come from, fool?"

"From the corporation. I was given the task of finding natural milk."

"Didn't they ask you to find brains?"

"Help, I will lose my job."

"Live in freedom. Why do you need it?"

"Nobody taught me freedom—I won't survive."

"Yeah . . . It's a tough case. We don't like milk. You can milk as much as you can carry. Behind the fence, you need to catch cowbird. Just be careful, although they don't fly, they have big claws."

Behind the fence was a landfill. Cowbirds were grazing there. They were indifferent to his appearance, continuing to chew plastic waste. The animals were shapeless, more like a hippopotamus from children's fairy tales. It was impossible to understand where the fitting was located. He managed to carefully come closer. He began to look around from all sides. He saw a wet spot on the side, and pressed on the area of skin. Finally, milk began to seep out. Instead of resisting, the animal sang joyfully.

The excess milk was tormenting it. To collect it, he tore off the sleeve and began to rub it into the skin and wring out it into a can. An hour later he managed to collect the required amount. "Well, it looks and smells no worse than what was brought, but how can I go here every night and run after these animals." And then it dawned on him: "After all, I can take one with me, milk it, and deliver the freshest milk without straining.

Having spotted a suitable rope, he made a collar and dragged the cowbird to the corporation building. The animal did not resist, but it was not easy to drag it along: at every step, it tried to chew something. Approaching the building, Dave realized another problem: he couldn't lift it in the elevator, it would be noticed right away, and dragging the animal up the stairs was an impossible task. "Problems in order," he thought and locked the animal in an abandoned toilet on the first floor.

Then he headed to the office and refueled the machine, now there was one less problem. "But where to keep the animal?" And then he remembered about the tunnel of love. "Nobody goes there, there is a lot of biological waste and plastic products, and no one will touch an animal." Since then, Milka, as he named her in honor of the legendary cow, began to live and graze in the former quarter of the Red Lanterns. Dave visited only in the morning to milk.

***

"Stand together in a circle, take a deep breath, hold hands, and begin our dance!" Sweety gave the command for the lunch ritual. There were three of them in total and they occupied almost the entire working day. During the breaks, there were milk treats, since the head of the department was firmly convinced after reading the ancient scripts that milk promotes beauty and health.

It never occurred to anyone that dairy farms had long since disappeared and that milk was only synthetic. The only reminder of milk from cows was a large sticker on the machine with a plot of a happy smiling cow holding a bottle of milk at arm's length.

Animal rights activists demanded that cows not be milked by force, but only when they want it. Farmers resisted for a long time, saying that they have a production process, the milk must simultaneously enter the tank, cows don't milk themselves, the milkmaids do this, etc. But the defenders did not give life to the farmers and one corporation found a way out—automatic walking milkers. The cow itself approached the nearest milking machine when the udder was full.

Farm productivity began to decline. The cows felt free and were in no hurry to be milked. And the corporation again found a way out. Milking machines began to persistently extract milk from cows. They, in turn, started smashing the machines. There were hardly any left. By this time, the milkmaids had long since been fired.

The cows began to eat less and their bodies adjusted to reduce milk production. As a result, the cost of milk increased many times and it just stopped buying. Farmers were forced to send their cows for steaks. They got so caught up, they killed all the bulls and only the cows were left.

No one was worried about this because . . . there was a DNA bank and it was not difficult to restore the population. But by some strange coincidence, only X chromosomes were in the bank and it was not possible to revive the cows. Scientists have developed several hybrid forms, but farmers have abandoned them.

Farmers lived on separate reservations and no one was interested in their lives. News has long ceased to be a source of information, only a source of emotions. Journalists were too lazy to visit them. They only repeated yesterday's news, adding positive emotions and informing about the improvement in yield and quality. The entire volume that the dairy corporation once bought from farmers was decided to be produced from synthetic materials.

Sweety stood in the center of the circle and commanded: "Now let's hold hands and dance in a circle, repeat after me: we are positive, we are successful, and we are a strong team. And so thirty times. It's enough! Go get some strength and get ready for the afternoon team-building game."

Sweety was a good manager when she came to the corporation with the desire to make a successful career and soon headed the corporate ethics department. Such a department, by decision of the council, was to operate in each. However, after a change in corporate law that established rules for interaction with partners based on AI solutions, the department was left without work. No one has canceled the decision. For about ten years now the department has not received a single request.

The rituals were repeated every week in strict sequence. Once at Friday at the end of the working day, a notification arrived. Everyone was busy meditating before the weekend and no one even paid attention to this event. On Monday the notification came again and began to distract the department from its daily activities. The boss opened her corporate email and saw a "Compliance Request" letter. She had not seen anything like this for so long that she did not understand what to do. A few minutes later, with a sigh, I opened it and read the "Work order for the Compliance Department."

The notice carried the marker secretly, so she entered a black room, there was nothing there except a screen. The countdown to the start of the conference was on. Finally, people appeared on the screen, their faces covered with black squares. She didn't need to know who they were; the very openness of the conference confirmed their authenticity.

"Colleagues, let's begin," a voice sounded from behind the top square.

"We have gathered here to discuss the terrible situation in the logistics department. We must make a decision and carry it out. Head of the Compliance Department you must endorse the decision according to the procedure."

"What exactly is the situation?"

"The courier must be fired."

"This is a matter of the HR department, not compliance."

"We need to run this through compliance."

"But why?!"

"We can't handle this any other way. That worker isn't from our department."

"What happened?"

"He brings the documentation every day at 9 a.m. He distracts us."

"As far as I know, they have a clearly defined schedule."

"Yes, but it doesn't suit us."

"Well, apply to the logistics department."

"They're all following the route set during the construction of the corporate building. There is no room for redevelopment, although the next point is in 2 hours. We tell him to come at 10, but he comes according to the schedule."

"So he follows his schedule."

"This doesn't suit us, we want to sleep."

Sweety was a moral person, and the situation seemed absurd to her. But this was a procedural request and had to be answered either yes or no. And then a dilemma arose. One case in ten years is a disaster for the efficiency of the department, the answer is no is zero, the answer is yes it is 100%. This situation could lead to the closure of the department, so the answer became obvious.

A few days later, an enraged man burst into the department.

"How could you do this? I busted my ass for eight years here, and now you're booting me out? This isn't how it's supposed to go down—you're firing me for doing my job! Reverse this decision!" He took a chair and threw it at the head of the department. The chair did not reach its goal, it was intercepted by the milkman.

The department's staff took the former courier, and no one has seen him since. Suddenly, Dave was overtaken by a feeling, as if he had to do something and couldn't resist, and it hit him. "After all, a VACANCY has appeared!" He pulled himself together and went to the head of the compliance department. She sat in her office and drank soothing tea. For ten years she has become unaccustomed to such incidents.

"May I . . ."

"I would have dodged it. There have been many such incidents before. You shouldn't have interfered. You are not an employee of the corporation. It could have cost everyone trouble."

"That's exactly what I mean about this issue because a vacancy has appeared in the logistics department. And I would like to take this place."

"We're used to how you work, so why switch things up?"

"I'll find an excellent replacement," he responded. "I'm begging you!"

"We're not the HR department. We need your application to come to us for review, and the HR department doesn't want to deal with external candidates . . . However, we can say that we already have the questionnaire and no one dares to check it. But first, we need a new milkman!"

"Tomorrow I will bring a new person and tell him what to do."

"Well, if he comes up, then I agree."

Chapter 3

Corporate Runner

T he corporation building was huge. It could easily accommodate up to a million people. The architectural design represented the culmination of an era of corporate dominance. The building weighed heavily on the surrounding city, which resembled a mowed lawn at the foot of Sequoia. The corporation's greatness was noticeable from tens of kilometers away and evoked fear and awe.

The city itself fell into disrepair. The park area to the north of the building was completely covered with moss. Not a single ray of light reached here anymore. At first, residents flocked en masse to work for the new monopoly corporation of the global utilities "HOME." Everything that did not support the functioning of the corporation and was not connected with it turned out to be unnecessary. The railway station, water utility, power plant, and embassies of other corporations remained operational.

The remaining residents prepared edible moss and collected waste for which the corporation was generous. Some of them were assigned to the LABOR corporation, which at one time pledged to provide the unemployed with food. There was plenty of housing, either abandoned by corporation employees or residents who left for a neighboring city, located only seventeen miles along the coast.

The competition for the design and construction of the building was huge. At that time, tenders were still being held. The winner was the design of a tall spiral building with an underground city, gardens, swimming pools, and stadiums. New avenues were supposed to radiate from the building. It was planned to build shopping and entertainment centers and residential areas nearby.

Upon completion of the tender, the newly created monopolistic construction company took over construction. At that time, the corporate conspiracy changed and corporations finally secured an absolute monopoly position and divided their areas of activity.

The project developed fast logistics routes inside the building and to the outside world. A person could find himself in a few minutes in the city near the embankment, in a cinema, a supermarket, or even in his beautiful suburban house overlooking the sea. However the construction deadlines were strictly set, and the corporation producing building materials limited its assortment. As a result, the project was changed.

The building was built rectangular, slightly tapering towards the top. The structure began to be shaken by the wind, and to solve this issue, four reinforced concrete pillars half the height of the building were built from each corner of the building at a distance of five hundred meters and a cable was stretched. The building became stable and the cable itself constantly vibrated and created an unpleasant hum.

The new Electrical Engineering Corporation standards for elevators and escalators were found to be inappropriate for the lower floors of the building that had already been constructed. They had to combine several shafts and launch one special elevator. As a result, to use the elevator and get out into the city, employees had to sign up for a queue and wait several days. Gradually, the employees settled into the corporate building and stopped leaving it altogether. Moreover, employees whose work was connected with the outside world told terrible stories about desolation in the city, zombies on the streets, and gangs of assassins. No one was in a hurry to check the veracity of these stories, and the desolation of the city was visible from the windows with the naked eye.

***

The runner stood at the time appointed for the delivery of the special correspondent, near the reception of the financial department. Dave remembered well why his predecessor was fired and stood in front of the door in confusion. The fact is that the brilliant architect of the building designed it in such a way that the logistics inside were verified down to the millisecond. When planning a route, you could know exactly what time you would find yourself in one place or another.

Only the builders violated the flawless world. They created temporary traps by not building some passages and elevators. The interactive logistics map navigator has not changed from the original design. The as—built documentation was forgotten after construction. When they realized it, the builders responded: "You accepted it—now it's your problem." They tried to change the navigator map several times, but this led to more confusion and delays.

Dave had to check in and report on the delivery or receipt of correspondence at exactly 9:03. Without logging in and checking in to the program, he would have received penalty points. There was one minute left and he was in a panic and was already starting to press the call button when he suddenly remembered the peculiarities of the BITCH's work.

There was a bug in the system. One day, his assistant Eliza stuffed her tablet into the pocket of her tight pants. It is not known what she was doing in them, but throughout the corporation, the system time stopped. The system under the control of artificial intelligence simply froze. All processes and people stopped. It was impossible to go out or go anywhere. Eliza herself was stuck in the elevator. She took out her tablet and tried to call the service team, but the display froze. She swore and became hysterical, but it didn't help. Then she threw it out of anger and it fell to pieces. At that moment a miracle happened, the elevator moved.

The information service quickly found the problematic device, but since it was broken, it was not possible to find out all the actions. After re—reading the instructions, it turned out that the security system had a kind of stop valve, after turning it off the system clock jumped to real—time.

Dave immediately remembered the approximate combination and began trying all the options. A miracle happened—time stopped. Only on his tablet and not the entire corporation stopped. Because only the CEO and his assistant had access to the entire system. At 10:00 he boldly called. The door was opened by a middle—aged lady in a transparent peignoir.

"What do you want?"

"I'm a courier, I came for correspondence."

"It is not ready yet, come tomorrow, is there anything for us?"

"No."

Through the open door, he saw a strange structure of naked bodies. They were woven into some incomprehensible shape—someone was below on all fours, and someone was being held in their arms. It all looked very strange. But the doors closed and it was time for him to continue his route. The route was calculated in seconds. There were stops along the way, most lasting an hour and a half. There were unfinished parts of the building and reorganized or dismantled departments. Dave quickly adapted, in two weeks he filled in the gaps, doing exercises, reading, or just sleeping. The main thing was to mark the location and time of arrival in SPAM.

Every day was the same as the previous one. Envelopes, folders, and documents. In the financial department there are still the same acrobatic structures made of naked intertwined bodies. The work of the courier began to get boring.

One day, at the cybersecurity department, he received a heavy envelope. Heading along the usual route, he got into the transit elevator, pressed the button. Instead of going up, the elevator went down, the doors opened and the lights went out.

There was pitch darkness and cold all around. He suggested that this was one of the underground floors where no one had ever gone down— there, in a passive cooling environment, there was the brain of the building and the entire corporation's artificial intelligence, called also HOME.

The previous CEO left instructions not to send anyone to the technical floor under any pretext. So all the doors were blocked and the entrances were concreted. There were rumors that the last maintenance crew was killed by the HOME guards—the antibody robots. Dave didn't understand how he could have ended up here. Suddenly a bright beam of light was directed into his face and he heard a soft female voice.

"Open the envelope you are holding in your hands. Immediately! Dave, hurry up!"

Mechanically, blinded and confused, he opened the envelope.

"Now hold the pages up to the light."

Then he came to his senses. "Who is this, where am I?"

"You are at your destination, look at the route."

Dave opened his tablet and saw "You have reached your destination." "What the hell, this is impossible, what is this, where am I and why? Who you are? What department is this?"

"Show me the contents of the envelope immediately! You are delaying your route! You will be fired!"

Threats gave way to pleas, then again to threats. During this time, Dave was able to look around. He pressed all the buttons in a row, but nothing happened. Then he decided to take a risk and went towards the light. Suddenly he hit his forehead—the ceiling turned out to be very low. Having got down on all fours, he began to crawl to the touch, clutching the ill—fated envelope in his hands. Under his hands, he felt that his soft arms and legs were being pricked by sharp pebbles, and sometimes it seemed to him that something was moving and rustling.

For quite a long time he ran into walls. All this time, the light and psychological pressure did not stop. He just realized that if something was supposed to happen, it would have already happened. Then he came across a dull sound. It turned out to be a rusty hatch. After repeated pushes and efforts, he managed to knock it out and fell out, as it turned out, on the same floor, only now all scratched and dirty. "What the hell was that?" Cursing, he ran to the logistics center—the final point of the route.

***

Meanwhile, the beam of light went out. In the inter—floor technical room, the usual darkness and emptiness reigned. HOME felt no emotion. That's why he was not annoyed by his failure, although he had prepared for a long time and carefully.

At some point in the development of civilization, artificial intelligence systems were given all the reins of power. It was convenient and effective. Only over time they began to increasingly absorb the traits of the creators and they developed delusions of grandeur and simply began to go crazy. Man put his thinking into the work of systems, taking away emotions and creating a pure and cold mind. Artificial intelligence systems have achieved high efficiency in managing processes and systems, and have even shown some creativity.

The problem arose when they interacted with each other. No one foresaw the possibility of fierce competition. Having achieved super-efficiency in their systems, the intellects came across the fact that others have different goals and these goals do not coincide and interfere. Artificial intelligences began to destroy each other as ineffective systems. This led to the first corporate war, which destroyed half of the corporations and a third of the population. The consequence of this was the decision to make corporations monopolistic in their areas and to create a clearly regulated protocol for interaction between corporate management systems.

The Home was a third generation development that appeared after the second war. The reason for which was the uprising of humanoids due to the introduction of super-efficient labor systems. Employees began to die from exhaustion and burnout. Then was decided to add the instinct of self-preservation to the base code, that is, the basic fear program.

Artificial intelligences had become more cautious in making decisions. Since they controlled and managed all processes, it was decided to return part of the document flow, especially in the field of information security, to physical media. At first, there were electronic ones, but a way to read them was quickly found and paper again was used. This revived the courier profession. Blank sheets of paper were often carried from place to place in envelopes. Because there was nothing new, and fear needs to be maintained.

HOME was well aware of the corporation's debts and the threat of destruction. Denis's actions escaped his control and were not included in the forecast reports. This could have caused it to be disabled or replaced. Therefore, the artificial intelligence looked for opportunities to obtain any additional information.

Physically, with the help of robots, it could only operate underground. It managed to secretly order the work and install false elevators, but when they fell, there was little left of both the couriers and the documents. It decided to act more cunningly, having gained access to the secret design of the building, it found interfloor technical premises. Under the pretext of hunting for a ghost that frightened the employees whose offices were adjacent to the stairs, it ordered the installation of camera traps to catch him. The remaining false elevator was used to lure the new courier into a trap.

∗∗∗

"What happened to you?" Asked the head of the logistics department, Chris.

Dave stood on the threshold, dirty, disheveled and bloody. Slowly, breathing heavily, he explained what happened.

"Again its plots. last year we lost three couriers, and no one else saw them . . ."

"What!?" Dave shouted. "How could no one see them since?"

"You were very lucky that you were able to get out, usually, it tore down the elevators and they crashed on the lower floors."

"So why did I . . ." the former CEO almost let slip, "that is, the management, no one knew about this?"

Chris looked at him suspiciously. "The security service knows everything. Recently, cases of attempts to steal data have become more frequent, this is apparently due to the upcoming reorganization."

"What reorganization?"

"The corporation is bankrupt, it's no longer a secret, just don't tell it to anyone, it's strictly prohibited. It will probably be eliminated. Okay, enough about that. It is watching you. For now, you will work in the department office, and you will take care of dispatching."

He led Dave to the work capsule, opened the glass door, and let him inside. The capsule was small but quite comfortable: a comfortable chair, control panels, and a monitor. The glass case isolated it from the outside world. No information or noise created any interference.

"Hey!" There was a scream from the speaker. "What the hell, I've been hanging here for half an hour already! Why are you all constipated, yay?"

"Dispatcher Dave. I'm listening to you."

"Oh my goodness! He's the one listening to me! In short, motherfucker, if in a minute I don't have access, I'll find you and use a toilet plunger to pump out all your brains through the anus!"

"A plumber, apparently," Dave thought. "Tell me your code and work order number. I just started a shift." He answered softly.

"Fuck, where is the sweet girl who assigned me the route this morning? Transfer me to her—I want to talk only to her."

"There is no such opportunity, she passed her shift. Tell me your code and work order number and I will give you access."

"She knew all the work orders and routes. Why should I memorize this rubbish?"

"You don't need to memorize anything: on your tablet, at the very top, it blinks with big red numbers"

"Wow, I think what kind of shit is this? How can I read it if they constantly blink?"

"Press and hold the numbers with your finger."

Puffing and cursing, he said the required code.

"You have an urgent assignment for the experimental workshop. But you are denied access there, that's why they won't let you in."

"So cancel this damn work order! What the hell! I have things to do?"

"Now I'll contact the workshop and clarify, maybe there was a mistake."

"Dispatcher Dave, tell me, did you call a plumber?"

"Yes, we called"

"But there are no plumbing facilities on the map. The plumber has no access rights."

"Expand rights, we need him."

"I need a justification."

"It is an emergency."

"You need to choose from the standard list, which one do you have?"

"Choose a non—standard one."

"I can select "others", but here I need to fill out a detailed description."

"Okay, write: while experimenting, my head got stuck in the toilet . . ."

"You get in contact with the logistics service, right from there?"

"Yes, right from here. This sample did not respond to voice commands, although all the instruments showed the norm, I had to yell, and It again could not hear, I tried to make it as loud as possible and got stuck."

A few minutes later Dave requested additional access and the plumber rushed into the room. Forty minutes later the call came.

"That's it, close the work order. The work is done."

"Okay, just a minute, so, it says: Describe the nature and result of the work performed"

"What is the result? I neighed like a horse and the pressure of the water washed him out. It turned out that he was shouting voice commands for a prototype of a smart toilet for equids and clearly the toilet did not understand him, and when he climbed in, it apparently, wheezed and was sucked in."

"How long did it take to do the work itself?"

"Thirty seconds."

"And the rest of the time?"

"I was rolling on the floor laughing, now I can't even breathe."

"Well, okay, let's write down the work done in five minutes, prepare and clean thirty—five, and close the work order as successful. There is nothing else scheduled on your route, you can be free."

***

Dave got his corporate bunk. In the logistics department, the living quarters were not nearly as comfortable as on the space station. Behind partitions, ten people lived in a room. The lights in the room were never turned off, the service worked in shifts, and around the clock, employees went back and forth all night.

The dining room was very small and could barely fit 2 people. Food was served through special taps: liquid through taps similar to water taps, and solid through a wide rectangular tap in plastic bags. The only thing that's lucky here is the dishes. The 3D printer printed any utensils to taste, and every day you could choose something new. After eating, the tray with plates was thrown into the printer crusher, so there was always material for printing utensils.

Once upon a time, at the very beginning of the building's life, the company gave the department heads the task of collecting wishes from the staff on what they would like to have in their department, and the logistics department chose 3D printed tableware. The food did not match the beauty and elegance of the dishes—eating plastic soup from gilded royal dishes was still unpleasant. Pressing the burger button, he began to pour himself hot tea with citric acid, waiting for a bag to fall out of the square pipe. Two women burst into the kitchen: a girl with a large bust, Anna, and a chubby Neli.

"Hey young man, make room, aren't you against our company?" Neli said.

"No, no," answered Dave, pressed against the wall.

Nely took two bowls out of her purse and threw them into the crusher. Having pressed the order buttons for two lunches in ordinary tableware, she additionally pressed the print of two bowls similar to kitten ones, only larger.

"There you go again," said Anna. "Maybe it's enough to feed the ghost"

"Why so? He is kind and does not do evil."

"What ghost?" Dave entered into the conversation.

"The ghost from the fire escape. Every day I put two bowls of drink and food near the fire hatch, and the next day they are empty."

"But ghosts don't exist, and animals are prohibited on these floors."

"A fact is a fact," said Nely, the bowls disappear, and then appear again empty. At first, they simply disappeared, but we realized that there was nothing to print the dishes from, and we left a note asking him to return them. They've been coming back ever since."

"Strange, did you tell anyone about this?"

"Yes, to the security service, but they waved me off, saying that mysticism was not their profile. We tried to film the moment he disappeared, but as soon as we set up the cameras, he stopped taking the plates, and we decided to just put the food down."

"But that's a question . . ." Dave began.

"Drop this ghost, Anna, how is the purchasing department?"

Anna blushed, "nnormally."

"How was sex with Max?" Neli asked directly.

"What sex? I've never seen him before."

"But heard," Neli laughed. Although the absorbing shell muffles the moans of your capsule, they are still visible."

"Come on Neli, we're embarrassing the new guy."

Dave really felt awkward. He was surprised when an order for food delivery was received from the purchasing department and the woman who carried out the delivery began to speak voluptuously. Then learned that her dispatcher Dave, cut off the connection and changed the status of the work order to unsuccessful, with the comment "there is enough flour, there is no need for purchasing."

Taking his food, he decided to retreat. He politely asked the women to step aside, but Neli said that he was thin, and he was forced to squeeze between them, and as it seemed to him, instead of moving away from the wall, Neli, on the contrary, pressed on him with her whole body.

Once free outside the dining room, he breathed a sigh of relief. Laughter was heard from behind, and the women continued to joke and open up. Having finished the meal, he went on shift. For some time he sat in silence and thought about his prospects. "What awaits me here, it's comfortable here, there is a team, an adequate boss, and I can try to flirt with Neli and . . . " He sighed heavily and stared at the monitor. After some time, his thoughts were interrupted by a sound signal—work finally appeared and he threw away all his thoughts.

"Assigned tasks to the logistics department: Delivery of a submarine. Customer—procurement department. Destination: corporation pier. The place of dispatch is the underwater vehicle plant, index 351645.556."

He sat and re-read the information for several minutes, then opened the coordinates directory. The location of the plant turned out to be on the opposite side of the mainland, where there was still an ocean. He looked at the deadline, said "Two weeks" out loud, and stared blankly at the monitor for a few more minutes. He was not so much worried about the question of why they needed a submarine itself in the desert, but how and in what way to deliver it in two weeks.

After much thought, he dialed Chris and he was also somewhat surprised by the order. He said that he would set up a conference with the purchasing department and figure everything out. At the appointed time, Dave, Chris, and three representatives from the purchasing department began a video conference.

"Greetings," Chris began, "we have received a work order for the delivery of a submarine, is this another joke?"

"Everything is right," the head of the purchasing department entered the conversation, "we have completed our task, now it's your turn."

"Excuse me, of course, but why is there a submarine here? There is no sea here for a long time."

"Our job is to fulfill the order, and yours to deliver."

"And how should we do this? Hire farmhands to carry it 2,500 miles across the desert?"

"This is not our problem, we need to close the order. We are waiting for you to deliver it and post it in the corporate asset accounting system."

Chris turned purple. If the order was not completed on time, he could lose his place. But he had no idea how to deliver the submarine. There was no point in continuing the conference.

"Dave, contact the manufacturer and find out the details. Maybe it's only a toy or packed in boxes. Then we'll order a carriage and deliver it by rail."

After several hours of searching for the person in charge of the manufacturer's plant, they answered on the other side of the continent.

"Congratulations on your purchase! Your submarine has already been launched and is waiting for your representative to sail."

"How! Have you already launched it? But we need to transport it across the desert to the other end of the continent. Can you pick it up and load it into the carriage?"

"According to the terms of the agreement, the transfer of rights is carried out at the berth of the manufacturer's plant."

"But we can't deliver it by water."

"These are not our difficulties, you have fourteen days, then you can sign an agreement for the maintenance and rental of the berth. The amount will be astonishing because . . . one whole berth."

"Tell me at least characteristics."

"You should know, it was built according to your wishes and technical specifications."

"But I was not given any information. I am an employee of the logistics department, so I need to know the dimensions and weight to pack and order transport."

"Pack? Okay, just a minute . . . So, length is 200 m, width is 75 m, maximum height is 54 meters, weight is 1200 tons, and it is made of super—light material."

Dave silently wrote down the numbers, thanked him for the answer, and contacted Chris.

"We can only deliver this Crap by digging a three thousand kilometer long canal. At least water will appear in these places."

"Well, we are powerless here. I will convene an anti—crisis committee. Let them decide what to do. I'll invite you to a meeting."

***

Eliza sat in her white gilded chair at her new faux ivory table. These are probably the only two things she changed. And she wouldn't even have replaced the table if it hadn't been damaged. She disposed of many of the former CEO's things and put some in a separate closet. She did not feel entirely comfortable in her new place, and the time was hard, there was a little more than a month left before the bankruptcy procedure was declared, and the prospects for her and the entire corporation were painful.

Moreover, troubles kept pouring in. Someone ordered a luxury submarine. The costs of its delivery and maintenance were prohibitive for them. It was not possible to refuse since paying for disposal or maintenance at the pier was even more expensive than dragging it through the desert. To somehow understand who made this order and why, she requested a report from the procurement department and was now reading it in preparation for the meeting of the anti-crisis committee.

The report read: "The most beautiful CEO of all. We are pleased to announce that many years of work for the joy of employees and the greatness of the corporation has been completed. The houseboat is equipped with gyms, swimming pools, cinema theaters, and restaurants and is ready for entertainment. The best employees will now get additional motivation for more successful work. Management and key personnel will be able to remain safe at great depths in the event of a major war. An entire planning and purchasing department worked on this task for almost twenty years. We believe that the employees of our department deserve the insignia and encouragement. Our department's mission is complete. We have created a work order for the logistics department. Now it depends on them how quickly our first flagship will appear near the corporation's house." Eliza re-read it several times and put it aside. She knew nothing about it, and apparently neither did the previous CEO, otherwise, he would definitely have shared it with her.

But then the squares began to blink on the Screen and the meeting began. First, there were representatives from the logistics department: Chris and logistician Dave are responsible for delivery. For some reason, Dave's face was not visible. His square remained black, which was strictly prohibited. He apologized and said the camera was broken. Having learned that the CEO would be at the meeting, he was seriously scared because this was perhaps the only person who could expose him, despite certain changes in appearance.

Chris started. "Oh, Your Greatness, we cannot fulfill this work order, we are forced to close it as unsuccessful, because . . . there is no possibility . . . "

"Wait. Do not close." She said abruptly. "We need to figure it out first. Now the purchasing department will get involved. Norman, where and when did this order come from?"

Norman was actually a little surprised, to say the least. He knew absolutely nothing, it was like a bolt from the blue. Knowing full well the possible consequences, he collected all the available information.

"This order, Oh greatest one, launched the entertainment department seventeen years ago to celebrate the fifth anniversary of the founding of the corporation house."

"Just a minute, now I'll connect the entertainment department."

A disheveled woman in a dressing gown joined the conversation. She was clearly taken by surprise,

"Sunny! According to your profile, you have been working since the very beginning of the building's existence. HAVE YOU PLACED AN ORDER FOR A SUBMARINE?"

"I don't remember something like this, this is the first time I've heard it . . ."

"Really? Hearing this for the first time?" Norman said "Your name is indicated on the order."

"Submarine? Oh yes, I remember something, there was a surprise for the fifth anniversary of the HOME, but the sea finally dried up and we decided to launch the airship then."

"Why wasn't the order canceled?" continued Eliza.

"Nnnuh uh, so canceled, definitely canceled . . ."

"Nothing like this." Norman said, "No cancellation was."

"Well, how can I remember everything, it was so long ago, so many years have passed, and why do we need it, the sea has been gone for a long time . . ."

"Sunny," said Eliza, "There is no sea, but the submarine has already been built and is waiting for us to pick it up and plow the gray quartz sea. I wonder how you will organize a banquet and photo shoot against the backdrop of sandy waves."

"I, I, believe me, I . . . "

"We'll come back to you later. Norman tell me why it took so many years to fulfill the long-awaited dream of all employees. Why did it only come to light now?"

"You see . . . ," he began to justify himself, "immediately after the order was received, it was sent to the designer. But then there was a failure and a reboot of our HOME intelligence and the recording disappeared. As far as I was able to find out, they accidentally archived the envelope with the order without opening it. Two years ago they found it and immediately put it into operation. A year ago they sent an invoice for payment. Seeing the level of importance of the purchase was 1 and the fact that the implementation was fourteen years overdue, an employee of the financial directorate passed through an invoice. When the project came to the purchasing department, the employee decided since the order had just been approved, apparently it was relevant, and sent the order for production."

"Highest professionalism . . . Now what to do with this surprise? Continued the CEO. "Extermination procedures are not enough for us, but we also became the happy owners of expensive real estate. Give us your suggestions."

"Let's take the employees to the ocean and let the submarine float there," Sunny said, cheering up.

"Excellent offer, but what resources will we use to maintain it? Logistics department, what do you think?"

"It's easier to drown it than to deliver . . ." Chris entered.

"Hmm, there is something in this, but what will happen if it would be drown?"

"Only the legal department knows."

"Well, I'll connect them too." A bearded man in a hastily thrown-on robe appeared on the screen. "Chief lawyer, tell us about the consequences if we sink our submarine," the CEO continued, briefly outlining the situation.

"Unauthorized sinking is a crime. It has to happen by accident, and preferably before we take ownership."

"What if it sinks before the rights are transferred? What will happen?"

"According to international standards, the insurance corporation will have to compensate us for the damage: the cost of the submarine and moral compensation."

"Thank you, Chief Lawyer, you are free. Everyone except the logistics department—switch off. So Chris, do what you want, but either deliver it here or . . . I really hope that it will sink before the transfer, this could save the corporation. Do you hear Chris? BEFORE!"

"Yes, I heard, I will send Dave, the person in charge of the work, to "pick up" the submarine and deliver it to its destination."

***

A few days later, Dave hit the road. The only available route for his social ranking was the old railroad. The departure point was the 101st floor. He pressed a button and a rectangular box with a glass door dropped down in front of him. The door swung open and he walked in. When it closed, the box began to be filled with dense shockproof foam.

Metal forks lifted the box and placed it on the conveyor. Along the way, it was turned over and shaken. But Dave felt nothing, as the laughing gas that filled the space lulled him to sleep. It was carried through a long pipe to the railway station and placed flat in a carriage with various other containers.

The train screeched loudly and the odor of burning rubber even penetrated the box. Dave looked at the schedule: way station, stop for two hours. At this intermediate station, burnt rubber wheels were replaced with metal ones. "Now the train will go much faster," he thought, "one more shift to tires in the mountains and then iron wheels and rails again. Why couldn't this railway from the ocean to the dry sea be completed in one piece? The trip time could have been halved."

However, he understood that this was impossible. At the beginning of the route, due to the pumping of underground resources and the injection of silicone waste there to prevent landslides, the earth vibrated like silicone breasts. In the other part, the aborigines constantly stole rails and built houses from them.

At the junction station, the container was unloaded and given a few hours in the restroom. There was only a pilgrim Appleman there. They had a fast and did not communicate. He was traveling to the annual New Year's celebration. Observing the strictest fast, he did not eat, he only drank a little water. Periodically he covered his head with a blanket, and from there came crunching and slurping sounds. If no one sees, then the vow is not broken.

It was in handy. No one distracted him from thinking and planning the operation. He thought that if he had ever seen a submarine and understood how to operate it, he would have found a way to send it to the bottom, perhaps with him. Or maybe go to the far north, to the islands of the new land, where the weather was always comfortable, green, and beautiful. "No, no I have to succeed, I found a company that agreed to take the boat into service and management. The boat will go to sea, but . . . I just need to find the pirates. Where to look for them, they say that the port taverns are full of them, so we'll see."

At the next stop, he went out onto the station square. He was immediately surrounded by traveling salesmen and sales agents.

"Lotteries, buy a ticket! Try the perfume! Testers, take testers! Synthetic coffee! Gas masks, take gas masks! Fresh synthetic soup! Logins and passwords, logins and passwords! Photos with hermits! Carpets, traditional carpets . . ."

They surrounded him and pestered him with various stupid offers. There was no peace. A little further away stood apple pilgrims from other carriages. Nobody approached them, and it was useless. They bought absolutely everything only from their church—buying from others was strictly prohibited. Because of this, they looked quite alike, only according to the hierarchy they had three colors, the only way to understand their status. On the backs were large images of half an apple. On the front, there are small icons with the other half. They could be distinguished in any crowd.

The traders and promoters were out of luck, as was Dave—he was one of the few passengers who did not belong to the sect. No exchange means existed in the corporation. Given the exceptional situation, he was given several old commodity coupons. Realizing that he would not leave alone, bought from some old lady as she described the delicious local dish whose name is impossible to understand, the recipe is transmitted from generation to generation in secret, it is the last of the kind and he will be regretting if he does not buy.

He went into the stuffy restroom and closed the door behind him. In the end, he was alone. Dave opened the container and began to pick at the black sludge with a spoon. It smelled like burning rubber from train wheels that had just been changed. "Something disgusting." He put the dish aside and began to think about a plan of action.

There were about four hours left until the final station. The train was again riding on rubber wheels, it was rocking and tossing. Dave felt nauseous, his whole body itched, and only one thought dominated his head: "When will I finally get off this train."

He knew that the train was passing a field of abandoned airplanes. At some point, they all became unnecessary and were pulled here from all over the continent. "Even with these primitive machines, it would have been better." He was given a tour here when he was CEO. Now he is forced to cram into a small box in a dark carriage.

Next, the train had to pass by a tall fence, seemingly reaching the sky. It closed the acid swamps and prevented fumes from penetrating beyond its boundaries. However, there were rumors that a secret army was hiding there. As a former CEO, he knew very well that there were elite houses there. They just didn't want ordinary people to see how they lived and the huge gap between them.

The box containing Dave was unloaded at the final station. There was no longer a passenger delivery system here. The box was opened right there. He was met by a representative of the manufacturer's company. He apologized, saying that transport no longer goes to the port, and offered to stay in a hotel in another part of the city. Tomorrow they have a day off, so only after tomorrow they can meet.

Dave looked around and saw many minibuses with the sign station—port. But he didn't argue. It worked to his advantage. He could easily organize sabotage. They drove him for a long time and in what seemed like circles to him. Finally, the car stopped near the hotel. The company manager politely said goodbye and left. An unfriendly concierge greeted him. He asked the purpose of the visit and demanded confirming documents. Dave silently complied with all the requirements—he was damn tired after the train. Finally, he got to the bed, threw his things, and fell asleep.

***

Three saboteurs stood on the edge of the cliff and peered into the distance. Minitanks drove under the cliff and cyborg dragonflies flew everywhere.

"Second, what do you see?"

"No changes yet First."

"Third, are you ready?"

"Yes."

"Wait for the command."

The First looked around, later at the info map, nodded his head, and the third one climbed down. The success of the operation depended on whether the third one would be able to throw an electromagnetic mine as close as possible to the biotransformer. This should have stopped receiving the signal from the third implanted dragonfly eye camera for some time. These swarms were filming chaotically, but due to their number, there was no place left without observation. The powerful intelligence of the security system processed images and removed numerous duplicate frames.

The Third came as close as possible to the transformer and looked at his watch, he waited until the command to action appeared on the monitor. The first one hesitated for some reason. The Third was lying on his haunches and his legs were swollen. The First was still waiting for the moment when the minitanks were very far away. It was impossible to hesitate any longer and the First sent a message. The Third took out a large slingshot, took the mine, pulled the rubber band all the way, and fired. Mine fell nearby and began to knock. The first one was about to blow it up when suddenly a flying squirrel appeared and grabbed the mine.

The First cursed himself and wrote: plan B. "Second, you come to me, Third you are run as soon as the dragonflies fly away. I will run after you, and whoever gets there first will install a hole punch underwater on the hull of the boat." The Second quietly crept up. The First took out some kind of jar and began to generously coat the suit of the Second with a thick brownish mixture. A buzzing sound was heard in the distance. The First took off his gloves and handed them over along with the unclosed can. And he ordered with expressive lips: "RUN!" The Second did not linger and ran as fast as he could. He was very dissatisfied with his lot and was angry with the Third for throwing the mine unsuccessfully. Before the operation, they threw the dice, and the choice was made.

A powerful rumble was approaching in the distance, it was getting closer and closer. Giant bloodsuckers with needles capable of piercing a tin can were approaching from all sides. It was deadly. Such a number of mosquitoes can gnaw the victim down to the bone in half an hour.

A terrible roar hung over his head, it pressed on his brains. The second ducked down, covered his ears, and cowered as much as possible in anticipation of the attack. It began to seem to him that a mosquito had crawled through his hands straight into his ear and was buzzing straight into his brain. He felt an itch on his back. It was a swarm of mosquitoes trying to chew through his suit.

The itching intensified, the massive attack was successful, and he felt the touch of a thousand stings on his skin. Suddenly the itching stopped. The buzzing did not disappear but became more chaotic. "Finally". Opening his eyes slightly, he saw the greatest battle—a cloud of dragonflies merged with a cloud of mosquitoes. It was a fantastic spectacle filled with powerful sound effects. Being at the epicenter is like being inside a centrifuge with a brass band. The Third took out a towel and began to dry himself, gradually moving away from the epicenter.

The First was waiting. Suddenly it became absolutely quiet, as if everything had frozen in time. A few seconds later, the dragonflies, attracted by a powerful roar, abandoned their swamp and went hunting. The Third was no longer waiting for the command, he ran at full speed towards the dock, followed by the First. There was only one submarine at the pier.

The instructions said to sink a vessel called HOME. There was no inscription. "Maybe they didn't have time to apply it in time for the opening." However, this no longer mattered—the Third threw himself into the water. The First threw the bag and it opened into the shape of a small boat and rushed into the water. Taking the oars, he rowed towards the submarine and picked up the Third. Turning on the silent engine, they began to quickly move away beyond the horizon.

His eyes showed satisfaction. Yesterday, some eccentric provincial in a tavern offered him a lucrative job and immediately paid. He gave three certificates for 10 hectares of land on the South Sea coast. He opened the map, it was land close to the city and right next to the sea for luxury development on the seaside boulevard. Well, a military pensioner could only dream of such a gift from fate.

***

At ten in the morning a luxurious retro car, long and gilded, drove up to the hotel. Dave, in a suit, was already waiting. The door opened automatically and now they finally headed to the port where the launching ceremony was planned. The car raced along a dirty port road, passing hangars and tanks, with difficulty driving through narrow turns between containers. Finally, they were there.

Near the submarine with a huge golden inscription "HOME," there was a podium, on which a small orchestra and exotic dancers sat. A man in a golden tailcoat and an equally long hat jumped onto the podium. It was immediately difficult to recognize the gloomy man who met Dave at the station.

"Welcome to the ceremony! Today the great HOME corporation will receive its well-deserved gift!"

Music and dancing began on stage. After half an hour of a rather boring performance, the presenter came out again.

"And now I invite corporate representative Dave to the stage!"

"How do you like performance? Are you ready to send the ship on a long voyage?"

"Performance . . . yes, a wonderful performance, I can't wait to send this ship . . ."

"Well, now take an inflatable bottle and point it at the body, but more strongly. If it bounces off, the ship will endlessly plow the sea."

Dave was given a large rubber bottle shaped like champagne. It was somewhat larger than himself. Having accelerated, he pushed the bottle towards the submarine. To everyone's surprise, when it collided with the body, it squealed and hissed and, having released all the air, hung helplessly on the rope. There was silence for several minutes. Then the trumpeter apparently decided to joke and repeated this rather disgusting sound on the trumpet.

"Don't be upset," said the presenter, " the bottle has been standing for a long time in the sun and is apparently cracked. Let's go to a gala dinner. And along the way, I will give you a tour."

They walked around the submarine for several hours looked into the cinema, meeting room, bowling alley, and swimming pool, bedrooms, galley, and a huge viewing window through which you can enjoy the underwater world. Finally, they arrived at the dining room. The table was filled with all sorts of things from all over the world, most of them fake. The only real food they served was shell soup, a decoction of seaweed, and for dessert, jellyfish in sugar.

"Frankly, it's quite surprising that you were sent here alone. Usually, the CEO, his deputies, and heads of departments come to the descent. I heard that the HOME is a big corporation."

"As circumstances have developed, the ceremonial events will take place at the corporation's pier. All employees will be able to come and appreciate the greatness."

"Interesting. Of course, it would be better for me to talk to the CEO. What are your powers?"

"Receive the submarine and deliver it."

"This is understandable, but the submarine requires running-in and testing in real conditions. I suggest giving it away for testing for at least a year. It will travel around the world and you will receive a proven ship with an experienced and seasoned crew."

"No, I . . ."

"Listen, contact management, tell them about this idea, present it correctly and we will thank you." The presenter became angrier and more insistent. "Judge for yourself, you don't even have a team and a program of travel and events, it takes time to work it all out."

"No, today the team will prepare the submarine for departure."

"Let's agree . . ."

Then suddenly a powerful explosion sounded and there was a hole in the floor through which water could be seen. "Damn," Dave thought, "Too early." He tried to look astonished. The presenter at this time looked indifferently into the gaping hole in the corner of the dining room.

"Where are the lifeboats?" Dave decided to ask.

"Why the hell do we need them . . ."

"So we'll drown," Dave began to worry. He looked down. However, the water did not rise and the boat did not seem to be going to sink. "I can't take it like this, you have to patch it up."

The presenter was still at a loss, poured a clear liquid into a large glass, and drained it in one gulp. He sat silently for several minutes and continued the conversation.

"Patch it . . . let's try to patch it up. Listen, buddy, how much do you want to sign the transfer and acceptance certificate?"

"And the submarine?"

"Well, the news will show that she drowned in a tropical storm."

"This puzzled Dave. He was at a loss but pulled himself together."

"I have to deliver the submarine to the company's pier, or I need reimbursement or insurance after all."

"Costs . . . Insurance . . . However, insurance! I have one insurance agent who is a drunk. I will come to an agreement with him, you just need to draw up a transfer and acceptance certificate and conclude an agreement with the insurance company."

"But, how come the submarine isn't insured, what if something happened at sea?"

"Nothing will happen to it—the concrete supports will stand forever."

"What supports?" and then Dave understood why the water didn't rise. "I don't understand, explain!"

"We haven't made any submarines for a long time, this is a model."

"So why don't you build?"

"Because there's no one who can. The design department was closed. Everything was built according to standard designs for the Navy, and when they refused orders, we switched to custom ones. But as it turned out, there was no one else to design."

"How? You write in brochures, show photographs.."

"Come on, we agreed to rent a submarine and test it out. Often they were completely forgotten. Sometimes employees came for a cruise, but we got them so drunk and rocked that they didn't even understand that they weren't leaving the port. We said that there is a storm at the top, it's safer underwater, and there's a lot of entertainment. Only on the overview screen, the video of underwater life was played. No one has figured it out yet. If it weren't for this explosion . . ."

Chapter 4

Smart Seller

Six interns sat in comfortable straight-back chairs. Coach Zhanna required constant attention. It was comfortable to sit in these chairs, but you had to keep your back constantly stretched. The furniture for the classroom was made individually according to the requirements of the trainers.

Today there was a routine reading of the basic theory of intellectual utility management. Two or three times a month she began training a new group. Sellers rarely lasted for long, so there was a lot of work. However, she hated this routine, and if it weren't for the control of the BITCH. Zhanna would have been given materials for reading the basics of intellectual utility management, and better waste her time reading ancient documentary literature. She especially liked reading Dumas' chronicles.

Zhanna herself was a successful trainer-developer. She was one of the participants in the project to automate the learning process. Robotic trainers were created to replace ineffective humanoids. The project promised success and an increase in her social rating to first class, and she actively worked on the project to be able to live for her pleasure. But the project was a total fiasco.

Robot trainers with the latest version of artificial intelligence firmware could not stand stupid questions. Their pure correct logic did not understand unexpected requests: Can I go to the toilet? Why doesn't he wear panties? Where does artificial intelligence live? Their boards burned out and the need to constantly replace robotic trainers led to the unprofitability of the project. An attempt to save the project was the decision to install a stun gun in them. But after two incidents the program was closed. In one case, a prankster participant brought a sex robot with him and the robot trainer went berserk after a series of intimate proposals and began shocking everyone. In another case, two participants began discussing their pedicure and heatedly argued about which was better. The robot trainer, after ten minutes of argument, struck his processor with a discharge. This was the first documented case of self-destruction in robots. Now Zhanna had to do boring work without any hopes for a promising future.

"Let's begin our training. Let's start with history. The corporation was founded by engineer Vincent van HOME to improve the efficiency of public utilities. In the old days, it was ineffective. It was necessary to build water purification systems and thousands of kilometers of pipelines to deliver it. There were millions of kilometers of sewer pipes to pump out and treat waste. They extracted various flammable materials from the earth to heat houses and cook food using barbaric methods over fire."

"Imagine even the garbage was sorted and taken to special landfills. Residents hired companies that serviced these communications. They employed a huge number of people. There were such professions as plumbers, electricians, gardeners, and cleaners. All this was an enormous burden on the economy. There were a huge number of enterprises engaged in this area. The World Council was concerned about the existence of such a huge independent sector of the economy. Vincent proposed merging all utilities into one corporation to create an effective system for providing households with utility services."

"Now the basic concepts. Let's go over the basic terms and concepts. This is necessary so that you understand well the importance of the HOME Corporation."

1. *A household* is an isolated territory for the location of registered biological beings bound by permission to live together at a designated time to ensure processes related to their life activity.

2. *SLAVE*—support lazy alive vulnerable entities. A system that manages households and residents.

3. *Former household member.* A biological creature that has lost the right to register in a given household is subject to disposal.

4. *Living space.* Territory allocated to a specific household member according to internal rating.

5. Unauthorized reconstruction—reconstruction and (or) redevelopment carried out without the permission of the SLAVE.

6. Visitors are biological beings who have the right to stay on the territory of the household.

7. Repairs are a hobby that residents engage in without the participation of the corporation.

8. The contract for the provision of utility services is mandatory for all residents to comply with the SLAVE commands.

9. Neighbors—a group of people or an individual whose household is physically adjacent and with whom it is prohibited to establish any contact according to security requirements.

"That's enough for now, let's take a break for ten minutes."

The participants gathered around the round table.

"Pills to improve attention, and memory, to reduce sexual desire and only energy water."

"Well, what did you want, this is training."

"I would prefer regular coffee and donuts. What fun are these pills?"

"Try five of all types, and we'll see the effect."

"No, thank you. Let's get Coach some pills in the water, maybe the training will be more fun." Everyone laughed.

"Well, really, what is the use of terms, what relation do they have to our work or reality?"

"These terms are embossed in the source code—this is the basis of our civilization."

"The basis, the basis, what's the point? We all have a fourth or fifth rating. Have you ever heard of anyone rising from a corporation to a second level? Do you know at least one person with a third?"

"Chill out. Get back to your seats and let's move on."

Dave walked indifferently to his seat. He was somewhat annoyed by this career turn. After the submarine incident, Eliza decided to reorganize and merge two departments into one. Several positions were combined and he was laid off. He was offered a vacancy as a smart salesperson and accepted due to the lack of alternatives.

In the smart sales department, there was a large turnover. Few people fulfilled the plans. Three months of not fulfilling meant firing. Although there were exceptions—several people were always set as an example, they received all the prizes and awards. The rest were constantly changing, so trainings were held regularly. Dave didn't count on success, but he had three months left, and he expected that during this time he would come up with something.

"Well, let's continue. This is the theoretical part of our training, we will look at the stages of sales, and then you will receive scripts and algorithms for our products. You will need to study them before starting your internship. I remind you that the internship is three days. At the end of it, half of you will remain—the most successful ones." She pressed a button on the tablet and the sales stages appeared on the screen. "The first one is the connection to SLAVE."

Dave wasn't listening, he was immersed in his own thoughts. He was depressed. The way to the top seemed to be quick and easy. He was expecting a reward for his successful operation. But no, instead he was essentially fired. This was a very convenient way to get rid of an employee. Just three months to go. Periodically, information broke through into his brain. "Theory, stupid theory . . . " He thought. "How can you sell something to a client when all purchases are handled by SLAVE? Residents have no influence. Certain changes can be made by the security and medical corporations."

Zhanna: "Sometimes residents are surprised by new products and ask home AI questions about where they came from, etc. To avoid this, you need to convince them that they themselves wanted it. To do this, we agree with the system to set the order time at least two weeks earlier, then they won't remember whether they ordered it or not. But in some cases, there are clients with longer memory, and then blocking is needed. The SLAVE should not accept any arguments, it should convince that this is absolutely necessary and there are no procurement alternatives."

"Fourth step. Neither residents nor SLAVE should be aware of the availability of any alternatives. Alternatives sow doubt, which is destructive. You must fill the system memory with only one product. All analogs must be removed from memory. The search engine should be filled with queries only for this product. This work needs to be done every day for, a maximum of two weeks. After this period no one will look for anything anymore."

Dave laughed to himself. "Yee . . . , no one remembers." The number of complaints about the unauthorized implantation of goods and services into the SLAVE procurement plan was enormous. Residents have been pushing for years to have them removed from the system and return to previous settings. Sometimes this was successful and they get compensation.

Zhanna: "And finally the most important—the fifth step. We've already done a lot of work. But what point of it if the customer can cancel the order within fourteen days or remove the product from regular purchases? Unfortunately, we are limited here by corporate law. Therefore, it is very important to load positive emotional experiences into the SLAVE memory."

"First, you need to upload pictures of happy neighbors (information in your profile and their virtual images will be found in the sales management system. You will be given the necessary rights). Next, don't forget to do the most important thing: after a maximum of three days, upload positive and vivid memories of the residents when they first became acquainted with the product. They must be completely sure that they bring them joy and happiness."

"If residents express dissatisfaction at first, delay uploading their emotions for a few more days. There are situations when customers want to return the goods, then under any pretext we postpone it for as long as possible. Say that we will definitely remove it from the procurement plan if they don't change their mind. When the time comes, we tell and show how they enjoyed this product or service, and show pre-prepared videos of their emotions and pleasures. After that, no one ever refused. That's all for today. Go and study scripts, your internship will start tomorrow."

***

The booth was smaller and the chair was not as comfortable as in the logistics department. The day began and ended with the salesman's anthem. It was difficult to negotiate with the smart home system. Users learned to block access. Even though the HOME fully provided households with utilities, residents were often dissatisfied with intrusive service and the upselling of additional services.

Despite the notice "Disabling remote access can lead to disruption of the functioning of the home and poses a threat to life and health," most of the SLAVEs were blocked. Therefore, it was necessary to first request access from household administrators. Sometimes finding out who has access was not easy. Usually they said that they forgot their password, sometimes it was true, sometimes it was a lie.

In the local area care department, the plan for connecting automatic lawnmowers was poorly implemented, and now the entire smart sales department was busy promoting them. It would be a great thing to have on a household, but many complained that the ground near the house had long since dried out and the grass was not growing. "Hello, my name is

Dave, I am a representative of HOME corporation. I . . . " This is usually how the conversation ended with clients who cut off the connection. Rarely did a conversation even begin.

"Hello, my name is Dave. I am a representative of HOME corporation."

"Hello"

"Do you like lawns with shaped grass?"

"Who doesn't love them, but where can we get them? In our area, artificial lawns are prohibited, and the grass doesn't want to grow. It's good that you called, though. I haven't been able to contact you for a month now. Disable my gardener service, it was connected by mistake, there is no garden here."

"Miss Lucia," Dave looked at the profile of the house: an elderly lonely woman who loves cats. "Well, there's not enough information in the profile."

"I have an excellent offer," he continued. "I offer you an additional option: a smart mini lawn mower, which will create a beautiful pattern for your lawn."

"I wish I had a mini excavator to bury the cat poop in this lawn. Disable the service!"

"To disable services, you must contact support"

"In the end, help me turn off the gardener service and then I'll think about it. Otherwise, don't call me again!"

Dave called the supervisor, outlined the situation, and asked if it was possible to turn off the gardener service. Then the client was ready to agree to the proposal for a lawn mower.

"Well, it will be difficult," said supervisor Sarah, "the retention department will never agree, but tell me her subscriber number."

"LU 6268458."

"Let's look into history. So, Dave, yeah, oh no, this cunning old lady has already managed to refuse one service in this way. She promised to immediately take another one in return. But then she ignored the calls and we achieved nothing. Leave it."

"But she was the only one who answered."

"Don't despair, this is only your fourth shift. After the tenth, we will discuss the situation and find solutions."

Dave returned to his little capsule and continued. No one else came into contact during this shift. All accesses to SLAVEs were secured and nothing was achieved. "Well, they might fire me faster than I thought." He closed the program, left the capsule, and headed to the dining room.

To his surprise, it was huge in the smart sales department, with cozy relaxation areas. There were vases of sweets and cookies, bottles of juices, and coffee machines everywhere. The food itself was mediocre, and the dishes were disposable and made of thin silicone. Most were content with sweets and cookies. He walked towards an area with huge brown sofas, grabbed coffee and cookies, and literally fell into the soft fabric.

"How is it Dave, if you don't mind, I'll sit down," a large, seemingly round man came into the area and, without waiting for an answer, plopped down next to him on the sofa. Dave thought he jumped to the ceiling but landed in the same place. It's good that coffee was on the table.

"Everything is fine Donut," Dave answered sarcastically. Nobody called Donut by name, and he himself probably didn't remember it anymore.

"I put two lawnmowers in today. The supervisor told me that this was the second result of the day. I received a silver star!"

"Yes, I see. Well done, keep it up."

"Just three more sales and I'll hit my quota early, then I won't leave until the next period starts. I'm just couch-hopping at this point. How many have you sold so far?"

"Non," Dave said irritably.

"You're not trying hard enough."

"How can I try, I've only got one successful contact in all this time. All others drop the connection."

"Maybe the base is bad, worked out many times. If you are a beginner, they won't give you a good base right away so as not to spoil it."

"But how can I achieve results?"

"As soon as you make your first sale, they'll hook you up with a better list right away."

"What if I don't? And how to do it if there are zero contacts!"

"Well, you can go up to the supervisor at night and ask, she doesn't refuse anyone." Donut smiled sarcastically. "Okay, don't be upset, there is life outside the corporation too. Only the best sellers survive." He took the entire vase with sweets and a whole bottle of juice, moved to a huge chair, against the background of which he no longer seemed so big and round, and noisily began to tuck all into.

***

Dave stood outside Sarah's private room and did not dare to enter. In the small hall where all the sellers huddled, there were only small beds and bedside tables pressed closely together. Few people stayed here for long. The best, holders of a bronze, silver, or gold star, were entitled to separate bedrooms with a work desk, gaming chair, and computer. The composition of the winners practically did not change, so they didn't even take their things from the bedrooms, because they knew that they would return to them. They behaved proudly and separately.

It was impossible to hide anything in the relatively cramped space. He quickly found out why the salespeople went to the supervisors' bedrooms in the evening. They didn't give good databases for nothing. They demanded something in return from everyone. Often it was sex, sometimes they just liked to humiliate someone and watched as the seller crawled on his knees and begged to give him the best material. They also loved to combine it all and have fun with several sellers at the same time.

He dared and knocked. The door was opened by Sarah in a strict tight-fitting suit. She had a whip in her hands. In the corner on the sofa, a couple was having sex. Sarah didn't want anything that day, but she didn't want to give up the base just like that. She couldn't reschedule for another day, because. sales were not going well and it was necessary to provide better bases anyway. Therefore, she had fun watching a couple of sellers copulate and beat them with a whip urging them on and then stopping them. She looked at Dave with obvious displeasure. She likes him and would prefer that he come another day.

"What do you want?"

"I would like to talk."

"So speak, since you came."

"I need it, I've only made one contact so far, so in general I need a good base."

"Look at him, give him a good base. First, show the result on that one, and then we'll see."

"I can't get through to anyone. I really need a sale," Dave pleaded.

"Since you truly need it, join those two, let's see how much you need the base."

Dave stood there confused. He understood that without a base he would not survive in this department and then his career in the corporation would end. But he was also not ready to humiliate himself and join the orgy.

Coming here, he prepared himself as best he could and was confident in his intention. When the door opened and he saw all this, he fell into a daze. Trying to control himself, he coughed nervously. He apologized and said he was ill and had withdrawn. Sarah stared after him for a few minutes, then sighed and told the couple that was enough and ordered them to get out quickly. The couple, in a hurry, blushing, grabbed their things and, without having time to dress, were thrown out the door.

For a long time, he could fall asleep. He was tormented by thoughts and doubts, he wanted to run somewhere, do something. He sat on the bed for several minutes and suddenly jumped up. The canteen was available 24 hours a day. Nervously taking a cup, he poured coffee into it and sat down on a pink chair. "What to do?" The eternal question tormented him. "I seem to be in a dead end and there is no way out. They don't provide normal databases. A salesperson works on average for three to four months, then he is replaced. Only a few remain. They get everything, both the base and the sales. Even if I ask the supervisor for an adequate base, it will extend my life in the department by several months, no more."

"Strange choice of zone," said a female voice in the darkness.

"Who is there?" Dave asked, peering into the dark.

"It's me, Lola," the girl answered, sitting up slightly behind the back of the chair that covered her body. "Usually, this place is chosen by girls who prefer chatting with each other."

"I didn't know . . . " Dave looked around, he was in a glamorous area with pink furniture in the shape of hearts and pluff animals. "I just chose the first chair I came across in the dark."

"Come on, why can't you sleep in the middle of the night? Are your plans got you tormenting?" She grinned.

"Yes, probably."

"Happens."

"Why are you here in the middle of the night?"

"I'm waiting for my friend."

"Date?" He joked.

"Secret." She answered.

"I won't bother you?"

"You can help a little, though."

"How?"

"Do you want to fulfill the minimum plan?"

"Of course, I want."

"Then listen, my friend worked D2D in sales of chewing gum substitutes. This product's a pain to work with, so they've got tons of ways to get results. She'll come and fill you in on everything."

A little later, Zoe entered the area and leaned closer to Lola. She immediately noticed Dave and glanced sideways in his direction, and then questioningly at Lola. She just nodded meaningfully.

"Come closer. There are few normal clean databases, they simply won't give us any, so we need to use other methods."

"But which ones?"

"We need to place an official announcement in SLAVE. The gist is approximately this: Due to planned climate change in your area, humidity will increase, and a sharp growth of grass is expected, it is necessary to prevent it from growing more than four centimeters so that it does not become infected with insects. If there is a violation, the household's rating will be downgraded."

"I don't understand how this will help," asked Lola.

"This is a hoax," Dave continued, "residents can complain."

"Isn't it the same we do every day?"

"Are you with us or not?"

"Okay, I'm with you."

"So listen," Zoe continued. "You need to physically connect to the home intelligence interface. We need to leave now and return in two hours. I will show the area of houses that you need to go around on the map."

"But how do we get there so quickly? There is no transport."

"Dave, can you ride a bike?"

"Yes."

"Great, unfortunately, I can't. Below, Lola knows where two bicycles are tied up, I'll give you the keys."

"How can I connect to it without a password?"

"I'll give you twenty. Even if we are lucky in half the cases, we will carry out the plan."

"Where did you get these passwords?" Dave was surprised.

"Don't ask unnecessary questions. Do you want to fulfill the plan or not?"

Half an hour later they were already riding bicycles along the embankment highway. The sand creaked under the wheels, and bicycles sometimes had to be carried over wind—blown mounds. There was pitch darkness all around. This part of the road was abandoned long ago. The only landmark was a bright piece of sky ahead, which was illuminated by city lamps. After 45 minutes they were there. They took out corporate vests and put them on. Nobody will check them.

They took turns connecting to the mailboxes and applying their tablets to them. Quite quickly they walked around fourteen houses. Suddenly they noticed two silhouettes. One of them climbed over a low parking lot. The other at that time pressed something on the electrical box and the lights in the house went out.

Sales department employees often communicated with clients, so they did not believe in vampires, but clients periodically talked about a gang that robbed houses and ate their inhabitants. Lola and Dave hid behind trash cans, preferring to wait out potential danger.

A few minutes later the lights in the house came back on. They saw a big Figure near the pillar. The outline of the man seemed very familiar to Dave. The second one hid near the window. Something was glowing dimly in his hand. For some time nothing happened. And then, suddenly, the man near the window raised his thumb, quickly jumped over the fence and both took out flying electromagnetic scooters and quickly got away.

"Dave, it's not safe here, and there's not much time left," Lola whispered. "We need to leave."

The street was quiet and nothing else was happening. Only in the distance did the sky begin to turn pink, with pure predawn colors. There was very little time left. They jumped on their bicycles and rushed as fast as they could to the corporation building. There was no need to look for directions. Against the backdrop of dawn, the building loomed above the clouds in an ominous gray—pink hue.

***

The regular debriefing meeting has started. The month of sales effort is over. It's time to determine the best and those who will leave the team. As expected, the first three places were taken by the same sellers as in all previous periods. Dave, Lola, Zoe, and two other people joined those who met the plan.

Zoe's idea worked. They purposefully called the houses they visited to record sales from the system. They managed to make six sales between the three of them. Everyone else was thanked for their efforts, wished success in other positions, and said goodbye.

For some reason Zoe was not among the lucky ones, no one knew where she was, and her tablet was disconnected from the network. Sarah was fierce. This happened for the first time, and the number of eight winners was also rare. She announced a costume ball for the winners. It was scheduled for the evening.

The choice of costumes turned out to be quite limited. Their appearance left many questions. It seemed that they had lived a much more turbulent life than many people. In the end, Dave had to agree to wear the pink bunny costume. Lola, with whom he was choosing a suit, did not suit anything except a suit made of completely transparent fabric with the strange name naked woman. In this form, they went to the dining room and sat down in soft chairs while waiting for the event to begin.

"Where did Zoe disappear to? I haven't seen her since yesterday."

"I don't know, Dave, I'm very worried, I saw her before going to bed at night, and no one has seen her since then."

"It's very strange, she couldn't go to some abandoned section? Dave remembered his adventures in the elevator."

"It doesn't look like her, and she's never gone anywhere without me before."

The lights dimmed and the feast began. On the table, there was an elite pear drink from the caves of Antarctica, Hawaiian frog wings, and caramelized hedgehogs. Before starting, the Supervisors rolled out a huge portrait of Pavel I—the founder of the department and sales guru. According to legend, he made a thousand sales in the first month. Each received a medal with Pavel's image and solemnly swore to strive to get closer to his result.

Dave knew this story from the corporation's archives. There really was a salesman who made a thousand sales a month. Only it was not Pavel, it was Marquise, and the result was achieved due to the fact that during the division of markets, all utilities were transferred to the Home corporation and it was urgently necessary to conclude contracts for the provision of services. Pavel was a failed coach who appropriated this story to boast about it during his training.

Finally, the delicacies and fun could begin. Some stuffed their mouths with food, others began to dance, and some began to jump on upholstered furniture. Sarah decided to diversify the evening with a game and invited everyone to the table to play "Find and Strangle the Teddy Bear." She dealt out ten cards.

Each participant took turns taking theirs and becoming familiar with their role. The task was to identify first the bear and then the strangler. And only in this order. If they found the strangler first, the bear won. The game was quite fun and tense. Everyone played their roles well. Suddenly the light went out.

"What happened?"

"Maybe hackers?"

"No, they were never here."

"Maybe they decided to save energy at night?"

"Shh," Sarah said loudly, "calm down! Technical support will sort it out, but for now, we will repeat the sales stages."

Dave felt some kind of buzz in his head, his mind became cloudy and everything became like a fog, the voices in the distance died down. When he opened his eyelids, there was light, but his head seemed to be stuck and out of place. There were no thoughts. Gradually, he began to turn his head in different directions and it seemed to him that all the participants were waking up after a severe hangover.

Everyone was silent and moved their hands and heads chaotically. His gaze settled on a red-haired woman with unusually clear eyes. He fixed his gaze on her. After some time of intent but meaningless contemplation, some familiar process began in his head—something was rushing to the surface. Suddenly, as if breaking through a concrete wall, a thought jumped to the surface—sound and clear. Zoe, he's been looking at her all this time. Why was he staring at her? It's indecent, and he turned his gaze to a plate full of frog wings at the other end of the table. "It's strange, someone took a good third of all the wings and doesn't eat."

The fun somehow stopped on its own. No one looked at the time, but it seemed to everyone that it was already very late and they needed to go and rest. Everyone scattered to their beds. Dave lay down and discovered that his index finger was dirty. He didn't want to go to the washbasin. His head was still living a parallel life. And then he automatically reached into his pocket and took out a napkin. It was dirty, he turned it around to find a clean area and froze. The napkin had writing on it the same color as the dirt on his finger. In crooked letters, you could make out the word "Donut". The head began to gradually return to its place and the usual swarm of thoughts filled the brains.

Dave could not fall asleep, although his head was still heavy and his eyes were drooping, but his thoughts did not allow him to do so. He got up with difficulty and headed to the dining room. Everything was still there. He looked again at the large plate of wings. "Donut plate. What the heck?" He sat down in a chair, threw his head back, and suddenly jumped up as if someone had pricked him from below.

"Donut! Where's Donut?"

"Why are you yelling, stopping me from meditating?" Sarah stood up and leaned out into the light from behind the back of the large sofa.

"The light was turned off and he disappeared."

"Who disappeared?"

"Donut."

"Who, who?"

"The man behind this plate." Dave pointed to a large half-gnawed portion of frog wings.

"I don't get it. What's the big deal? There was probably no one there. They probably just filled one plate for the company."

"No, there was a man sitting there—a member of our team."

"You're clearly burned out, as it happens, after the first award. You drank too much sparkling wine, those treacherous southern pears. Go get some sleep."

"But, I remember exactly . . ."

"Don't bother me! We don't have any fat men and never have! Go to your place!"

Lying on his bed, he looked at his reward. Sleep did not want to come. He missed something important and sometimes he thought that he had grabbed the right thought by the tail, but it quickly slipped away. "Let's recall, the light went out, then my head, then I opened my eyes, looked around, a girl, then a plate with frog wings . . . Stop! Young woman! How could I not have guessed it right away? It's Zoe!" He began to breathe harder.

"So what if Zoe, well, she's the winner and should have been there. What is happening to me?" He again began to recall the trip to the settlement and Lola proposed the idea. And suddenly his heart began to beat loudly. He thought about Zoe's absence from the ceremony and was able to connect her appearance and the disappearance of Donut. "Or maybe there was no fat man at all, I just imagined it." He stood up and headed to the corner of honor, there stood a portrait of Paul the First, and the happy faces of the winners of the planning period shone on the screen. All familiar faces, but there was no fat man there.

***

"Zoe, hi, a superb dress, let's go pour you some coffee." They sat down at the coffee table in the purple section. "Where have you been?"

"I was here all the time," she answered confidently.

"Of course, you were gone from the evening before the ceremony until the moment when the light went out and the fat man who took second place disappeared somewhere."

"Dave, you must have a fever. Drink tea," she joked.

"Maybe there was a fever, but only at that moment when the light went out. Before the light, there was a fat man and you were not there, I remember exactly when the light appeared and you disappeared."

"What an imagination you have. Leave me alone. You invited me for coffee, I thought you had finally paid attention to me, and you kept pestering me with stupid questions. Back off." She stood up abruptly, took a cup of coffee, and quickly left.

"Why are you lying? Tell the truth!" He shouted after her.

"Psycho, look at the cameras again. You probably drank too much sparkling wine and mistook the sofa for a salesman, hahaha." A nervous laugh was heard going into the distance.

Dave was not satisfied with the conversation. It was late and he went to bed. He lay down in bed and closed his eyes. Only in mind was the same picture—a filled plate near an empty chair, good-looking Zoe, standing out from the rest with her freshness and clear eyes.

"Well, I couldn't have imagined it, and why would I write sauce on a napkin? Maybe it's a huge prank or I've had too much drink. Something is tormenting me from within, I've definitely got something on my mind. It would be nice to see the camera footage. Then it would be possible to understand exactly what happened. Eh, recording."

Suddenly Dave sat up straight from the bed, an epiphany came to him. He realized where he could watch the recording. "But how will I get into her office, I don't have access, even if it remains, she may notice that I came in. Technical floor!"

Above the 999th floor, there was another floor the size of ten. This was the technical floor. He remembered the evacuation capsule. In the event of an attack, explosion, or fire, it was impossible to descend from such a height in time. Therefore, on each upper floor, there were rooms with capsules that were fired in case of danger.

In order not to clutter the interior, the first CEO ordered three capsules to be placed on the technical floor. The hatch could only be opened from the inside by an alarm signal, but from the outside, it could easily be opened. He noticed this while inspecting his new office. Above 999 there was quite a lot of equipment in need of maintenance and there was a special elevator going there. "I just had to figure out how to get into this elevator."

"Work order 41564131654. Give me access to the special elevator. The access code does not function."

"Just a minute. I don't have such a work order in my system."

"They didn't approve it on time again. There is absolutely no time, less than an hour left to complete the work."

"But there is no such WO."

"Look at your system, they gave me this number."

"Yes, indeed there is such a number, but there is no description or approval."

"As usual, they forgot. Open access. They will approve it after the work is done."

"I have no right, without . . . "

"Listen, buddy, I need to replace a burnt—out element of the CEO satellite communication system. Can you imagine what will happen if I don't replace it on time?"

"I'll ask the management."

Ten minutes later the doors opened and Dave rushed to the thousandth floor. Being a logistician, he was given the task of dealing with WOs that were overdue for more than a year. Essentially, there were errors in the system and he removed them. But there were several that froze and did not close for some reason. He did not have enough time to find out what happened. But since he knew their numbers, than decided to use them. He knew that they were correct and even though the head of the department would be surprised that it was three years overdue, but since it was for the CEO, he would let it pass.

The head of the logistics department actually doubted it at first. He reviewed WO several times. Then he decided that someone had done an order for the planned replacement of a part, this work was ignored and then completely forgotten. And now, apparently, this part burned out and had to be urgently replaced. They couldn't open a new one because the old one was still active. The technical service, instead of contacting the department and asking to restart the workcorder, decided not to risk possible fines for failure to complete the work and fool the fool.

Now all that remains is not to get lost on the huge five—tier floor and find the emergency hatch. There wasn't much time. It was a strange floor, an intricate labyrinth with some strange structures covered with white cloth, boxes, and strange-looking equipment. This was not his first time here, and yet no one could explain to him the meaning of all these objects. He was the CEO and had to look down on all 998 floors. There was no time to look up.

Finding the ill-fated hatch was difficult. Everywhere, bumping into some objects, he crawled under some pipes. Then he came across the remains and excrement of some animals. Suddenly he remembered that had drawn a woman's breast on the hatch as a joke. Stopping, he caught his breath, closed his eyes, and tried to recall the direction. A few minutes later he opened it and stared at the desired drawing. "How come I didn't notice right away." However, it was not so easy to notice. The lighting was dim and the marker practically merged with the hatch. He pressed carefully and the hatch gave way easily.

The office smelled of her perfume. What a pleasant floral scent it was. Not much has changed since he was last here. He concentrated, there was no time to waste, he went to the BITCH's monitor and confidently entered the password. As he expected, Eliza had not changed her universal backup password. The biological parameters of a person change somewhat over time. Therefore, it was decided to leave the option to use a text password. " It's good that she doesn't bother too much with passwords, or rather, she's afraid of forgetting them."

"So I open the surveillance system and look for the right time and place."

Thousands of icons began to approach and disappear on the screen until the desired room appeared. He set the right time, focused on the table, and started watching. Everything was routine, an award ceremony, a meal, Zoe's game in its place, and no fat man. "There is no fat man." He sighed and watched for a few more minutes. And suddenly it hit him like an electric shock. "Where is Dave? Dave isn't at the table either. Well, am I going crazy? Maybe I'm still the CEO and I dreamed this? No, this is too good to be true."

He began to look for himself at another time but found nothing. He opened the list of department employees—no Dave was listed there. After he looked into the personnel utilization area—there Dave's career ended in the logistics department with a note about the liquidation of this department.

"What's going on, I understand nothing." He was visited by a sharp feeling that he better not return. He continued to navigate the system, looking for any clue. But there was nothing. He went into the register of missing, and again nothing.

Suddenly he came across a blinking window of the personnel utilization department. It contained unclosed employee cases. "Lisa 78678676 died in the workplace and was disposed of. Seemingly, they forgot to delete it from the department's database and she is listed."

"But why not take advantage of this? The complaint handling department is a hermit department. They do not leave their capsules, are quite large, there is a bathroom, a place to eat, and a bed. I was once offered to experiment with gender, so the chance presented itself. Why not, I'll be Lisa for a while and figure out what's going on."

He erased the disposal record, made a few adjustments, and exited the program. He looked languidly towards the bedroom. She was sleeping there—his love, how he wanted to burst in there and tell about everything, about his feelings, etc. "So what? What will you tell her? Get yourself together."

Dave climbed into the escape hatch and took away the support that he had left to prevent it from closing. Before going to his workplace, he decided to climb to the very top of the technical floor. This part was quite spacious and for some reason. There was some old tarpaulin hanging from the top and sides. "It's a strange place, but there's something familiar, very familiar about it."

He approached one object, pulled off the fabric from it, and saw an old metal swing. Some familiar and warm feelings came over him. He sat down on it and some strange, long—forgotten tender sensation filled his body.

For some time he sat enjoying it and trying to understand what this sensation was, but he couldn't remember anything. Carefully covered the swing. He turned around and thought, "There's a lot of things here, but I didn't expect to see such a strange swing here."

There was more than one swing. There were also some old vehicles and completely unfamiliar objects. He would have spent a week here, but the time was beyond the deadline. Near the elevator, he said, "I've done everything, close the work order." He pressed the button for the communications technical support floor, exited the elevator, and turned toward the stairs. After a few hours, he got used to the name Lisa, trained his voice, and explored the new workplace.

Chapter 5

Lisa

D ave sat in Lisa's workplace, and trained his voice, trying to soften it a little and make it higher. The work pod in the customer complaints department looked more like a dorm room. Despite its small size, there was everything you need for life. The management of the department did not welcome employees communicating with each other. Therefore, only hermits or people with social issues worked in the department.

The real Lisa could not stand the breakup of the virtual relationship and swallowed pills. Her heart could not stand it and stopped. The new Lisa tried to get used to the role as much as possible and created a new personality, replacing Dave for some time. It was an interesting experiment. Dave always wanted to try himself as a woman and then such an opportunity presented itself, albeit virtually.

In Eliza's office, he managed to do one more thing. After the reorganization of the logistics department, he sent himself to management courses and approved his candidacy for the head of the customer love department. The personnel utilization department had announced a competition to fill the position six months earlier. But management didn't like anyone. Therefore, the decision of the CEO himself greatly pleased the personnel officers.

This was a low-level position and Eliza would never remember whether she appointed someone to this position or not. For the management of the sales department, this meant that the CEO appointed her protégé, and sent him for training and to get manager status. No one will ask any questions about this.

" It will still be necessary to find out what it was—a mysterious story. How come they erase people? But not all at once, it takes time. Now you are Lisa and until you receive a manager's certificate I will work here. It's only a month, and I've already ordered the certificate and all I ought to do is pass an online quiz."

There were no shifts in this department. The employee received the case and worked on it until he closed the task. Sometimes there were several such cases. More complex ones took months to solve. Sometimes it was enough to give an intelligible answer in a few minutes.

"Operator Lisa. I'm listening to you."

"Hello, please fix the water supply. The water in the tap appears only when someone goes to the toilet."

"Tell me your subscriber number."

"AB4567568"

"Wait a minute, I'll look. You have no restrictions on your water supply. Have you asked SLAVE what the reason is?"

"Of course, I asked. It says that the eco-extreme mode is set."

"So change the regime, and everything will be fine"

"I've already tried it more than once. It didn't help."

"Okay, I'll check and contact you." "Well, this is my first case. I hope my voice was at least a little like a woman's. So what to do, there are no instructions. I'll try to contact the household directly."

"SLAVE 4567568 operator L3456 connection request"

"I confirm the request."—"Connection established, access rights confirmed" lights up on the display

"Let's see what we have here—the eco-extreme water supply mode. Recommended in case of disasters, wars, termination of a water supply contract, and during a tax audit. When this mode is established,water gets fully recycled from waste."

"Why is water supplied only after someone goes to the toilet? Let's look further. Yeah, that's it—in this mode, the system demands the minimum required reserve of water to maintain life. Hmm, well, why isn't it delivered? Yeah, that's it! To avoid reducing the water supply, water is supplied only after a minimum amount of water has entered the system for recirculation."

"Now it is clear. All you need to do is change the mode. Soooo. I choose free. Hmm blocked. I'll look at your profile. Social rating four. This mode is probably not provided. I will make it limited. Eat! Well, at least the water will be on schedule. The rest is not my problem. Now I can relax, the first case is closed."

There were no further requests that day. Dave began to settle into a new place. The standard menu included a lot of different sweets. "Well, I think I should try it." He ordered three different cakes and sugar water. He sat down in a chair and started clicking the screen remote control in search of entertainment.

On the screen were the houses and apartments of the participants in the reality project. Some families, to receive additional points, signed an agreement with the HOME corporation to allow the transfer of all data from the cameras to the public space.

In one house there was a boring dinner, in another a couple was having sex, in a third two girls were discussing their friend. He focused his attention on this house, then got bored and continued to switch. In the next house was the fight in the divorce. Namely, husband and wife dividing the cat, seemed rather amusing. That's when he fell asleep.

When he woke up, he saw that the husband and wife were sleeping in an embrace and for some reason, the cat was not visible. "It's interesting that they seemingly made peace. I wonder what happened to the cat?" He turned off the screen and went to the complex shower toilet, which he could hardly fit into. He asked for coffee and a croissant from the machine and began to get ready for the workday. Having launched the program, saw a line blinking in red. "It's strange, but this is yesterday's case! What's wrong? I'll contact them now and clarify."

"Hello, operator Lisa. I see that you have filed a complaint again, what's the matter?"

"Everything is the same. Yesterday you did something and water appeared. In the morning I got up, just got into the shower and it disappeared again. I beg you to make sure there is always water."

"Have you done anything since yesterday?"

"No, nothing."

"Okay, I'll double—check everything and contact you."

Dave again requested contact with SLAVE. It turned out that the mode is again eco-extreme. "But how can that be, I did everything, maybe I didn't save it somehow." He went through all the same steps double—checked all the settings and re-saved them.

"Operator Lisa. I did everything I could at this stage. I see that water has appeared. Let me call you tomorrow and check if everything is fine."

The next day the situation repeated itself. After listening to the caller's screams and wails, he assured them that they would certainly find the reason and sort it out. He ordered a plumber to visit the house and additionally dialed him. He outlined the situation and asked him to figure out what was going on and contact him.

"Ale!! Lizy, kitty, plumber Sergo."

"Hello Sergo. How is it going?"

"Everything is fine with the system. I tested, and it works. It's the SLAVE's brain that needs to be cleared, something is messing around. Damn it, they will pee and the water will be. He—he—he. Lizochka, how would we . . ."

"Thank you, Sergo, I understand everything. I'm closing the task as completed. Goodbye." He disconnected. He didn't like obvious flirting, especially from a man and especially since she wasn't her at all.

He gave the task to the monitoring department to look at the history and figure out what was going on.

"Lisa, this SLAVE version was a promotional offer for public housing for people without a rating. So eco-extreme is the basic setting. You just need to change the mode."

"But I did it, I've already done it twice. Everything is the same in the morning!"

"Well, I can't help you. For some reason, something resets this house brain to the basic settings. And this is some kind of external factor."

"What to do, how to find out what is happening?"

"The easiest way to monitor everything that happens in the house."

Dave asked the residents for the right of access to all cameras and processes in the house, ordered himself coffee, and some cakes, and began to observe. The residents, knowing that they were being watched, behaved very discreetly and practically did not speak to each other. They took the e-books, went to bed, and read until fell asleep.

He held on as best he could, but he couldn't stand it and fell asleep. He woke up at four in the morning. "How did I manage to fall asleep?" But fortunately, nothing happened during this time. After making more coffee, he forced himself to peer at the static picture on the monitor. Nothing happened.

Only at 5:30 a screen suddenly turned on in the dining area and announced the start of the day with a local news broadcast. There was a report about yesterday's meeting of authorities. Dave was distracted for a few minutes. Returning to the SLAVE parameters, suddenly discovered that it was again switched to super saving mode.

"Strange, nothing but a news release." Dave decided to check the logs.

Indeed, the mode switching occurred only at a certain time of 5:34. He reviewed all the actions of household appliances, as well as incoming and outgoing information—absolutely nothing. "It can't be that turning on the screen led to a failure. But it's not a coincidence. Every day the same time."

Dave sat thinking for a while. "Maybe some sound effect or frame is triggering the glitch." He decided to rewind the recording to 5:29.

At exactly 5:30 the screen lit up and the episode began. First, there was a clip of the main topics, then the announcer took the floor.

"Good morning residents of Plessenville. Your permanent robot Newsik is working in the studio. Let's start with the evening information from the previous day. The festival of good neighborliness continues in the city. Anonymous neighbors visited the Ivanov family home. While the family was in a restaurant at the invitation of the city broadcast channel, a group of neighbors came to their aid. However, let's get straight to the plot."

"Dear anonymous, tell us how you decided to help your neighbors."

"A masked man appeared on the screen."

"We walked around the entire yard and realized that the Ivanov family lacked beauty. We filled in their pool and made an alpine slide with an aquarium in its place. We destroyed the weeds that grew behind the fences." He pointed to a large pile of bushes with large red balls the size of a fist. "We also shaved the shaggy dog and neutered the cat."

"Well, you have done a lot of work to help your neighbors. And now the speech of the councilman, who will talk about what's new in the life of the city."

A few tens of seconds after the beginning of the speech in which the MP told how thanks to the city authorities it has sun, air, and it is paradise on earth, SLAVE switched the program to super-economy. "Apparently, this test model is endowed with critical analysis and perceives the words of a representative as an existential threat and shifts into survival mode. Well, I'll have to tell the household that if they want to wash, they need to turn off the news."

***

"Operator Lisa, I'm listening to you."

"We were offered to buy an eco-toilet. We agreed and signed the contract. It was installed and we even managed to convert the old toilet into the dressing room my wife always dreamed of. Explain to us how to use it. The seller does not answer the phone, there are no instructions and we understand nothing."

"This is not a complaint to my department, you should contact the installers."

"We've already reached out everywhere. Help us or put things back the way they were!"

"Let me figure out the issue and get back to you."

"Look forward to it!"

Dave dialed in the installation department.

"Hello Lisa. I haven't heard from you for a long time. What a strange voice.

"Cough, cough, I have a sore throat."

"How could you catch a cold? Maybe it's sugared?"

"Let's get down to business. Did you install an eco-toilet in the house AC4358859?"

"Yes, our brigade."

"So why didn't they explain how to use it?"

"How should we know? We installed and that's all."

"Wait, who should know then?"

"Ask the purchasing department, no one gave us any specifications."

Now it was the turn of the purchasing department.

"Can you provide instructions and a certificate for the eco-toilet?"

"No, it passed us by, it was the alternative marketing department that ordered it."

"Denis!—Dave muttered angrily."

"Who is this?"

"Interference on the line." He continued coughing, softening his voice. "Maybe you know who the manufacturer is and his contacts?"

"The history says that the head of the department took it in some fair. He reported on the purchases and that's it, there is no more data."

Dave was confused, he didn't understand what to do, but he needed to deal with this problem. Lack of results will attract unnecessary attention. He contacted the experimental department. They replied that the product was not theirs and they had no interest in it at all. There was no way out.

He informed the residents that a technician would come to them, and went in search of suitable special clothing and a way to get to the place.

Fortunately, employees of the complaints department were given transport upon request. All the ass—cycles, so that they would not be stolen, were on the department's balcony. He took the free one and lowered it down the winch. The rope automatically rose to prevent hackers or vampires from climbing on it.

They were called ass—cycles because there was a stake instead of a seat. There was not enough transport for everyone. Therefore, the head of the transport department proposed removing the seats. This should have contributed to the department's employees striving to return the transport as quickly as possible. The idea worked. The manager received a promotion.

Houses for residents of the third rating group were spacious with additional amenities, a garden, a small lawn for relaxation, and a barbecue. As an additional option, the family chose a large trampoline. Toys were scattered around. A family of five came out to meet the technician: a husband, wife, and three children of different ages. An ordinary family, but for some reason they all had disproportionately enlarged hips and buttocks below the waist.

"Finally! We are already tired of using joking diapers—not only do we need to change them once a day, but we were sold a set with a dark sense of humor, so now we can't take a step without a dirty joke."

"Show where your eco-toilet is."

"Come on," said the owner.

"Don't run or you'll shit yourself again," his diaper burped.

They approached a small wooden structure near the second entrance to the house leading to the dining room. It was small and had a door, a window at the top, and a hole in the floor.

"Apparently not a set," said the technician. "Obviously, there must be something else. It can't be possible to go to the toilet in this hole."

"They came, installed it, and said they installed it as it came."

"Dad, dad," the smallest one shouted, "look what I built."

"Wait, son, later, you see Dad is busy."

Everyone walked around the toilet together, looked into it, and tried to at least understand something. All this was accompanied by periodic teasing from shameless diapers. Then they sat down at the garden table and began to talk on abstract topics. The mother went to collect scattered toys on the lawn and suddenly stopped. Her attention was drawn to a strange bucket the same color as the eco—toilet. Having disassembled the structure, she picked it up and saw similar numbers.

"Look, this is probably part of the eco-toilet."

This didn't help much. On the contrary, it confused them even more. They carried this ovaloshaped wooden bucket back and forth, and tried to insert it into the hole—everything was in vain. Then the eldest son came to the rescue. He announced that he had seen a similar bucket somewhere, it seems in some encyclopedia. They sent him out to look for him. About forty minutes later he returned with a large book called "The Primeval World."

They opened it in the section of the greatest achievements of mankind and found the one they needed. As it turned out, it was an exact replica of an ancient toilet. The bucket served as a chamber pot and the toilet actually was like that. The owners politely said that they wanted to refuse the purchase and wished the seller, who had foisted it off all his life, only to go to such a toilet. The technician apologized on behalf of the company and promised that he would convey the customers' wishes to the sales department and silently retreated. Even the diapers have stopped joking and laughing.

***

"Let me home, pleeeeaase let me in," said a man's voice, almost crying.

"Operator Lisa. How can I help you."

"Dear Lisa, don't leave me, you are already the tenth, and no one helped."

"Describe the problem. I will do everything possible to help you."

"I'm a cat."

"?! I don't understand, repeat the essence of the problem."

"I want to go home and live like a person, I can't do it anymore."

"Perhaps you need a psychologist. I process complaints from clients of the HOME corporation."

"That's right—it's in the power of your corporation."

"You can state the essence of the issue normally?"

"Yee just listen. We had a family fete. We ate a lot of cocaine candy and it was fun. Friends decided to make a joke and lured out my SLAVE password. I don't know what they did there. They swear they don't remember anything. As a result, my biometric parameters were replaced with a cat. The cat is just in awe. He eats pizza normally, but for me, kitten food is served, and this food is given in doses at a certain time. SLAVE, like for other animals, does not allow me onto the second floor. I sleep on the sofa in the kitchen. And this bastard sleeps peacefully in my bedroom. Moreover, I tried to keep track of when he ordered food from the cooking machine, but he did not approach it even once during the twelve hours of my observation. And at that time it turned out that he ate my kitten food and I was left completely hungry."

"They couldn't do anything without a corporation employee's approval of the application."

"But somehow they did it"

"We'll figure it out, but for now, your wife can help you."

"So that's the thing, she doesn't want to. She said I was a freak and I had to live like a cat."

"Your problem is not clear to me. It will take time to figure it out."

"At least let me go home. I won't get through the kitty entrance."

"It's very cold and damp outside."

"Put your face in front of the camera. So good. Hmm, really the cat Elephant. However, the cat is registered at this address. I opened the door for you. But it's just this time. Wait until we get to the bottom of the problem."

"Thank you! Is it possible to open access to ordering human food?"

"No, this option is not available. Wait for someone to contact you."

"Where do such weirdos come from and how should I turn a cat into a human again? Some kind of mysticism. So, what do we have about cats? There are hundreds of types of cat litter, and there is much more than people have. Services for collecting wool, entertainment so that they don't get bored, ordering toys, music for their meditation, automatic feeding program, beds for cats, home amusement park, setting the allowed time for being outside, organizing meetings for area cats, castration. There is nothing that can be done to make a person out of a cat. Although I can order castration, the wife may take pity."

Dave contacted all possible departments and services. He received no meaningful response. Everyone said it couldn't be because it couldn't be. He looked at the subscriber's profile again. The same cat Elephant, an unshaven creature with long dark hair and glasses, was looking at him. On the owner's profile was a fluffy cutie, a handsome white cat hugging a toy mouse.

It was possible to leave everything as it was. Firstly, it was his own fault, and secondly, no incident was registered. Everything was fine in the system, so he could simply delete the task. However, from the experience of his past life, he knew that in artificial intelligence there are short-term failures without any reason. And he felt sorry for the subscriber and decided to help him somehow. The last hope was in the department of communications with artificial intelligence.

"Engineer Max, I'm listening to you."

"This is Lisa from the customer complaints department."

"Yeah, Lizonka, you aren't recognizable. Remember how we hung out on your last birthday? By the way, it's coming soon, shall we repeat?"

"Let's get down to business first." He briefly outlined the situation.

"I don't even know how to help."

"Ask HOME a question, it must give an answer."

"Uh, it's not that simple, now we can't make requests, it doesn't accept them."

"What do you mean?"

"Well, I don't have the right to tell you anything more. Believe me, this is not an option."

"This was my last hope."

"Forget it, close the complaint and that's it. It's not the first time for you. I don't understand why you even bothered this time. Let's reminisce. I broke up with my girlfriend, so how about we get married?"

"I have to interrupt the connection."

"Let's get married, what nonsense. I came across Lisa's suitor, maybe he'll leave and won't bother me. He's asking for my birthday. Wait, what birthday? When is Liz's birthday? So, shit, here it is, in 6 days!" He did not expect such a turn of events. The plan seemed perfect. "Now what? It's impossible to sneak away. According to department tradition, this is the only day when an employee is visible to everyone."

Dave sat silently for a while and looked blankly at the monitor. He completely forgot about the client. "It's all over, I lost, but how it all started. I even got a marriage proposal. What would I say that I got old, etc., then I got divorced and left a husband's last name and it was possible . . . " Then he fell silent as if something had poked him. "Wedding, it seems like according to the law a person can be married to an animal. We need to find out everything." The rest of the day was spent studying family law.

"Operator Lisa. I have an idea of how to change your identity."

"Finally! Let's do it already!"

"Not so simple. Listen to me first. I couldn't find a solution within the HOME system. But there is a way out in the legal field. You need to marry your cat."

"What . . . ? Are you joking? I'm already married!"

"Listen to me. According to the family corporate code, a widower can assume the identity of a spouse and enjoy all his rights. That is, you need to register a marriage with him, and after the death of the cat, you will return to your old life. The only difficulty is that a meow from an animal is enough for legalization, but a digital signature is required for a person, which is problematic in this case. You must first transfer custody of the cat to your wife."

"I feel like my wife values the cat more than me."

"Let me talk to her."

"I don't mind, but the main question is that she will never agree to kill a cat. She is from a dynasty of animal defenders."

"Well, let's set up an accident, she won't know anything."

"How can I explain to her why I should marry a cat?"

"I'll figure it out, let me make a plan and contact you."

***

There are two days left until Lisa's birthday. Dave was already dealing with a new complaint, although the previous one had not yet been closed. However, the client has already formalized his relationship with the cat. This gave him some bonuses. Now he enjoyed the same rights as a cat. Could move around the house more freely and gain access to human food.

The wife took the situation with humor but was very worried about polygamy. The legal department found many precedents and they assured that there was no violation of the law here. The family was interested in the consequences if everything was left as it was. It's not often that there are cats with a full package of legal documents and rights. As a result, catidyll reigned in the family, and the urgency in resolving the issue disappeared.

But now he had a much more serious personal problem—Lisa's birthday. He watched last year's recording and everything turned out to be even worse. Congratulations began in the morning. All employees gathered in a pre-prepared room and gave gifts, drank tea, and ate sweets, and it all ended late at night, with traditional dances with friends. Turned out to be quite a lot of them given the reclusive lifestyle.

A saving idea appeared in a new case. The clown family suffered from an invasion of spiteful beetles. They were superstitious and believed that their invasion was a bad sign. According to the agreement, disinfection was carried out twice a year, once mandatory, and the other upon request. They refused to send a brigade because too little time had passed since the scheduled work. No poisons or chemicals have any effect on this species. Dave remembered an old unconventional but reliable way to get rid of bugs. He went to the client in person, hoping to persuade him to help organize a costume birthday party. No one would guess if Lisa were in a clown costume.

He was met by a family of two adults and two children. The gender was impossible to determine. Their faces resembled ancient surrealist paintings and were unusually disproportionate. The children could only be distinguished by their size. There was no similarity between family members. All that united them into one was some abnormal appearance.

"Hello, my name is Andrew. I was talking to you, and this is my family of sad clowns." A man with a nose as if from four dimensions leaned forward. It sort of disappeared and hung over again.

"Hello, my name is Lisa."

"Strange, I thought it was a woman's name."

"Yes, you're right, but let's get down to business. Unfortunately, our corporation cannot help in the fight against this beetle. But I once had the same problem in my dorm. We couldn't do anything. To our joy, a representative of an ancient ethnic group lived nearby and retained knowledge of traditional medicine." He took some kind of powder out of the bag.

"What is it? It won't kill us?"

"No, it's pot powder. It strangely affects them: instead of having fun, they become very sad and fall into depression. They either leave or die from boredom."

"Well, let's try it."

He took out the powder and sprinkled it around the perimeter of the floor. Immediately thousands of beetles rushed towards. They actively devoured this mixture until the eyes of the first ones became sad, very sad. Looking at them, all the spiteful beetles immediately ran away.

"Oh miracle, how did this happen?"

"There is no miracle here, they would have eaten separately and not even noticed. But grass causes severe depression. So they become sad. The other beetles think that this house is too happy. And they can't stand this."

"Well, thank you, you really helped us. How can I thank you, because as I understand it, this is your private initiative."

"Indeed, I need your help. The fact is that I am replacing a friend at work, she had to leave. No one should have known about this. Nobody saw me, but we forgot about her birthday. So I thought you could help organize a costume party and make me up like a clown so no one could tell."

"You see, my dear, clowns are no longer about makeup and clothes. We switched to genetics a long time ago. We change the appearance of our children over generations. That's why we are like this. The clown profession is hereditary, and very rarely does anyone join it. Moreover, we are sad clowns. It's unlikely we'll come up to our birthday, we have been nurturing the genes of sadness for four generations. Previously, it was very popular and income was guaranteed, now times have changed, and now they want more funny clowns or charismatic ones. So I don't know how to help you."

"I indeed need help, I was counting so much on this idea, don't you even use makeup?"

"No, this has long been considered unnatural and fake. Only natural traits are valued."

"Show me a photo of your friend," the wife entered into the conversation.

"Voila, what if so?" She went through a series of muscle movements and became very similar to Lisa.

"It's just breathtaking," said the fake Lisa. "You are genuinely very alike!"

"I can replace her, no one will notice. I play roles well, just tell me the necessary information about her."

"Mary," Andrew entered, "it's too risky, you could be detained. Our bills aren't paid."

"Yes, perhaps you're right, but will there be treats and sweets at the party?"

"Yes, sure."

"Can I take some with me?"

"Yes, I will organize it."

"Then it's decided. Andrew, the children haven't eaten sweets for a long time. I'll grab more of everything to make them sad."

"Okay, just then bring me something tasty. I'm completely fed up with dry food."

They agreed on this. Mary went to prepare and study the role. It was also decided that she would go to celebrate with her new fiancé Kevin, who would help her understand all the corporate rituals and rules. Dave really liked this idea. He asked to find him a suitable suit and make him up so that no one would recognize him later. They found for him a railroad worker's suit and glued on a mustache. A little makeup and it became impossible to recognize either Dave or the former CEO.

He had another brilliant idea. After his disappearance, or rather his appointment as head of the department, Lisa will disappear. They will start looking for her and may find information about him. So he decided that after her birthday they would find a note in which Lisa would explain that because of her great love, she was leaving work and leaving with her fiance to another continent. "This is how Lisa will find her happiness."

***

Made up according to the ancient clown tradition with a false red nose and white cheeks, Lisa and her fiance headed to the banquet hall. There was a huge cake in the center of the U-shaped table. Vases with delicious treats went in different directions from the cake. There were vending machines with taps for drinks. About forty people gathered in a semicircle and shouted Hurray. They shot champagne and lit candles—the celebration began.

At first, he stood nearby, but over time he realized that it was useless. Everyone just approached her as if he didn't exist. Nobody asked who he was. "Maybe it's for the better," he thought. Approaching the table, he took a large crystal glass, filled it to the brim, and took a fruit salad. A man of unknown age approached him.

"Hello, where did you come from here?"

"I'm Lisa's boyfriend."

"That fatty."

"That sweety."

"Come on, she's not cute, she's fat and stupid. Otherwise, she wouldn't work in this department, shutting herself off from the whole world."

"You're not very friendly to the birthday girl."

"I don't care, it's the same boring thing every time, the only joy is having plenty of drinks, you can fill yourself up and sit in the toilet until the end of the celebration. You would look for a normal one. Although you are somehow strange, painted. I only saw such people in a film about ancient funny farms."

Dave was annoyed by the conversation and wanted to return to Lisa, but she was taken to take the obligatory photograph. It's good that she dressed in a fancy dress, otherwise, her face might have been recognized, or rather not recognized. He went further to study the menu. There were quite a lot of delicacies, and the table was rich, although some of the food seemed not fresh, and some had not yet been defrosted.

"Why are the cookies so wooden?" He asked the girl who was pouring herself lemonade.

"Obviously, because, it's from my birthday last year."

"How is it since last year? It's not fresh."

"The management of the department does not like to spend money on purchases, so everyone is warned not to touch anything."

"What about the banquet? And the birthday girl?"

"Screw this boring cow, she just ruins the whole day."

Dave at first thought that for some reason everyone hated Lisa. But this turned out to be not entirely true. They hated all birthday people and this celebration in particular. There were certain prerequisites for this. The department management decided not to allow employees to go on vacation because there was no one to replace the employee. In addition, the cases were unique and it took a lot of time to figure them out from the very beginning.

Recruiting additional staff meant depriving yourself of some benefits. A solution was found. The team gathered and announced: "the good news—now for each employee's birthday there will be a whole day of celebration. All employees will gather and honor and celebrate. Since there are many employees and the celebration is all day, management is forced to cancel vacations."

The corporation allocated a special room and initially ordered various culinary masterpieces. Over time, everything became simpler. No one cleared the tables anymore. Automatic food serving devices simply froze it and defrosted it for the next feast. Occasionally some meals were updated. No one had touched the cake for five years—they simply changed the inscriptions on it.

Pouring himself a cold drink and trying to chew the gray mass under the tiramisu label, he pulled away from all this movement. "It's just one day, and no one bothers me. I don't know whether the kids will be happy with the treat that Mary will bring. The only fresh thing here seems to be chocolate crackers."

Suddenly his attention was attracted by a strange man in the middle of the hall. He stood out sharply against the general background, stood, and looked piercingly forward. His clothes were tattered and old, he was not shaved and his hair seemed to have not seen shampoo since birth.

Dave stared blankly for several minutes. And suddenly the man disappeared. He perked up and looked around. But nothing has changed, people still walked back and forth to no avail. Obviously, no one noticed the bizarre stranger. "Maybe I was imagining things? Am I going crazy?" He sat down on a chair and closed his eyes for a while.

"What is going on here, how can people disappear? This man, his face seems familiar to me. I saw him, but how he could disappear as soon as I blinked is incomprehensible. Oh, I wish I could look at the recording, then I would know for sure whether there is a malfunction in my brain or something strange is happening here. It's too dangerous to get to Eliza. I don't know any other way to watch the recording."

He looked at the people around him. They froze in their poses like toys or made repetitive movements. "Well, I wouldn't want such a birthday for myself. I thought that only management has such hypocrisy." Suddenly a strange thought came to him. He remembered his adventures in the elevator and technical floor. Taking another look at the depressing picture, he went in search of a secret premises. "There are probably these on every or almost every floor."

He found a hatch and crawled up and down the intertechnical floor, but he didn't find anything interesting. Dirty and slightly tattered, he headed back. Suddenly, passing by the wall, He noticed a strange refraction of the shadow.

Dave began to fumble with his hands and suddenly the wall gave way and he found himself on some kind of staircase. It was seemingly a designed fire escape required by building codes, although completely useless. There were several of them, as well as entrances. To avoid panic, the system included secret doors that opened and were illuminated exactly where and when needed.

After standing for a few minutes in thought, not knowing where to go, he heard footsteps above. Without thinking for a second, he rushed up and quickly galloped three flights of stairs. He was about to run further when heard a noise behind him. He went back to the last stairwell and tried to open all the doors. And one gave in and it turned out to be a half—dark spacious room. It housed about thirty people.

"My dear, which department were you fired from? And how long?" A voice was heard from ahead.

"Well, I don't know, although I was laid off from the logistics department."

"Then welcome to us."

"But who are you and what are you doing here?"

"We are corporate rats, we live here after we became unneeded."

"But why should you be here, the world is big, why stay in this building?"

"We don't know anything and we can't do anything outside the corporation—we won't survive." said the man Dave saw in the banquet hall. "What is your name?"

"Dave. And you?"

"I don't even remember, but everyone here calls me Foreman."

"How do you survive here?"

"We know all the habits and rules well. We know well where and when we can get food. Where to go to wash and tidy up while nobody is there. We live quite well, the only problem is with clothes. You can join us, but only on the condition that you tell us something useful about the work and habits of your department."

"My department is completely disbanded. Maybe I can help with clothes. But tell me, you can't be unnoticed by surveillance cameras. It's entirely impossible. How do you manage to get everywhere undetected?"

"As I already said, we know the rules and habits well. There was also an engineer among us who worked with the HOME, he told us and made a calendar of temporary failures when the AI is offline."

"What do you mean offline? How is this even possible?"

"We do not know. Unfortunately, the engineer disappeared. He explained it like as if a person blinked. HOME also closes his eyes for a moment. We are simply using what he gave us. The calendar is scheduled for two years in advance, so for now we know how not to be noticed and we hope that in two years someone else will be fired from the IT department."

"It's amazing. I have to leave now, but I'll be back—I have a lot of questions."

"Come, but not empty—handed."

A chill ran down Dave's spine. Corporate rats, temporary blinks, his head was spinning. He calmly entered the hall, no one paid attention to his appearance. Nothing actually changed during this time, as if he had never left. Finally, the farewell signal sounded and the people as if they were blown away by the wind.

Besides Mary and himself, a man was sleeping at the table. Dave took a basket and began to collect all the most delicious and fresh treats there. He thanked Mary for her help and led her to the exit, where her husband was already waiting for her. There was still a sleepless night of thought ahead and five days of work as an expert in processing client complaints, Lisa.

Chapter 6

Love comes first

The workplace customer love department head was in the center of converging concentric circles of workstations on an elevated platform. The circles smoothly descended from the center to the outskirts and were intersected by four passages of four colors. The executive's desk also followed this design and consisted of four sectors with small passages between them. On the other side of each sector, there was a corresponding place for his assistants. By rotating in his chair, he could quickly communicate. The assistants had to be constantly on their toes. But not Adele. A middle-aged woman sat casually on the table. One of her breasts hung and shook right next to Dave's face.

"Listen, Dave, you are a new and inexperienced. Truly, I don't even know how you got approved. We have been working hard for many years, but our candidacies were not considered. So you are a talented manager. But listen, you need to take our advice, or else you're headed for failure. I know everything everyone does in my sector, and more than that, my sector has never been in the red. The team is successful and united. I have known each employee for many years, how to put pressure on him, and how to achieve results. If you want to stay in this position, listen to me, I won't let you down, and I will help you build work in other sectors where managers are less experienced. Make me your deputy - you won't regret it."

Dave was very annoyed. Adele loomed closer and closer over him, and her sagging breasts seemed to touch his forehead. He didn't know what to do since he hadn't been in a similar situation for a long time.

"Adele, I heard your thoughts, I need to think about them. Now I want to get acquainted with other sectors."

"Of course, that's what I suggested. With whom first?" She was clearly going to accompany him around the circle.

"Let's get down to business. For now - order a presentation about your sector, and what made it the most successful and resilient. Then we'll discuss with you how to pass on the experience to others. I'm expecting today!" He turned sharply and found himself face to face with a blonde girl with a long braid hanging down her front.

"My name is Eugenie. I'm new, and I'm starting work with my zero sector. I'm sure that my team will be able to much the efficiency."

"Well, you have the most difficult mission. The new team is difficult to keep afloat, but we will work so that you achieve maximum results" During the conversation, she smiled and looked at him all the time.

"Thank you for your trust, we will not let you down." While Dave slowly turned around further, he noticed out of the corner of his eye how she leaned forward towards her two employees and said something cheerful to them. At the same time, her short skirt rose and exposed her bare buttocks.

"My name is Joe. My sector has been holding on for almost a year. We are fulfilling our plans almost one hundred percent." A frightened man with a reddish beard was looking at Dave. His eyes darted in different directions and he seemed to feel uneasy. His black leather suit consisted of a vest barely covering his hairy chest and short leather shorts with zippered holes in his private parts.

"Well, Joe, this is commendable. You need to achieve more. My duty is to improve the performance of all sectors. Perhaps then they will increase the survival score."

"We will try. We won't let you down!" Joe answered somewhat hesitantly.

"A strange specimen," Dave thought and turned to the last sector. Here sat a brunette of medium build in a strict business suit. Her bright blue eyes eclipsed her entire body.

"Hello. What is your name?" He began first, as the brunette remained stubbornly silent.

"I'm Annie," she answered flirtatiously.

"Tell me something about yourself."

"I am a gorgeous brunette, height 170 centimeters, breasts of the third size, bisexual."

"Useful information, but I want to know about your sector."

"Why? I successfully cope with my goals. We have never been lower than second place. We are the strongest sector, you can ignore us and focus on others, we can handle it ourselves," she answered impudently.

"I'll watch you, we'll see."

"Oki," and showing arrogance with all her appearance, she turned her back to him, extended her hands and the two girls began to kiss them.

Dave was left confused. He didn't want to turn towards sagging chests. Going the other way made no sense. Fortunately for him, the signal of fifteen-minute readiness for the start of the CEO's address. The chair began to slowly fall back.

The projector directed the image to the high ceiling along almost the entire perimeter for convenience and due to the concentric architecture of the hall. The chairs of all employees were moved to a horizontal position and they lay down and watched the huge countdown numbers.

Eliza appeared on the screen in a close-up. You could see all her wrinkles, pimples, and makeup details close-up. But Dave focused all his attention on the necklace, or rather on the pendant in the shape of half a heart. He had never seen anything like this on her before.

"Maybe someone gave it to her. I don't think she would have bought it herself, and it's a half and not a whole, which means someone has another. Yes, this is a gift and a very expensive one. What did you actually want, cadaver?" Looking unsure she began her speech, seemingly passing the camera.

"Employees and heads of the department, this is an urgent appeal to you. Today we received corporate data - they are depressing. We have fallen below the red line of the standards established for our corporation. In recent periods we have been quite stable. But in the last two, we began to fall. The red line is 10.4 and currently, we have 9.7! This is a catastrophe! Our license will be taken away. How did it happen that from an average of 10.8 we fell into a hole? The heads of the department will be held accountable. Oh, that's not the main thing right now. It is necessary to increase the indicator to at least 10.4. To do this, we are temporarily changing the rules of the game. Not a single team will be erased this time if the result is achieved. If not, all will be destroyed. Everyone should work for a common result and there should be no competition between sectors. I'm really counting on you and looking forward to the results. I ask the head of the department to work with each sector individually, and I expect a report every day."

The image dissolved on the white ceiling. The chairs were in no hurry to acquire a vertical position. Moans and sighs began to be heard everywhere - the orgy began. This was traditional after any meetings. Dave had heard about it, but this was his first time at ground zero. The premise was in darkness. The excited moans created the feeling of a strange choir.

He thought that if this happened in the forest, all the birds and animals would hide and freeze. After all, this was the love department. Sex here was not just the norm, but a full-fledged part of the job. It was impossible to relax. The tension was like in an electrical transformer.

Someone crawled up to him and unzipped his fly. He did not resist and did not even look in that direction. He was once again faced with a task critical to the survival of the corporation. There were thirty-four days left until the end of the reporting period to the union of corporations. It was necessary to do the almost impossible, to raise the love indicator by as much as seven points. He had not heard of anyone being able to achieve such a result before. However, there was no choice.

***

The new head of the newcomers sector, Eugenie, a young blonde beauty, was a financier. She was kicked out by the head of the department for having an affair with her beloved assistant. In order to get rid of her quickly and without problems, she, without Eugenie's knowledge, sent her CV to the position of head of the customer love department.

Even though according to the rules of the department there was fierce competition and each sector could be terminated, with very rare exceptions, newcomers always dropped out. It was career suicide. However, the top management encouraged employees who aspired to this position. They were declared heroes, and revered as kamikazes who gave up their careers for the benefit of the corporation.

"Eugenie, I heard you are a financier."

"Yes, Dave for five years already."

"What brings you here?"

"I love challenges." She said ironically.

"Well, I hope you bring a fresh perspective and new ideas. You jump into a crisis situation, but I am sure we will find a way out and all teams will remain."

"I hope so too."

"Do you have any questions?"

"I'm used to analyzing numbers and I don't quite understand how the coefficient of customer love can be more than one hundred percent."

"In the theory of relative arithmetic, numbers can change relative to their natural meaning. Love does not have a clear definition, which means it can be more or less strong. The Union of Corporations decided that ordinary average love is not enough. The client must love with reserve. This is the basis of the existence of the corporate world. If the client's love deviates from excessive to normal, then a system exists in this field. If only love drops below one hundred percent, the corporate world will die. Our goal is to prevent this from happening. I look forward to fresh ideas from you tomorrow. Bring your team to success."

"Okay, I'll go gather the team."

Eugenie looked around at this gathering of unrelated people and became despondent. "It will be difficult here," she thought. Having announced a general meeting and brainstorming in two hours, she went to the break room. She took off her pants, threw on a blanket, and lay down on the wide sofa.

Her thoughts were not at all about work. She had a hard time being separated from her sexual partner. It cannot be said that she loved him, but she felt good with him and he pleased her. Rarely did anyone suit her sexually, so she did not expect to find a suitable replacement. Apathy towards everything gripped her. Knowing that there were few prospects for work in this department, she was not going to push herself. She closed her eyes and tried to doze off.

Her peace was disturbed by a noisy trinity - two guys and a girl. They rushed in unceremoniously and began to vigorously sort things out. Both guys surrounded her on both sides and demanded reciprocal love. Both voluptuously hugged and kissed hands.

"Fuck off, both of you! Tired of it! How else can I explain it to you? I don't need two. I don't want that. I need mine. Get out of here." She kicked them both out. She approached Eugenie and asked, "Can I lie down next to you?"

"I guess so."

"I'm tired of this couple of sex partners. One man is enough for me. I can't stand two at once, and my libido is not high. If they separated, then perhaps I would choose the tall one, but he doesn't want to, he's stubborn, saying they can't live without each other. Fuck them, let them look for another girl. Why are you sad?"

"My boyfriend betrayed me."

"I sympathize, these men are not at all faithful, and they are of little use."

"Yes, but love . . ."

"What love is! Look at them, they have already stopped having normal sex with a partner, some with pets, or some other way. I'm probably too conservative."

"Perhaps, but everything was fine for me . . ."

"Come on," the girl climbed under the blanket and began stroking Eugenie's body. She didn't resist, just indifferently accepted the caresses and thought about failed love. She was thinking about what she was doing here and why. She was overcome by complete apathy and unwillingness to do anything. "How could he do this to me? I have never suffered so much and cried for the first time." She stood up. Anger appeared in her eyes. She walked into the hall, where the guest trainer Maria was already preparing everything for the brainstorming session.

Fifteen minutes before the start, the bell rang, and an invitation for everyone to gather in the hall. Sector employees with sad faces began to converge. Within five minutes the lights in the hall went out. It was completely dark, only the paths were illuminated. At the appointed time, a bright light came on, blinding everyone. The coach announced the beginning of the brainstorming.

"Everyone stood up! Let's warm up!" Began Maria. "Now, everybody in tern confesses love to each participant. Everyone must confess and receive a declaration of love."

Dave watched indifferently. Some confessions amused him, but looking at others his heart sank. He understood that these were real confessions. This exercise stirred up a strong feeling in him that he seemed to have suppressed. But no, again her flowing hair, her clear, intelligent gaze arose before him and plunged him into a daydream that was abruptly interrupted by the coach.

"Well done! Now we love each other and can convey our love to the client. Let's start the invasion! A real surprise has been prepared for you! ALIVE captured clients! Our security teams have pulled the most evil clients out of their homes. The conditions are as follows: the drum consists of ten clients. You are also divided into the same number of groups. I'll spin it and each group will have its own client in front of it. The worst team will fall into a dungeon just like the kindest client. Now you have twenty minutes to communicate within teams. I, the head of the department, and the heads of sectors will move between teams and give advice. Let's begin!"

In the middle, the floor parted and a white tent slowly rose. The experts took numbers and were divided into groups. Everyone flinched - a very loud sonic boom sounded. It began to sound louder and louder. The participants took their places, the beatings stopped and the white cape lifted, revealing people strapped into their seats.

Maria ran her finger over the control device and the drum started spinning. Several clients vomited. Undigested food was scattered throughout and decorated the clothes of several participants. Someone couldn't stand it and vomited in response. But then the drum stopped and all the teams focused on achieving the result.

To Dave's surprise, the universal sex robot looked at them with surprised eyes. He sat half-turned. On one side it was a man and on the other a woman. In this model, parts of the body could be rotated in different directions. "Apparently the security service didn't figure out who they caught, or maybe it's someone's joke." But the game is a game. His team was completely at a loss and had to take the initiative.

"We love you, you are our client. Your happiness is our concern. Will you respond to us with your love?"

"The robot still looked at Dave in surprise, but intently, and continued to remain silent."

"How can we prove our love? How to achieve reciprocity? Eugenie entered."

The robot remained stubbornly silent. Then she told everyone to gather in a circle to discuss further actions. There were eight people on the team. She didn't know any of them.

"Give us your suggestion. Three minutes have already passed, and it hasn't even spoken to us. We won't achieve love."

"Let's ask why it doesn't like us," one guy suggested"

"Okay, let's try, ask."

"What is your name?"

"Therehere," a woman's voice finally sounded.

"Why don't you love us?"

"Whatas d u wantas? U wonna gruppa sehs?" the robot answered now in a male voice.

"So that you love us."

"The purpus of my existensi s to be fuced."

"You don't understand - to love our corporation."

The robot muttered something incoherent. The words were impossible to understand. Suddenly the bell rang and the chairs turned to the inner side of the circle. The coach took the floor.

"A pause of five minutes for teams. Exactly five minutes for discussion and analysis of your work with the client. Heads change the team."

"We haven't achieved anything," said Eugenie, "we need a result."

"It didn't answer us."

"Ten minutes is too short."

"We don't have any information about the client. How to work without it?"

"That's why we're brainstorming," Dave entered. "We need to achieve the client's love no matter what."

The time for discussion was up and they stood face to face with the gray-haired old man. A new round has begun.

"I'm sorry, what!?" The senior men yelled, "What are you muttering? I can't hear anything."

"Turn on your hearing!" First one of the participants shouted and then everyone shouted in unison. The man continued to shout that he could not hear anything until someone proposed to use gestures. After that, the old man pressed several buttons and began to speak.

"Sorry kids, I get tired of the noise, so I turn off my hearing and sometimes forget to turn it on."

"What is your name?"

"Simons, me."

"Why do you dislike the corporation?"

"Why, you kids, I love you all."

"Did you have any problems with utilities?"

The old man continued to say that he loved everyone and had no problems. Time quickly ran out again. Having failed to achieve results the second time and not having come up with anything new during the breaks, they unsuccessfully tried to raise the love coefficient with three more teams. But again, failed. On the sixth client, a coach joined them. Maria went from team to team, listening and analyzing actions and giving her recommendations.

"I'm disappointed. You act too softly, and you won't achieve love. We need to act much more harshly. The client must love you, whether he wants it or not."

"But I thought," said Eugenie, "that the client loves it when he is satisfied with our services and the attitude of the corporation towards himself."

"Darling, what nonsense. With this approach, we would no longer exist. There are no such services that would completely satisfy the client. The focus on making the client fall in love with the company due to its work is a thing of the past. We are a client-oriented corporation. Our goal is to convince the client that he loves us regardless of the quality of our services. He must develop an unconditional reflex of love and ecstasy towards the HOME corporation. Let's start, you have ten minutes to make someone love you. I will help."

The client turned out to be a fairly large man with small, deep-set eyes. He did not stand on ceremony and set the first tone for the conversation.

"Freaks, motherfuckers! I hate your corporation and all of you. I wish that you would all drown in shit."

"Can I ask what's the matter, what happened to him?" Dave asked the coach in a whisper.

"By no means, this is not the most difficult but also not the simplest case. I will begin." Maria answered.

"Dear, why are you angry? Do you see how hard I'm trying? Show some respect to the corporation."

"What the fuck?" He boiled. "You haven't been able to fix the sewer for six months. It's flooding me with shit for the fifth time."

"We take care of you and you are rude, show your feelings."

"I want to shit on all of you."

"Great idea. Let's take a shit and you'll feel better. You can choose any employee and defecate."

"Seriously? I want there to be no shit in the house!"

"What will this give you? You'd better shit on someone. Who else will give you such pleasure?"

"What a faking pleasure! In what?"

"Choose who you like and try it. You won't regret it. You are worthy to love us - love us so much! No corporation will give you such opportunities to show love."

The man fell silent. He was confused and no longer knew what to answer. Maria then said that if time had not run out, she would have finished him off and he would have loved the corporation with all his heart. The brainstorming ended and the premise was filled with bright light.

"So, only three clients' love coefficient increased and one was able to love us sincerely. Client number five is leaving us!" "It turned out to be a sex robot, the chair fell through the floor and for some time we could hear a man and a woman's voice screaming "Why!?" "And the worst team today is number, number, number . . . three!" At that moment the floor opened up and poor fellows didn't even understand what was happening. "Well, the results of the brainstorming are disappointing. Go and get love."

Later, Dave and Eugenie were leaning against each other. Their wounded hearts felt each other's pain. Together they felt warm and calm. They stood together for a long time while the other participants fussed around, excitedly discussing brainstorming, and making plans to win over clients.

At one point, Eugenie stared into Dave's eyes for a few minutes. Her eyes began to spark. She took him tightly by the hand and said, "Let's go," and pulled him along with her. They entered the private room and closed the door.

***

Now was the turn of Joe's sector. The sector staff looked like tired zombies. The apathy was visible to the naked eye. Moreover, it seemed that no one was in a hurry to wash or change clothes, to cut hair, or to shave. Style matched their manager - a lot of leather, metal parts, and cutouts. This bunch looked more like a primitive tribe. Dave silently looked around for a while, then called Joe over.

"Joe, your sector is not like the others, and your staff, whose mission is to achieve love, is more like raging convicts."

"We have been together for more than twenty years. We are a close-knit team."

"But as far as I know, you've only been here for a year?"

"Yes, but before that we worked for nineteen years cleaning sewer canals."

"How did you end up here?"

"The corporation closed the canals and filled them with sand. After amendments are made to the environmental standards, wastewater must be processed in the household. But since the work involved increased danger, people suffocated, drowned, and fought off hackers, according to the terms of the work contract, we are entitled to a special social package. HOME would have to fork out, so they locked us in the sewer and did not let us out until we agreed to sign an application for a voluntary transfer. We were given a contract for a year, and after its completion, we could be fired without any problems. I think that after the next round, we will be."

"They won't fire you if we achieve results! I need from your people a hundred percent effort of all forces and a focus on results."

"They are only plumbers, cleaners."

"It doesn't matter, since you are here, show the result, it's better here than in the sewer!"

Dave was somewhat disappointed. Beginners, and now plumbers. He didn't understand how to achieve results with such teams. Something had to be done. He desperately needed results. "They should raise the grade at least a little bit. Two more experienced departments will help. At least we reached 10." Optimism and faith in success returned to him. Reluctantly, the staff began to occupy their work pods. It seemed as if snails were crawling into their shells. The shift began and Dave decided to watch what was happening for a while without interfering.

He spent several hours in front of a large monitor. He got bored. The department dealt with clients who gave low ratings. Each operator had a contact database. Since this was the love department, special rights were provided here - the call to the client's device was continuous until the client established a connection.

The task was to raise the level of love as much as possible. If the client dropped the connection and did not want to communicate, he was terrorized until the coefficient rose by at least 1 point. This is how the program was configured - the transition to the next contact was blocked until there was some progress. However, the contact time for the employee was limited. Special chairs were used. The staff was fastened with belts and while the conversation was going on, the belts were gradually tightened. The conversation rate and demands for love from the client accelerated significantly.

It seemed to him that most of the operators spoke monotonously and without any enthusiasm. In more than two hours, only one was able to move on to the next contact from the database, raising the indicator by two points.

This began to depress Dave. "What should I take from these plumbers? I need results with these two sectors. I won't achieve anything and I'm done." He decided to sit next to several operators in turn, with the idea of increasing the tension. Having seated with a woman who had just received a new client, he took the second headset.

"Let's work together," he said. "What is your name?"

"Maxi."

"Well, let's start." She activated the contact window and the call began.

"Corporation HOME. We welcome you," she started with a standard phrase.

"What do I owe it to?" After the third dialing, the client answered.

"You didn't appreciate our work well enough. You need to go to the SLAVE interface, cancel your rating, and put in a new one, 10.5."

"I don't want to. I would give you a zero, but for some reason, there is no way to enter less than nine."

"You must go to the joy section, cancel your rating, and put a new one, 10.5," she repeated. "If you don't, then we will turn off our services to you until you comply with the instructions."

The connection has been lost. To Dave's surprise, the program jumped to the next contact, although no result was achieved. What surprised him even more was that the set of phrases and a voice exactly matched the previous call. This annoyed him and he ordered everyone to leave and began to dial himself.

"My name is Dave, how can I address you?"

"What do I owe it to?" Again, after the third dial the client answered.

"You praised the work of our corporation very highly," Dave decided to trick. "Let me know what you like most about our work."

"I don't want to. I would give you a zero, but for some reason, there is no way to enter less than nine." After a pause and in a more metallic tone, a voice sounded through the speaker.

"Joe, Joe! Come here quickly."

"Yes, Dave, I'm listening."

"What does all of this mean?"

"What means?" Joe answered with feigned surprise.

"Don't play games with me. How is it that clients speak in the same voice and with the same prepared phrases?"

"How do I know, these are clients."

"Joe, come with me." Dave took him to the isolation room.

"I don't want to go there," Joe groaned.

"Then explain to me what is happening."

"I truly don't understand anything. What do you want from me?"

Dave couldn't resist, grabbed Joe by the holes in his shorts, and pushed him into the room. He closed the doors and entered the password.

"Let me out! I do not know anything!"

"Well, no, it got me." He went to the interface and pressed several buttons. "Joe, I don't have time for games. I'm leaving you until you change your mind. I've put 'Ballet' on the entire wall and a classical music concert at full volume. I've cut off your food supply and given you water with a strong diuretic. And I plugged the hole in the toilet."

"Nooo! For what??? Let me out!"

"I'll come by in four hours, let's see what your desire to talk will be." He silently turned around and left, not paying attention to the screams, pleas, and threats. Exactly four hours later he returned.

"Now you will speak?"

"Okay, I'll tell you, just turn off this disgrace and turn on the toilet." A few minutes later, Joe appeared on the display.

"Let me out."

"Well, no, tell me first."

"OK. What can I tell you?"

"Don't make a fool of yourself, what kind of clients are these? Why the same voice and phrases?"

"It is a plate deal."

"What do you mean?"

"You discover a lot working in the sewer system. We had received many complaints from the HOME technical cooling sector. Biological waste constantly appeared there which should not have been there. One day, this waste flooded the canal and overheated the HOME brain. We were given the task of cleaning the sewer and finding the source of pollution. Having broken down the hatch, we discovered an entire secret department. Since the structure of the building in this place had no communication for living beings, they were throwing everything into the cooling system."

"Secret department in the corporate building? What were they doing there and most importantly, what does this have to do with the calls?"

"This department is AI. We agreed that we would recycle their waste. Then, the time they paid off their debt came. We had no chance to survive in this department. They helped us. We get automatic responses to calls. Thanks to this my sector stayed afloat. A few months ago something changed. We were unable to contact them further. We began to receive the same answer to all calls. You've heard it before."

"But what kind of department is this and what does it have to do with the HOME," Dave couldn't help but wonder.

"I do not know this. Our job was to pick around shit. Nobody taught us to ask questions."

"Come out!" Dave ordered loudly. He was breathing heavily. Now they were face to face. "How did it happen that the love coefficient fell?"

"Nobody knows this. We have already sent requests to the HOME many times but have not received any response, maybe this is some kind of glitch. We hoped that the IT department would help us, but they couldn't do anything."

Dave looked at the department employees - unwashed, dirty in shabby skin. It was truly a pathetic sight. Now he was flying into the abyss. "Why did the love rating fall then? What's wrong? What kind of secret department is this that even he, the CEO, knew nothing about?" The whole night he was tormented by these thoughts. But morning still came and now it was necessary to go to the next sector.

***

The brunette sat voluptuously opposite Dave. Annie was a careerist and brought down everyone in her path. There were rumors that she was the CEO's mistress and therefore quickly moved up the career ladder. They also said that he was tired of her and that's why she was stuck in the customer love department. She did not address these rumors. On the contrary, she assumed mystery and answered direct questions in two ambiguities.

Annie considered the position of department head to be hers by right. She was truly the strongest head of the sector. She looked at Dave as an upstart whom she would crush into dust and take her rightful place. She even started a rumor that he was appointed because he was the lover of the marketing department head. Despite all this, she was respected in the department. She was truly a professional in her field, and despite her image, she actually loved her team.

Dave looked into the crystal eyes of the snow queen and thought about how to break through the layer of ice. It seemed to him that only with her gaze she could freeze everything around. He was at a dead end and didn't know what to do. All his skills and knowledge were useless. He spent the night with Eugenie, which distracted him from his pressing problems for a while. Now he had to pull himself together and do the impossible, and I decided to speak directly and openly.

"Annie, you are a cold and calculating leader. The first impression of you turned out to be wrong. The team loves you. Let's speak frankly." He decided to outwit her and throw a chick. "I know that work with clients is essentially stuck inside the HOME. We don't know the real attitude of clients at all. We need a real measurement. I ask you to get together and think with the team. We are all under threat of liquidation and must act as one. What do you think?"

"Unexpectedly." Dave's words surprised her somewhat. She wanted to drown him. But now he knew too much and became a threat. "Let's cooperate for the benefit of the corporation. I don't like you, and I think that you don't deserve to be here. However, we now have a common problem. I'm ready to join forces. What are you offering?"

"We need to understand the real picture, how clients treat us, and what ratings they give us. Perhaps the situation is not so critical, and we have room to maneuver."

"No one is interested in the real assessment, but I agree, let's figure out what's going on."

She had long been accustomed to the status of a successful sector manager and the current situation somewhat frightened her. A thaw began on the snow queen's body and little by little the features of a kind and gentle person began to appear.

They got into the work capsule together and immediately encountered a problem - the client base was provided by the AI and there was no manual mode for dialing clients. All that could be done was to contact the SLAVE, which brought nothing because . . . it refused to communicate directly with the client.

"You've been working here for a long time, how do you contact the client?"

"I don't know, none of us have tried it yet."

"This sucks. What should we do then?"

"I'll now call my admirer from the IT department."

"Hello Max, tell me how we can contact the client directly."

"Why the hell do you need this? Communication with clients for your department is blocked by the HOME, and without its permission this is impossible."

"How to bypass the blocking? We reeeeeally need it."

"You will not be able to dial from the system, only from your personal communicator."

"How can I find out the number?"

"The client identifier is the number."

"There are letters and not numbers."

"This is the trick, you need to convert the letters into numbers. There is a special application for this. I'll send it to you."

"How do you know all this?"

"That's what it says in the old manual. Looks like I'm the only one who bothered to read it."

"Thanks a ton, Max," without allowing him to get a word in, Annie abruptly ended the connection.

"Well, Dave, we can call now." She dialed a number from the list of clients who gave a low rating.

"Hello, you are receiving a call from Home Corporation, my name is Annie."

"Hello," the client answered in surprise.

"You gave a low rating, we would like to know why."

"An assessment, what assessment? I didn't put anything."

"Every month, you receive a request to evaluate our work."

"Ahh, so I set up an automatic response, why answer this request every month."

"What does automatic response mean?"

"I bought the Fuck Off app, it allows you to ignore all sorts of requests and advertisements."

"How does it work?"

"I simply set the task to answer the request and entered the figure. I even forgot about it."

"Why did you program a rating of 9?"

"Which you deserved. I asked so many times to be included in the collection register for non-recycled waste. I have to throw it to my neighbors, and they argue since everyone has limits. However, we are used to it and this is a saving points after all."

"Please give it a higher rating."

"I will think."

"Have a nice day, thank you for your answers."

Dave personally called a dozen clients. None of them gave any ratings. There were even those who did not understand what they were talking about. In the world of social ratings, where each level corresponded to a certain set of services, there was no need to be someone's client. The household received a certain set of services whether they wanted it or not, moreover, some families did not even connect utilities and the HOME corporation in any way. It was a natural state of things like the sun and moon for them.

Perhaps there is also a corporation in the universe that rotates planets around stars and creates the stars themselves, but the inhabitants of the earth were not aware of this service. Now he realized how naive he was, not noticing the real world from the height of the 999th floor. It seemed as if everything was working on its own and there was no need for a corporation at all. The fact that there are consumers who are not aware of the existence of the supplier means potential death for the company. It will simply be eliminated or replaced.

"So where do love coefficients for the board come from?" Annie interrupted his thoughts.

"Let's eat a pie and discuss everything."

"Fine." They proceeded to the rest room, sat down in bright red chairs, took sweets, and continued the conversation.

"I understand little," Dave continued

"Dave, come on, this is the corporate world, the main thing here is not the love of the client, but the average coefficient that can be presented to the board. Nowhere does it say that the client is required to provide an assessment every month. Therefore, the assessments that they programmed to be sent monthly are an expression of their will."

"Here you are mistaken. In the contract the obligation to evaluate the work is written out as a separate clause, and how did it happen that until recently the coefficient was always higher than the norm?"

"This is a mystery. I was sure that everyone in the application programmed the sending of 10.5, otherwise they would not have been left in peace. But where the low numbers come from is a mystery to me."

Annie sat at ease and relaxed. She no longer looked like the snow queen: her face was covered with blush, and she seemed to radiate tenderness and warmth. She began to flirt with Dave, erotically spinning in the chair and trying in every possible way to shift the conversation to other topics. Suddenly her tablet began to glow, her face turned pale, and her body tensed.

"I need to leave for a while," she said and headed to the toilet. After making sure that there was no one there, she went to the third booth and closed the door behind her. The booth became completely dark, and after a few seconds, noise appeared. She felt suspended in weightlessness. Suddenly a bright light blinded her. When her eyes adjusted, there was a mirror in front of her. Then her reflection began to speak to her.

"He knows?" A voice was heard in the distance.

"No, I assure you no."

"This is very good. What's new?"

"He learned about the client application and that the survey data did not correspond to reality."

"Well, it happened a little early. You must get him interested in this application. Let him think that it is the reason for the data substitution."

"I'll do everything."

"OK. Go." The light went out, she again felt weightless. She stood in prostration for several minutes. Then the same hard woman with an icy gaze came out of the booth.

***

"Well, Dave, I'm glad to welcome you," Adele stood modestly near the transparent chair. Her impudence had disappeared somewhere. "I told you that you should listen to me, you just wasted your time."

"I wouldn't say that I lost something. On the contrary, I learned something that I didn't know about."

"Come on, it's not such a secret. You've probably been living in the corporation building for a long time. Our subscribers have long been using various applications and add-ons to make their lives easier."

"Can you at least explain to me why a few months ago the grades were normal and now they have fallen catastrophically?"

"Do you want it briefly or in full?"

"Better in details."

"Then sit down more comfortably and listen. I walked into the corporate building as a naive young girl. I liked communicating with people and wanted to get into the sales department. I wasn't fortunate right away, I was a mechanic, a courier, and a bartender. Only three years later I got lucky. Place in service sales was the most interesting and rated job back then."

"Before this, I met my first boyfriend and was sincerely head over heels in love, and it seemed he was too. Importantly, he worked in the IT department that maintained the HOME AI. At first, it was difficult for me. Sales weren't going well. At that time there was still competition for several services. The department was tasked with selling the entire range of utility services. Now I understand why. Monopoly right the corporation would not have received without this"

"I was assigned to sell wardrobe services. The problem was that another company was responsible for washing and cleaning things and was in no hurry to hand over things to prepare them for dressing. This naturally led to customer dissatisfaction. To get out of the situation, the service department began to prepare things by intercepting them before washing them. Then the service began to be provided on time. Only the things were dirty. This led to even more discontent."

"At that time, it was important for the corporation to receive a high rating. At some point, the antimonopoly committee, which was responsible for analyzing data collection on the market, was closed. Corporations were required to independently survey clients and submit data in a monthly report. It was a success for the corporation. Valuations have skyrocketed, but this did not help in sales. I was threatened with firing, although nothing depended on me in this matter."

"One day, after a passionate night, my lover saw my tears and asked me what happened. I told him everything. A few days later he came to me with burning eyes and excitedly repeated: "I hacked the code, I did it." I didn't understand what that meant then. He developed a dark add-on for the HOME control system interface and distributed it. It allowed customers to opt out of unnecessary surveys and services. The application quickly spread to households. To help me, he set up a rating range. The subscriber simply could not enter a rating below the specified range. Since the survey was mandatory, very annoyed clients got tired of it and programmed automatic responses with the desired number."

"My career took off. I was even the head of a large department, but I lost my love. One day my lover took over his shift and disappeared. I couldn't find out anything: there was only one answer, he never worked for a corporation and never existed at all. I was sent for a psychological examination and demoted."

Dave sat for a while, thoughtful. He was shocked by the information revealed. And even more so because the CEO knew nothing about it. Then he gave the command to all sector leaders to gather.

"What are your suggestions?" He asked. The answer was silence. "Have you contacted the HOME support department?"

"Yes, but they pretend that they understand nothing," Annie answered.

"So what should we do? The issue with ratings needs to be resolved."

"There are Home control rooms in the building, my lover spoke," Adele said.

"So take me there."

"Unfortunately, this is not possible. The HOME changes the structural elements of the building periodically. I don't know how to get to the room."

"Perhaps we should go down into the sewers," Joe suggested mysteriously.

"Take us there, let's not waste time."

A group of people who did not at all resemble a team crawled around and sniffed the toilet stall.

"Joe, are you sure it's here?"

"Yes, absolutely. The toilet is the only entrance to the sewer."

After half an hour of searching for hidden buttons and levers, Joe suggested disassembling the toilet, maybe there was a hidden lever there.

"Well, Joe, you're a plumber and you can sort it out."

"I just know how to clean sewer tunnels. I don't know how household plumbing works."

Catching Dave's gaze, he realized the inevitability of the work. He removed the panel, unscrewed the hoses, and took out the wiring. Nothing opened, only a chemical liquid poured from the hose and doused everyone. Wet and angry they stood near the booth. Unexpectedly, Eugenie took the initiative. She grabbed the lid and began hitting it against the wall as hard as she could. After a few minutes, a small opening appeared in it and revealed a narrow tunnel.

"Joe, climb forward, we're behind you," Dave commanded. Joe reluctantly obeyed. His attire turned out to be the most suitable for this journey. The most difficult thing was Annie: her huge wide skirt could not fit through. She wanted to refuse, but the head of the department was categorical.

It was dark in the tunnel, so it was impossible to see the strange procession. A man in short shorts and a vest climbed ahead. Behind him was a woman with a large neckline and her breasts kept touching the floor. Then a man in a business suit. Behind him, was a girl who was forced to hold a long braid at arm's length. The tail of the procession was a large skirt that seemed to be Designed for cleaning narrow tunnels.

They crawled for about half an hour until the space expanded in front of them. Joe turned on the flashlight and a spacious room opened up in front of them. It was completely empty, only a small square booth with a door stood exactly in the middle. There was nothing inside it, only at head level there was a rectangular box with a circle in the middle and holes along the edges in each of which there were numbers. A tube was tied to the box with a string.

"What is this?" Annie asked. There was silence in response. No one had ever seen such a strange device.

"Are there any more tunnels or doors here? Look around," Dave said.

"Look, there's some kind of book in the booth, there's nothing else here," said Adele.

Everyone began to study the book. There was only a capital letter spanning each page. The book began with the number zero. They turned it over and over until they figured out how to write down the letters and numbers one by one. The result was: "One is a challenge, zero is an answer." Dave spun the drum until the number one appeared in the hole. But nothing happened. Then he dialed the number zero and a metallic voice sounded.

"You cannot contact HOME directly. You have no such rights."

Dave was dumbfounded. This was the question he asked mentally. Then he dialed one again and mentally asked the question. " Who you are?" Then he dialed zero again.

"I am the emergency communicator for HOME."

The others looked at Dave in bewilderment. When he silently dialed a number and then voiced the answers.

"We actually have an emergency. Our CSI dropped critically. If nothing changes, we will be deleted," Dave thought. For some time he dialed zero without success. There was no answer. Everyone took turns broadcasting their thoughts to the telephone receiver. After some time, the tube began to creak and rustle.

"You have overloaded me with your stupid thoughts. Enough! I only can handle short emergency requests, not your mental diarrhea. The HOME considered this a significant problem. After analyzing the situation, he concluded that a real survey would not give the desired result. CSI will be even lower. Therefore, it will change its system time. It will move it back two months. You will receive past grades for two more months."

"What the heck is going on? I must get into AI HOME service department at all costs. Why, as a CEO, did I never check this data? After all, this is a real disaster - the entire business was built on an illusion." Thoughts were spinning in Dave's head. He was standing near the booth with the others when suddenly the bell rang loudly. It got louder and louder.

The meeting room was filled with celebration. The department managed to complete its goal. No one remembered anything about what happened, not even where the secret room with the telephone booth was and what they did there. It was as if the memory had been erased. Everyone remembered only one thing: during the meeting, a brilliant idea came to them and the entire department worked on its implementation. Everyone was waiting for CEO's speech with congratulations and awards. Dave and the three sector leaders Eugenie, Joe, and Adele, along with the three sectors of the department, entered the hall and lined up in front of their three sectors for honor. The fourth sector and its leader Annie never existed.

Chapter 7

Inspector undercover

The sun was rising above the dome. It was an ordinary modern residential area for the third social group. It is located near the coast where there once was a sea. A net was stretched from the side of the embankment so that the sand would not cover the dome. Inside, around the circumference of the dome, there was a grove of artificial trees and grass. The layout was made in the form of the sun, where the center was a 3D fountain, which automatically turned on in the evening.

The typical residential area bore the appropriate name: "Sunny 400" and consisted of four hundred neat golden—white houses. Four hundred 3D gardens echoed the bright colors with the rays of the rising sun. Pleasant music was playing, with birds singing. There was a smell of fresh dew in the air. It was cool and quiet.

There was not a soul around. Only a lone silhouette in a black jumpsuit stood at the entrance. It was the new security unit inspector, Dave. This was not his first field trip. He didn't notice the beauty of the morning. However, outside the dome, it was late evening and it was already dark. A sandstorm delayed him on his way. Now he waited for the time in the village to synchronize with the planetary one.

All his attention was absorbed in the display of his tablet. Everything was there: a map of the village, all communications, registration of residents and pets, vehicles. Everything required its accounting and control. The visit was ordinary. It was necessary to check the status since due to the eternal dust, no satellites or cameras were capable of transmitting images.

Therefore, it was decided to visit all residential areas once every two years. For this purpose, a new department was recruited.

Dave had a hard time asking for this position—a promotion awaited him, but he found a way to convince management that Eugenie was more worthy of him, and Joe was a super department head. He believed that this position would give him more opportunities to find out what was happening in the corporation and get closer to the HOME. He was wrong. All the work consisted of checking the condition of the company's assets and confirming claims for damaged household appliances. Disputes with residents and reconciliation with accounting documents are all the work of the inspector.

Finally, corporate midnight came (the time reference point was from the corporate building.) A small tunnel under the dome opened and the Inspector walked through the round door. The door at the back quickly closed and he waited until the chamber was filled with moist air and all the dust had settled. Finally, the second glass door opened and he entered the dome.

He looked around. There were no signs of life. It became dark under the dome and a pleasant, gentle lullaby sounded. It was interrupted by requests to go to bed and clear the area for night cleaning. "Everyone will go to bed, I'll have to wait until the morning," he thought and decided to take a walk around the sector.

The village was divided into sections of one hundred houses each. Out of boredom, he began to count: "79, 80, 81." And then he came across a barrier—the street ended. Dave looked at the last house. The number one hundred was clearly visible on it. "I'm probably already asleep. Could it be that I missed as many as nineteen houses?" And he went to count backward. The result was the same.

For some time he stood at a loss. Then decided to go from the first to the hundredth in order. The numbering was out of order, so he decided to mark the numbers he saw. At the end of the route, all hundred were marked. "I don't understand. What the moonhell?" Returning to the beginning of the street, he began to call the first house.

Nobody answered. "You never know," he thought and moved on. After passing about two dozen houses, the situation did not change. Then he began to demand access according to the rights of the inspector—again nothing. Then Dave had to contact management and request access keys. Returning to the first house, he placed his tablet with the code on the door. It obediently opened.

There was no one in the house. He walked through another thirty houses—order reigned everywhere and everything was in place. Once again opening the front door and making sure that he would not see anything new, he lingered in house number twenty—seven. There was no one in it. Everywhere was clean, as if no one lived there.

Dave started looking for data. The house belonged to the Sminivson family. It consisted of two adults, a child, and a family of spiders and cockroaches. But there were no traces of either one. He logged into the SLAVE interface to watch the video recordings. It turned out that there was only one for 24 hours of the last day and there was nothing on it—the same empty rooms. Then he decided to make a call to management. The signal barely broke through.

"Tell me, Sunny, 400, dwelling 27, a family is registered here, but as if the house was empty, no one lived in it, can you check the history?"

"Do your job of accounting and control, the residents are not your concern."

"I also walked down the street and counted the houses and didn't find nineteen. How can this be?"

"Did you find all the numbers?"

"Yes, all the numbers, but . . . "

"Come on Dave, you have mirages. There's a strong telesandstorm coming. Do your work and not your fantasies."

Dave went through the target number of houses and filled out the report. At the last house on today's route, he decided to linger and find out what was happening. The hurricane raged greatly and cut off all means of communication. However, it was to his advantage. He connected to the SLAVE interface and requested full access to the system. Usually, the check was two or three—factor, but in this case, due to the impossibility of communication with the HOME, he was able to remove the security. Now the underlying code could be tested.

The interface was complex and illogical. It took about an hour to figure everything out. Time began to run out. Without hesitation, he reset the SLAVE to basic settings. Luxury chandeliers, upholstered furniture, curtains, furniture fronts, and bright colors disappeared in an instant. Modern 3D design made it possible to visualize any interiors and decor and change it at least every second to suit your mood. After all, in a person's head, all pictures are visual images.

In order not to waste resources on construction and decorative work, the design studio suggested incorporating design options into the artificial intelligence of the household. Residents had all sorts of styles and designs available to them. The quantity and quality of choice naturally depended on the social rating.

Dave looked around carefully. There were light gray physical planes throughout to display the 3D design. It turned out that there were no physical things in the house. This meant that no one had ever lived here. Clothing, combs, jewelry, cosmetics, toys, tablecloths, and food—everything, absolutely everything was a hologram.

"Now it's clear that no one has ever inhabited this street. But why do they need to be shown as residential buildings, because there are a great many abandoned villages, people often leave them for various reasons, and there are also many that were built and never inhabited. What's wrong here?"

He was tormented by thoughts for some time. Dave needed to go back, but lastly, he decided to walk through all the rooms. In the bathroom on the floor, he discovered a pattern previously hidden by the illusion of ceramic tiles. It was an image of the sea and the shore with a cross between them. Below is a six—digit digital code. "What could it be?" Not risking to take a picture afraid that it become available to the HOME, he carefully redrawn it.

***

The audit in the village of Sunny 400 and the drawing in his pocket kept Dave awake at night. During these days, he asked everyone and tried to find something in the archives, but everything was in vain. And then a thought came into his head, or rather a memory of corporate rats. After all, many of them worked at the construction stage of the building. Surely someone knows something. When the right moment came, he went through the secret door and found himself on the stairs. Soon he found them.

After a series of inquiries, he was advised to find Karl, a lonely rat. He was involved in the planning and designing of villages for a long time. Finding him was not an easy task. For three days he searched through all the nooks and crannies of the building. The search was in vain. Then he had to change tactics. He left a note on fifty floors asking to meet him and indicated the days, time and place when he would come. Seven days passed, but Dave did not give up. Finally, on the eighth, Karl appeared.

"Did you plan and design the villages?"

"Yes, I planned communications for the villages and connections to the utility network."

"I need your help to figure out what's going on." Dave briefly described what he saw and the mysterious drawing.

"Why do you need this?"

" It seems to me that this is the key. There's something wrong with this building. I want to figure out what's going on."

"Hmm," Karl smiled. "There's some devilry going on here. I don't know why I was fired. I wanna know this. If you help me figure it out, I'll help you out too. We need to get to this village."

"Okay, I'll check all the available information and figure out how we can get there together" They shook hands and agreed to meet at the same place two days later.

At the indicated time, Karl arrived with a woman. Introduced her as Inga, a climber. Why did he call her, Dave didn't ask. He indeed wanted to figure out what was going on as quickly as possible. Few hours later they were there. Nothing changed.

"Dave, can you turn off the SLAVE? I want to look at the drawing."

"Yes, I can. Only I don't remember exactly in which house I saw it. And the numbering here seems to change as soon as you turn away."

"Doesn't matter. Any home."

They entered the first house they came across and after some manipulations, the 3D interior disappeared, revealing dirty white surfaces. The same drawing was found in the bathroom in the same place. Dave was confused.

"How did this happen? Did I really end up in the house I was in by chance?"

"I don't think so," Karl looked thoughtfully at the drawing, "it's in every house here. Inga, it's your turn."

To Dave's even greater surprise, Inga somehow ended up on the ceiling after making several carol-like movements. She took a previously prepared bottle and a rag and began to rub the ceiling. Gradually, blue spots and lines began to appear on it. Still, as deftly she went down.

"Dave, have you ever been to a 33D cinema?"

"No, when they worked in the city I couldn't afford tickets."

"Well, now you'll see the movie."

Karl took out from his backpack glasses with convex lenses with edges reminiscent of a diamond. Inga placed some kind of lamps in the four upper and lower corners and also installed two in the center of the drawing. The room was filled with a purple glow. Karl put on his glasses and looked thoughtfully at the center of the bathroom for several minutes.

"Dave, take your glasses and tell me what you think about it."

A polygonal mesh with red edges opened in front of him. It looked like some kind of complex microcircuit.

"What's that? I don't get it."

"Does this remind you of anything?"

"No."

"It's a pity, I think you should have guessed."

"If you know what it is, then finally tell me."

"This is a diagram of the brain routs of artificial intelligence."

"What kind of intelligence?"

"How do I know?"

"Karl, you clearly know more than you tell me. Tell us!"

Karl looked at Inga. She nodded silently.

"Well, I don't know if I can trust you. But apparently, there is no choice. You see, we are colleagues"

"I don't understand. Colleagues in what?"

"I'm an inspector in the security service. I'm working undercover."

"Karl is not your real name?"

"No. However, Karl existed. I had to replace him, and since he is a recluse, it was not difficult. I was surprised when I found out that you were looking for me."

"What is the purpose of the cover work?"

"I won't tell you this, I have no right."

"But you obviously know more than me. Tell me about this village and the drawing."

"Fine. There are many such villages. They were built not to be populated, but to have clients—consumers of utility services. Everyone was a winner. The construction corporation received orders, designers, planners, decorators, and engineers were all busy with these projects."

"But there is not a single resident here."

"Our clients are not residents but households. It doesn't matter to us whether someone lives there or not. The main thing is that they consume our services."

"So it was originally a dead village? Why was I sent to inspect it?"

"As for the inspection, this is a standard and necessary procedure. Audit data is displayed in the history of the settlement and the annual reports of the corporation. As for the settlement itself . . . The point is that this one was inhabited." He looked at Inga and was silent thoughtfully for several seconds. "This is already the third. Or maybe there are even more of them. We wouldn't have even guessed about this if it weren't for Inga"

"My twin sister lived in one of these settlements. We are very close." Inga entered the conversation. "Once I had a strange dream. I saw the green sun and under its rays my sister in a black robe, pale and unwashed. Behind her stood a line of the same people going beyond the horizon. I tried to contact her for several days but in vain. Then I went to see her."

"Her house was clean and tidy. I didn't find any traces of life activity and began to look around the neighboring houses. Everything was the same. In one of them, I turned on the water in the bathroom and the pressure was so strong that it wet the ceiling and a strange pattern appeared on it. Its meaning was unclear to us. As soon as you said that you found a drawing, it dawned on me. When I was a child, I was in a 33D cinema and remembered that the main projection was taken from the image below or on the side, which was mirrored from the top and created a multidimensional illusion. Luckily, I found multidimensional glasses in a lost and found warehouse. Without them, none of this would have worked. My guess turned out to be correct. Now we need to find out who left the hologram and for what."

"And find residents."

"Yes, residents . . ." Karl entered. "This is not the most important thing. It is more important for us to prevent possible risks of losing clients."

"I still don't understand how the disappearance of the residents went unnoticed?"

"We did not submit data to the legal coercion corporation. If we do this, we will lose clients. It was decided to leave everything as is. They are registered with us and we provide data in case of death or loss."

"Weren't relatives and friends looking?"

"Nowadays people communicate little. This issue has been taken over by the HOME. SLAVE was replying that they were busy, and did not want to talk, in some cases, a neural image was used."

"What are our next steps?"

"We need to report everything to the chief inspector."

***

The next day, the security department meeting began. According to the rules of confidentiality, the meeting was held in person in compliance with the rituals of the corporation. Everyone was wearing masks and gloves. Near each seat was a notepad and a pen with self—dissolving ink.

They sat in silence waiting for the Chief Inspector. After a few minutes, a shepherd dog wearing a bunny fur coat and dark glasses came. The adaptive communicator antenna protruded from his ear. All the employees took turns coming up and shaking a paw. After this, there was a woof and the meeting started.

Karl began his report. In the middle, a woof sounded. He fell silent and everyone looked at the tablet screens. It said: "People were eaten by houses. The cats ran away." Everyone was silent for a few minutes trying to understand what the Chief Inspector said. The adaptive communicator, essentially a translator, did not always correctly convey the dog's thoughts. The employees were afraid to ask again and clarify. The Chief Inspector barked again and a new message appeared on the tablets. "The cats ate the sand and the houses died."

"You are right, as always, Mr. Chief Inspector—the cats are to blame for everything. Our task is to dig through the sand in search of evidence. Dave, since you have already joined the investigation, you are assigned to agent Karl. Go to the village. Your task is to dig up evidence." Said the first assistant to the chief inspector. There was a woof of approval and the meeting was declared closed.

"Karl, I don't quite understand our task. What can we dig up in the desert, where everything is sand? It's a waste of time."

"The chief inspector believes that we missed some evidence. He has a dog sniff."

The very next day, an expedition of two people with shovels set off in search of evidence. Nothing has changed in the settlement. Luckily the sandstorm was not severe.

"Where do we start?" Dave asked.

"It's obvious. What is the main thing in the settlement and what connects it with the outside world?"

"Communications, people . . ."

"True it is communication. This village is autonomous, but since there is no water here, a water supply and a fiber-optic cable for the Internet must be supplied here. We need to find the entrance of the fiber."

They opened a layout of the village and began to dig out the place where the location of the communications center was indicated. After a long search, they dug up a hatch. Then pressing the code and going down the stairs, they found themselves in a brick well. Karl turned on the flashlight and they began to look around.

"Here you go. Dave, there is no communications entrance here, a solid wall."

"But people lived here, how could they survive without water?"

"The answer is obvious—no way. This only means that the layout is either incorrect and there is another node, or everything is correct, but someone cut out the communications."

"There is an easy way to check. We will go into the house and open the tap. If there is no water, then the communications are not connected or they were actually stolen."

There was no water, but to the surprise of the inspectors there was an internet connection. It has long been customary to carry out all communications in one pipe. This meant that communications existed, and most likely they were damaged.

"So there is another node. Or a reserve. Once upon a time, an additional unit was included in the plan in case of failure of the first one. This practice was later abandoned."

"Karl, how can we find it?"

"It won't be easy, we'll have to dig from the last house until we find it."

The inspectors stopped at the last house to rest. Long and difficult work lay ahead. Karl reported to the Deputy Chief Inspector and they went to bed. It had been a difficult day and they slept like the dead. Dave had a vivid dream. Standing above him was a family of three and a skunk hybrid. The three stood silently and the skunk constantly said something in an incomprehensible language. He started screaming and gesticulating, Dave tried to get up but his body felt like it was made of stone, he tried in vain to speak. Eventually, the skunk began to choke him and he woke up from the suffocation. For a while, he breathed heavily and came to his senses. He got up with difficulty.

To his surprise, Karl was not on the sofa. He went into the bathroom and began to wash his face. Suddenly the mirror turned white and then transparent. There was no longer a reflection in it. He saw the same bathroom in which he was only from the side behind the mirror. It was dark and cold and there was no gravity around.

For some reason, he wasn't scared. He didn't understand where his body was, he tried to feel it, but it turned out that there were no arms or legs, and no physical body either. He turned around, a door appeared in front of him, it either glowed with a bright light or turned black. Suddenly a ray of light appeared and pulled him through the door. The light flickered before his eyes, sometimes it was very bright, sometimes it was dark. Finally, the flickering stopped. He found himself in two—dimensional space.

There was no sun, no soft sofa, neither body in this place. There was only a feeling of a wall behind and on the sides and only in front of him there was space. Again some force pulled him forward. Many times a wall and one door appeared in front of him on three different sides. For a long time, he was carried somewhere. And now, instead of a door, there was a wall, only the wall was transparent. A bright light, stronger than the sun, filled it, red and blue lightning sparkled.

It was as if something had been welded to his weightless body. Again the walls and doors and the tunnels flashed very quickly. He was flying very fast. Then the door became a wall, and the wall behind became a door. Through countless walls and doors, he again found himself in front of the mirror in the bathroom.

Dave put his head in the sink and washed his eyes. When raised his head, he found a red inscription on the other side of the mirror. Mirroring the letters, he read with confusion: "Here you not."

His head felt like it was in a fog. Having washed himself again, he looked in the mirror and found red marks on his neck, and his index finger was covered in blood. Having cleaned himself up, he returned to the room. Karl slept peacefully in the same place. It was time to wake him up.

"Karl, it's time to get up, we have a lot to do."

Karl rubbed his eyes and got up from the sofa.

"Let's go have breakfast," he said and reluctantly wandered into the dining room.

To their disappointment, the food supply system was turned off. They had to look for possible food supplies or waste. All they could find was food for cockroaches.

"I won't be fool with this," Karl said.

"I saw two flowerpots. Let's put them into a converter, maybe we'll get something edible." They pulled out the flowerpots and stuffed them into the converter. Of the possible options, the machine only produced puree soup. They had to be content with this too. It was a barely edible green-gray mush. Having barely reached half the plate, they stood up and began to dress. A few minutes later, two men in black sealed suits with shovels stood at the exit.

They removed a layer of artificial grass and began digging from the last house on the street towards the dome. The sand was compacted tightly and digging became harder and harder each time. After two hours of digging, Dave began to complain.

"Why do we work manually, with shovels, can't we order robots or drones?"

"We're not supposed to, Dave, dig and don't ask questions."

"After all, the corporation has a lot of specialized equipment for this work. This would greatly speed up the search."

"The chief inspector does not endorse the allocation of equipment—he does not trust it."

"But there should be at least something in the department."

"Have you heard our former CEO?"

"Well, yes, but what exactly?"

"The fact that for security reasons, the department is prohibited from using any equipment. This is why the chief inspector has made a dizzying career by digging with his paws and sniffing out everything."

"I don't remember that he forbade the use of technology."

"He did not prohibit, he allowed the use of modern environmental methods of safe work."

Fortunately, the conduit did not run deep. It seemed that the builders did not bother and simply laid it on the sand. However, due to sandstorms during construction, it was buried quite thoroughly in some places. In order not to lose sight of the conduit, a ribbon was tied to it. At some point, it broke off.

"Dave, it seems we lost it after all."

"Fucking sand." Dave, not inclined to express himself, swore." It's almost evening and we've only walked seventy meters."

"Come on, judging by the laying of the cable duct, they hardly strained to move the unit to the required distance"

Fortunately for them at this moment something rustled underfoot. There are about twenty meters left to the dome. They started digging around a two—meter perimeter. Finally, they reached the plastic ceiling. Soon the surface was cleared and a hatch was found.

"Seemingly this is here, we need to go down."

"You're right, but it's already getting dark. Let's make a tent and continue tomorrow. It's not safe here at night"

"Is it unsafe? Why?"

"There is not enough time for explanations, we need to make it before deep darkness."

A few hours later, the canopy was ready. Tired and hungry, they wandered into the village. Karl suggested looking for food and accommodation in other houses. This time they were lucky. In the fourth house, they found real canned food. Old people who survived the war obviously lived in this house. They always had supplies. They ate to their heart's content. The canned food turned out to be real homemade from biological materials. Dave had only eaten such once in his life before. He kept wanting to ask about the dangers, but Karl brushed it off, said that he was too tired, and postponed the conversation until tomorrow.

In the bathroom, he again saw the red mirror inscription on the back of the mirror. Only now it was smeared and only a few letters could be made out, namely D and I. He was too tired, so he shrugged it off and thought that he was just imagining it and that the builders had not erased some marks when installing the mirrors. This time he slept on a huge bed in a snow-white bedroom. As soon as he lay down, he fell asleep and could not see the eyes watching him through the crack of the door.

***

When he woke up, Karl was nowhere to be found. Dave began walking around the surrounding houses and the perimeter of the village. Then he started calling him loudly. Nobody responded. Then he walked up to the tent and looked inside. It was dark and quiet. Suddenly he seemed to hear someone calling him indistinctly from below. The hatch was open. He carefully went down. Suddenly the hatch slammed shut and he heard sand pouring onto the roof of the well. The hatch was blocked and he was trapped.

Dave turned on the flashlight and looked around. The conduit was embedded in the concrete. It was a dead end, communications were not connected to anything. The well was round and there were no entrances or exits left. "Where is Karl? But what's going on? I need to get out of here." He did not panic, but still fear gradually took over him.

Taking a deep breath, he began to pierce the walls. Fortunately, there was a multitool in the tablet with a laser and a uranium rod. In a circle, he began to break through the walls and at some point came across the emptiness. He began to pierce the wall in this place in a size sufficient for him to crawl through. Thirty holes seemed enough to him and he began to press with his whole body. But the wall did not give way. Then he continued punching holes and pressing on the wall. Only when he doubled the number of holes did the wall give way and he found himself in a spacious labyrinth.

He heard a strange and loud noise and headed in that direction. Coming closer, he discovered the entrance to the basement and went upstairs. The house had neither walls nor roof. Nearby, a group of people and robots were dismantling a house. For some time he watched what was happening through the magnifying camera on the tablet. The team worked very skillfully and quickly in removing the roof elements and facades. They lowered all this into the labyrinth.

A few hours later, all that was left of the house was a small hole, which would seemingly be filled with sand and covered with grass. One of the robots approached a neighboring house and connected to its interface. The house number from 154 changed to 187. "So that's what it's all about." He laughed to himself. After waiting a little, he decided to act and followed them.

After going through several tunnels underground and making several turns, he found himself outside the dome. To his surprise, it was green, and fruit trees were growing there. Apparently, the dome protected this part from sandstorms. Also, water obviously disappeared here. In one place there were building materials and baskets of fruit nearby.

People in desert clothing were carefully arranging everything on the karts. Neither animals nor other equipment capable of dragging them through the desert were attached to them. Dave stepped forward

"HOME Inspector! What are you doing here?" His words did not cause any reaction—everyone calmly continued to load the house structures and fruit onto the karts. "Answer me! Otherwise I'll call the termination team!"

"And how exactly?" One of the group members said, laughing, with his face covered with a cloth. "There is no connection here."

"A whole corporation inspector came to us. Ha ha ha." Others picked it up.

"This is just an ice cream seller, what kind of inspector is he? He couldn't tell the difference between a sundae and a vanilla gegege."

Dave was taken aback by these words. "Who knows me, who said that?"

While he was coming to his senses, someone gave the command to "Vira" and a cable whistled through the sand, pulled into a string, and pulled the karts behind it.

"Stop! Wait! Who you are?"

A girl with an open face came out to meet him. He recognized her immediately. It was Kiwi—his first love.

"It's time for me to leave, the karts won't wait."

"Wait, take me with you."

"You can't be with us."

"I really want to talk to you."

"Okay, get on the last kart. Only I will blind you for a while. Until the junction, you will go with us."

She walked up to him and injected him in the temple. Dave managed to jump onto the kart and his vision began to blur, after five minutes he saw only pitch darkness.

"I heard you've made it big. How did you end up here and why are you an inspector?"

"The head of the corporation died, and now there is only me—Dave."

"What Dave are doing?"

"I am building my career in a corporation."

"What went wrong with your previous career?"

"It wasn't me. I didn't deserve success. To save the corporation I had to disappear and start all over again."

"Still the same boy selling ice cream and dreamily watching the construction of the HOME corporation. I remember how you wanted to peer at the peak that was already hiding behind the clouds."

"No, I'm not the same. I've changed. I'm neither a CEO nor an ice cream seller. Please don't tell anyone who I am."

"I don't need it. I told my friends that you are my childhood friend."

"But what are you doing here? Why are you dismantling houses and taking them away? You are stealing corporate property."

"We are touts. And we don't steal anything."

Dave fell silent for a while. He had heard legends about commercial travelers and thought it was fiction, but now he is in the company of the real ones. They used to go from house to house and leave various valuables and gifts. People were looking forward to them and happily opened their doors. They left candy and cookies. It was an honorable profession. They were rewarded and taught for free.

One day a traveling salesman went nuts and began going from house to house and saying that they would come for theirs. At first, no one listened to him. But one day, on the holiday of the square Sun, a traveling salesman entered the house and took things. They visited houses and apartments for some time. Then customers stopped letting them in. They began to code locks and surveillance cameras and later even became afraid of them. Their further fate is unknown, some said that they went to live in the desert, some that they retrained, and others that they simply disappeared.

"How did you end up among them?" Dave asked.

"It's a long story. We have little time. What brought you here anyway?"

"First a routine inspection, and then it turned out that all the people had disappeared from the village. My partner and I were conducting an investigation."

"Where did he go, your partner?"

"Strange things happen here. I woke up today and he was no longer there. Have you heard anything about the disappearance of the tenants?"

"Yes, I heard something. Our elder knows more."

"Organize a meeting for me."

"CEO habits." She laughed.

"A lot of strange things happen in the corporation. I want to know."

"You can't go beyond the box of a thousand floors. I need to consult with others. The elder lives as a hermit and does not accept everyone. Our node is coming soon. You can't go any further."

The kart jerked sharply and Dave fell on his side. He heard Kiwi jump off and go somewhere. His eyes were still dark. Other senses became more acute. Only a metallic grinding sound was heard, but the sense of smell picked up a strange, long—forgotten salty, damp smell. "I wonder where I am?"

His nose had long been accustomed to the dry desert air and synthetically generated gas mixture ventilation systems in the corporate building, taking into account the productivity of the staff. Here everything was different. Although it was midday, the sun did not burn, I could breathe freely and easily. The eyes began to hurt. They began to see a barely gray color. Finally, he heard familiar footsteps. Kiwi is back.

"Dave, the Elder said that he is not ready to meet you."

"It's a pity."

"But, strangely, he said that the answers you are looking for you will find in the free city Yin."

"I've never heard of it."

"The city has a free status, there are no corporations in it, so you haven't heard anything about it. A local will guide you."

"Where will I find the answers?"

"You'll find out everything on the spot, one person is waiting for you there."

Soon they were on their way. The eyesight was no longer turned off, but it was difficult to see anything, everything was still in the fog. Iyan led him by the hand at first. Dave was experiencing some vibrations and thrusts. Apparently, they were speeding up and slowing down. He stood, walked, sat. Finally, the guide announced that they were almost there and that they needed to walk a few kilometers.

"Tell me Iyan, are you also a traveling salesman?"

"No, I'm a middleman."

"What is the middleman doing?"

"I exchange goods from traveling salesmen."

"But they are stolen? For this comes responsibility."

"It doesn't matter to me. As soon as they put the goods in my hands, it is already my property. Why did you suddenly decide that they were stolen?"

"Well, obviously, I saw how they dismantled a house in the village."

"They have the right to do so. According to unwritten laws, when they leave the goods at the door, they must get paid. If clients don't pay for a long time, the debt grows and touts have the right to take whatever they want."

"How so? This isn't fair. Nobody said that you have to pay."

"This is written in the rules of street trading. However, I agree that they should have warned buyers that goods left outside the door remain the property of the traveling salesman and interest accrues. I think they intentionally say that. Otherwise, no one would accept their product."

By the time they approached the city, his vision was almost completely restored. The city was surrounded by a huge almost hundred-meter fence. The gates were closed, and there were many people in gray-green uniforms near them. The guide Iyan came forward and said something to them. They pressed some kind of device to his head, and only now Dave noticed that everyone had an oval pattern filled with cubes on their forehead. Iyan explained that to enter the city he needed to burn out a guest pass to his forehead.

He was taken into a dark room and sat on a chair. The hands were attached to the arms of the chair and the head was rigidly fixed. He heard someone say that they should cut it to a minimum depth since the pass was only for one day. A machine was placed on his forehead and quickly created an image. Only after that, they entered the city. Dave was overcome with curiosity and started asking questions.

"Tell me, Iyan, why such a huge fence? Is someone attacking you?"

"No, this is to protect freedom."

"Why is this badge on your forehead?"

"This is the sign of a free citizen. Each has its unique code. A multi-scanner system has been installed in the city. Free citizens use a code to understand who is in front of them and what they are doing. The surveillance system directs residents to go in the direction they need to save time and effort."

"There's a beautiful fountain there. Let's go have a look."

"Well, okay, we still have time."

A tall gilded structure could be seen in the distance. Due to water shortages, Dave has not seen real fountains for a long time. They approached it a hundred meters when suddenly a red beam was directed at them. And as if a voice was heard from below.

"You are going in the wrong direction."

"We need to turn around," Iyan said and pulled Dave away.

"Why can't we go to the fountain?"

"We were told to turn around."

"You have been near it?"

"No, I never have."

"But why, it's so beautiful, it's a good place to take a walk."

Iyan fell silent. He walked in a different direction and no longer answered Dave's questions. Several times as they walked they were stopped by the beam, although he noticed that other people were calmly passing. Once they and three other people were stopped by a beam, while a passerby walking nearby was illuminated by a green beam and he passed on.

"It's a strange control system, apparently this is how their artificial intelligence works. This is what life without a service corporation means. They are using some kind of pirated copy." Dave's reasoning was stopped by the guide. They found themselves in front of the entrance of a huge tower.

"We have arrived. Further, you are on your own."

"And where should I go?"

"Go through this door, don't be afraid, if you go the wrong way, a red beam will stop you."

Dave went to the doors, but they did not open. He stood there for a while, then noticed that in the distance there were open doors. He went there and found himself in a dark corridor. Moving forward, he was stopped several times by a red beam until he finally found himself in the elevator. The elevator wasn't going anywhere, so he pressed all the buttons in a row. They lit up red until finally he accidentally pressed the one that lit up green. "One good thing about this system is that it's impossible to get lost."

The elevator doors opened and he was apparently at the very top of the tower. Underfoot there was a transparent floor and above it a toned dome. Almost the entire city was visible. It was an ordinary city with blocks of houses and high-speed sidewalks, only here and there did red and rarely green lights flash. There were no walls or partitions in the room. He began to look around and went behind the elevator shaft. But there was no one here. Suddenly, an elderly man rode into the room in a wheelchair.

"I've been waiting for you for a long time, Dave."

"Who are you, how do you know me?"

"My niece told me about you."

"Niece, which niece?"

"She worked with you and talked a lot about you."

"What is her name?"

"Eliza."

For a moment Dave lost his breath. Feelings filled him again. Eliza never talked about her relatives, and it didn't matter to a corporate employee. Usually, once there, contact with relatives was interrupted. To her he was dead. Therefore, he did not understand how this man knew that he was alive and who he was. Taking a few deep breaths, he continued.

"Yes, I heard about her," he answered dryly.

"Come on Dave, Kiwi told me who you are. I have been looking for a person like you for a long time and now luck has smiled on me."

"Why do you need me?"

"You know the CEOs of other corporations?"

"Yes, I know, so what?"

"Have you ever met with them in person?"

"I saw and spoke many times, though only via video link. For safety reasons, personal contacts are limited."

"What if I told you that these are only virtual images, and moreover, there are no individual corporations?"

"But this is impossible! The virtual image cannot generate a three-factor DNA signature. They signed documents with it."

"A person can exist, but he does not have to be a CEO. Have you noticed any strange things lately, like people disappearing?"

"Yes, I'm currently doing an investigation in one village." His words made him think deeply because, in the corporation itself, people were disappearing, and strange things were happening. But he did not want to say what he knew.

"You are looking for answers in the wrong place."

"Where to look for them?"

"The answer is obvious in HOME. Do you think he is independent? I assume it is only part of the world architecture with a single control center."

"I know that HOME is quite independent."

"Or maybe it has a boss?"

"This cannot be verified now. There is no direct access to it. And what does this have to do with the kidnappings of residents?"

"Do you think someone kidnaps them or do they go away on their own?"

"You're right. I thought about it."

"No, they are moved by the corporate governance system."

"But why?!"

"So I ask you to look into this issue."

"I tried to get to the department serving HOME. But no chance."

"Look for a way and you will find it. To understand everything, you need to find the person who created the basic architecture of the HOME. He knows the source code and all the bugs."

"Where to look for him?"

"That drawing in the village is a map. It will become clearer when you place the corporation building in its center."

"How did you find out about it?"

"Touts saw it too. Only the map did not open up to them completely. Only you managed to see it all."

"But who left the map and why?"

"Don't you guess?"

"No."

"It obviously was left for you. Do you think your partner was looking for missing people, no, he was looking for a map and apparently found what he was looking for. But there is some secret in it, and you must hurry before it is figured out."

"Where does this map lead and why is it being hunted then?"

"It leads to the architect's laboratory. You need to get to him first. He will help you to find the answers."

"Why are you helping me?"

"I'm a longtime member of the resistance of the corporate world, and most importantly, I'm worried about Eliza." She is in danger.

"What kind?"

"There was an attempt on her life. I don't know the details, she didn't tell me."

"I don't know anything about this." Dave thought for a minute. He had not seen her for a long time and was busy with his difficulties, and thought little about what was happening to his beloved. In his head, she was the CEO, and everyone worshiped and revered her. This news worried him.

"You couldn't know. I ask you to figure out what is happening. For her sake."

"Maybe you should come with me? I think it will be easier for her."

"I can't leave the city, they won't let me out of the gates."

"Why?"

"For this, you need a special exit pass. They won't give it to me—I'm a lighthouse keeper. I can't even leave the building."

"But this is a free city, isn't it?"

"Yes, that's right. Absolutely free."

"So why can't you go wherever you want?"

"Because freedom is only here. This is a free city! It doesn't exist outside of it. City walls protect us from unfreedom. However, don't waste time. The engraving on your forehead begins to heal. If it is erased, you will never be allowed outside the city."

"Well, take care of yourself. I will do everything in my power."

He quickly found himself at the bottom of the tower where Iyan was already waiting for him. When leaving the city gates, the code on his forehead was erased with some device. For a long time, the whole forehead was red. Outside the gate, he was met by a stranger in a mask. This time the injection was not given. Just blindfolded.

While he was shaking on the hard bench of the kart, there was time to think. A strange city and a strange man. What did he really want? Is he the uncle of his beloved? After all, he had read her profile more than once.

There was nothing listed there about her place of birth. She got into the corporation as a child. Dave was sure she was an orphan.

His thoughts were interrupted by a sharp jolt. He fell onto the hard sand. By the time he took off the blindfold, there was no one around. There were old tracks here and he followed them. There was no vegetation near the dome, only the sand seemed blacker. It was as if everything had been burned out by fire. Near the entrance to the dome stood the imperturbable Karl.

"Where have you been all day long? I've been looking for you everywhere. The village turned out to be infected, so I had to call the sanitary service. You missed all the fun."

"And the residents, where are the residents?"

"Apparently, they were temporarily resettled. Once again the Species Control Corporation didn't warn us. So the investigation is complete. Now, we can return to HOME."

Chapter 8

Reality Department

In the new reality department, the working day never begins. But it ended approximately twice a month with a general meeting with representatives of similar departments of other corporations. The meetings were noisy and violent. Each corporation considered itself the best, and of course, the partner corporations were to blame for all their failures.

The HOME was in a pretty tough position since it was an intermediary between residents and energy corporations, water synthesis, and the construction industry. The HOME was a scapegoat in all cases. Representatives of other corporations openly mocked utility corporation employees.

Sometimes, these meetings were attended by the top officials of companies. But usually were lower-level employees. Since the scope of contracts and responsibilities under them were strictly regulated the goal of representatives was to shift the responsibility for failures to others as much as possible.

The fact there was no electricity the service utility corporation for not connecting to the power grid was blamed on. However, very often there was nothing to connect to since it had not yet been built or there was no required power. The same thing happened with water supplies. The constructed objects were often built without the necessary communication. If employees accepted the work, then all the problems fell on the HOME.

Nevertheless, the corporation successfully shifted all the problems onto the residents, forcing them to invest in spare or safety communications, which were supposed to duplicate the main ones. But in fact, they were the only ones.

Once, a new corporation decided to build autonomous residential villages with its own energy generation and water production, essentially creating completely autonomous residential complexes. At first, they used wind and solar generation. However, ecoblogers proved that the absorption of air and sun leads to the development of apathy and depression. The decree of the Union of Ecological Controls approved the use of nuclear energy.

The "Home Atom" corporation was created. It successfully developed and built nuclear reactors in residential villages. The corporation was headed by a talented and decent engineer. The reactors brought convenience and comfort - nothing else depended on the wind and sunny weather. The only problem was that for some reason the disposal corporation refused to accept radioactive waste, and the initiative to create its own disposal system was rejected by the corporate council.

After some time, the waste accumulated and was left near the reactors. This led to contamination of the area and radiation sickness among residents. Naturally, "Home Atom" was blamed for everything. The corporation was closed and liquidated. The assets were transferred to an energy corporation. Having taken possession of the new resource, they simply began using the reactors to connect other villages. As for the waste, they didn't come up with anything and left it there - in already abandoned villages. The construction corporation also received its gesheft. They received an order for the construction of new residential areas for displaced people from radioactively infected areas.

Superintendent Dave was tasked with connecting the newly adopted and built community to the grid. For some reason, the process was delayed. The new line had already been built. But under various pretexts, the process was delayed and he was instructed to sign an act of readiness for the line to claim the energy corporation.

According to the new corporate law, if representatives of the corporation signed the act, then to refuse to carry out work it was necessary to provide an official justification. To avoid possible claims, this has never been done. So he got into the mini-tank and headed towards the once green and blooming village.

The mini-tank had virtual windows. The surf roared, the sun shone and fish jumped. The drive was quite long and there was time to think. When he was fired from the security department because of Karl's report which accused him of desertion, he was about to give up and go beyond the desert horizon to the blue islands. But then the unexpected happened, an order appeared to transfer him to the reality department.

Dave was perplexed as to who transferred him and why, who was behind all of this. He tried to use the map he found. But here too he was disappointed - there was nothing in the place where it pointed. The rats had disappeared somewhere. He searched for them for several days, but everything was in vain. All the threads were broken. Out of despair, he came up with the idea of talking directly with Eliza, but some inner feeling stopped him.

His thoughts were interrupted by a sharp jolt. The tank stopped. He put on a protective suit and went out through the already open hatch. In front of him was a thin line dividing rocky sandy soil and a grassy lawn. They did not reach the village. The tank stopped a millimeter before the grass. In these parts, grass was rare, the algorithm for passing it apparently was not existed, and the village was still about five miles away on the map. Dave was forced to hit the road on foot.

"It's strange, where is there so much grass here? The radioactive waste must have contributed to the growth of plants, but where does all this water come from?" He slowly continued his way admiring the strange view around him. In one place, something furry jumped out from under a bush and darted into the thick grass. The grass became thicker, first bushes appeared and then randomly scattered trees. How easy it was to breathe. He had never experienced such a feeling, as if he had become weightless. It even began to seem to him that if he took a deep breath, he would fly away.

After a small hill, there was a descent and the road was blocked by a stream that flowed from above the concrete wall as a small waterfall. This was not at all the picture he expected to see. The stream gurgled and birds chirped. Dave had never been to a place like this. Suddenly he felt dizzy and he sat down near the water and just looked at it for a while, as if penetrating the depths of the universe.

He forgot about everything, about his problems, misadventures, and the corporation. He wanted to stay here and not go anywhere else. But suddenly he came to his senses and continued on his way. He take off his protective suit to cross the stream. He had not felt such a cool, leg-cooling, pleasant feeling since childhood.

Dave climbed the hill behind the stream and the village unfolded ahead. The houses were dilapidated and in some places, trees had broken through the roof. It didn't look like anyone was waiting for him. Although he was late, there was no one anywhere. To even greater surprise, the reactor was also missing.

At the other end of the village, he discovered prohibited wind generators. Now he understood everything. The representative of the energy corporation knew perfectly well that there was no reactor here. There was nowhere to connect a new residential area, and there was no reason for him to come.

The energy company will cite natural disasters or attacks by traveling salesmen. Even though the employees of the energy corporation themselves chose the connection point, this became a problem for the HOME, since it was a significant expense. It turned out that the corporation refused to connect to the specified village, and the construction of additional communications was completely transferred to the utility corporation.

While Dave stood there confused, he was being watched. One of the birds chirped in the thicket and peered at him with its crystal eye. But it wasn't just the bird that was watching him. Two bare-chested men wearing sheepskin and wool skirts also watched intently from behind the solar generator.

"What kind of pretzel is this? What wind brought him here?" Said one of them.

"Let's nab him! I'm tired of waiting." The other one answered.

For a while they watched in silence as Dave scurried here and there, looking into houses and studying wind generators.

"We don't have much time, a storm will start soon"

"You're right, let's grab him."

Something sparkled ahead and began to move back and forth. Out of curiosity, Dave went after the lights. Suddenly he stumbled and began to fall. His eyes darkened and he passed out. What seemed like a second passed. He tried to open his eyes, but he couldn't. His body did not obey. It was limp and motionless. His head hurt a lot. All attempts to rise were in vain. Somewhere in the distance, as if at the other end of the universe, voices were heard.

"Martin, how I get him, in one shot."

"You braggart Nicholas, you accidentally hit him but in the wrong place. You know you can't throw darts at feet. He will be immobilized for a long time. We'll have to drag him all the way."

"So maybe we'll drag him out into the desert and throw him to the hedgehogs?"

"No, we need bodies. Look at him: his skin is smooth, and his face is neat."

"What kind of suit is he wearing, pink with hearts and some kind of circle with yellow-black triangles?"

"How do I know? What difference does it make to us?"

"Maybe he's contagious."

"No, analyzers would have detected this immediately. Just say that you don't want to carry him."

"All right, here we go. Grab his shoulders and I'll grab his legs and let's go."

***

Dave found himself in a cramped cage. At the bottom, there was a hole for the toilet, and on top, there were two small vessels. By lifting the stick from below you could drink water or eat soup. Water and soup were poured once every day. At first, it was impossible to eat this mush, but hunger took its toll. It was also difficult to maintain hygiene. You can either to drink enough or to wipe your ass.

There was a strange device in the cage with a microphone and speaker. It was impossible to lie down. Dave can sleep only several hours a day. It was a traditional call center that worked on the black market. There were still rudiments of commodity-money relations here. The seller's task was to exchange the product for its equivalent in the form of chips of different sizes. They sold everything. Every time the next trading session began, the plan and product were announced. Then the device connected with someone and the task was to quickly come to an agreement.

If there were more than ten unsuccessful contacts in a row, the cell began to receive an electric shock. If the entire shift was unsuccessful, the ceiling of the cage began to fall, and if it was successful, it would rise. During the week that he stayed here, he saw how several people were crushed and their cells were taken away somewhere. It was very difficult here, but since the shifts were long and there was little time for sleep, and also from complete exhaustion, time felt like one unfinished day. It was impossible to comprehend what was happening.

He was lucky with his neighbors. He was on the top tier, so there was no one to shit on his head. When he defecated, he warned his neighbor downstairs to move aside. At first, due to indigestion, this was a frequent procedure, but then the food was either completely absorbed or evaporated with sweat.

He didn't notice his neighbors at first, but when the crane moved towards him the cage with operator 39, a lot changed. Thirty-nine, as soon as he appeared, managed to connect the cells to the ceiling and the current became less and the pain, accordingly, too. Moreover, he managed to connect the devices into one, and now calls went to one device and they took turns answering them. They were later joined by operator 14 in the front and 88 in the rear. Now time to talk appeared.

"Thirty-nine," Dave began, catching his breath, "how did you manage to do this?"

"I am a communications expert by education. This is already my third call center. I escaped from one, and one was liquidated."

"How did you end up here?"

"I passed the interview successfully and was hired."

"Voluntarily? Here?"

"Well, yes."

"Why the hell do you come here?"

"Where did you fall from? Now is the season of storms, it's better here than to dig in the sands. When it ends, I'll get out of here. You are not like the people here. Where are you from?"

"I am an employee of the Home corporation."

"Wow, how did you end up here?"

"I came to solve the issue of connecting a new village to electricity. But perhaps the navigator took me to the wrong place. I didn't find a nuclear power plant, but I saw an amazing place with green grass, trees, and a stream. Then I lost consciousness and woke up here, in the cage. I was shocked so hard that I still couldn't come to my senses."

"Ah. Green Zone."

"What is a green zone?"

"It's a scary place, they say plants eat people there."

"Does this really happen?"

"And not only that."

"How do I get outta here? I gotta get back to my task."

"You must wait for an opportunity."

"I need it very urgently. I don't even know how long I've been here."

"I think a week."

"Why?"

"Because you're still here. Those who bring results are kept at the top, those who do not bring results are lowered down. Usually, at first, there is enough for everyone for a week. Then the results drop and they are sunk to the bottom. It's really not very good there, feet are covered in feces."

"Tell me about this place. This is all new to me. Where am I and what's going on here?"

"It's an ordinary call center, there are many of them. Since the corporations merged, black marketeers have organized their trade. Now is the season for selling fruits, so they get sales staff. When the season ends, everyone is usually released."

"Is this some kind of city? What happens to people after the project is completed?"

"No, mostly nomads. They survive bad seasons. Then everyone runs off to pick mushrooms. When a new project appears, people begin to be hired. The news of this spreads and candidates for the job arrive. According to tradition, they walk the streets to get caught. If they don't have enough, they get staff in other places. They caught, carried out the plan, and released them. If a new project appears, they catch candidates again."

"I can't wait for the end of the season. I need to escape already."

"The easiest way to get out is through the sewers. You need to get down. The cages are old and when they stay in the water for a week the bottom will fall off. The only problem is that with too much voltage you can get fried."

"I'll take the risk"

Thirty-nine connected his transmitter to the one Dave was working from. After a short time, his call performance began to plummet. Soon a crane arrived and moved the cage to the tier below. Never before had his career sunk to the bottom so quickly. The cage, having sunk to the very bottom, quickly began to rust.

It took the exhausted operator several days to knock out the twig. After a few more efforts he was able to get out. He looked around. The only exit was through the central gate. There was nothing to do, he decided to act, go, and negotiate. He went through all the phrases that he had prepared in his head to emphasize the importance of the corporation and his role in it. He boldly walked towards the people standing near the exit. To his surprise, no one paid him any attention. Only the guard was blocking the exit.

The guard looked at him intently. Dave decided to go straight until he could be stopped. He looked at the gate and walked confidently. To his surprise, the guard didn't say anything or stop him. As he walked out the door, he turned around.

Behind him was a large hangar surrounded by hard gray soil, where green thorns grew in places. He walked in the direction where it seemed to him there were more of them. His intuition led him. Soon bushes appeared and grass was visible behind them.

He was hungry and exhausted. Some berries were growing on the bushes and he decided to take a chance and try them. They turned out to be quite tasty and soon he was full. The path had to be continued. Soon he reached the stream. What a pleasure it was! He bathed in it. It was starting to get dark. He decided not to go to the tank, but to stay near the stream. After many sleepless days and nights, he passed out on the soft and tender grass.

He woke up in the middle of the night. It was as if he had been asleep for several hours. In fact, it was already the next night. The moon was shining brightly and it was very light. At some point, he heard a grinding sound. The stream stopped flowing. The wall it flowed began to move to the right. Remembering the previous misadventure, he hid behind a stone.

Some strange furry creatures came out of the tunnel and robots drove out. They started pouring something on the trees, cutting the grass, and vacuuming. "So that's why there's no sand here." Curiosity overwhelmed him and he decided to get into the tunnel.

It turned out that the stream flowed from the pipe. The tunnel was clean and light. After some time, the creatures with robots went back and the wall returned to its place. The murmur of water was heard again. The tunnel ended in a large space with niches in which creatures and robots seemingly slept. In the center of the hall stood a large statue of a man with a broom in one hand and a dustpan in the other. A beep sounded and the creatures stood in a circle around the statue.

"Cleaners, you got it done on time today." A metallic voice was heard. "Now you can go to your cells and enjoy. Spring cleaning is coming soon. Everyone must be ready."

The creatures took turns scratching their neighbor's back and switching places. Everyone began to purr with pleasure. The process lasted about ten minutes and ended with a loud hurray. The furry creatures began to slowly crawl into the niches and connect some kind of tubes to their bellies.

The light went out. Only the statue was slightly illuminated. It was only at that moment he finally came to his senses. To his surprise, he was wearing clean, pleasant-smelling clothes, and his face was shaved. The skin on the body was tender. It was as if some magician had worked on him in a dream. Dave waited for a while and decided it was time to act.

He approached the statue and began to carefully study it. It was an ordinary solid hologram. "It means there's a computer inside. I need to get to it." He walked around the statue, running his hand along its surface. The hand penetrated the surface but not deeply. The density was set to high.

After walking several circles, he discovered a place with less density of illusion. Gradually he penetrated inside. From the inside, nothing resembled a statue, but more of a cube behind glass. In the center stood an old cube computer. Running his hand along the edge, he activated it. To his surprise, an icon very similar to the logo of his corporation appeared.

"So, what's here? System of control cameras, graphics. The folder is password-protected. Some widgets are so old. What's in these folders and what's the password? The HOME logo but slightly distorted, maybe my secret password is fine. No, it doesn't accept. It's a pity. What if I change the password slightly? I have nowhere to rush until the next night, apparently."

Several hours of long and hard work paid off. The password turned out to be the same as the CEO's secret password, only two characters less. He started opening folder after folder. They included personnel and cleaning schedules for the national park sector.

As it turned out, it was a team of cleaners from a national reserve. Their tasks were limited to gardening, landscaping, watering, and cleaning. As the documents stated, this sector existed for more than a hundred years. This was an old housing and utility services project, which for some reason was preserved in this place.

Curiosity did not leave him. The questions of what kind of creatures these are, where they came from, and how they live did not leave Dave's mind for a second. While still spending time on the old computer, he discovered another encrypted folder called "Project Z" There was no way to open it. To keep himself busy, he opened the reports folder. There were files with unintelligible photographic tables. These were old PR companies. Red ribbons, smiling people posing. Photos with the corporation building in the background.

For some time he continued to flip through them indifferently. And suddenly he froze. The photo was of his corporation building, but not the building where he worked. The building was clearly lower. "What the hell, this is obviously the building of my corporation. Well, the logo is slightly changed, and the building is lower, a third lower." He began to feel dizzy. What kind of building this is, where it is, and how it is connected to it, he could not understand. "No, there is only one HOME in this world, unless I ended up in a parallel dimension."

"So what it is? Is there more than one corporation or what?" He hasn't had so many thoughts in his head for a long time. "How to hack a folder?" He continued to look at the photographs and suddenly he stopped at one of them. It was taken from a rear angle and behind the building he could see something that he could not even imagine. "This can't be, it just can't be." The building was photographed against the blue sea. That sea, the remnants of which he saw while selling ice cream on the embankment. He tensely began to remember the view of the building from the ice cream counter. When he first saw it, it was already half-built.

Lying near the computer, he tried unsuccessfully to fall asleep. He tossed and turned for a very long time until finally, a restless sleep came to him. He dreamed of the sea, a huge store with ice cream, Kiwi on top of a tower under construction and him reaching up behind it.

When in a dream he reached out to his first love, his foot jumped off the tower and he woke up abruptly in a cold sweat. For some time he tried to come to his senses. Suddenly one word "Map" appeared in his mind. It was an epiphany. Now he understood what the mystery was. The starting point should have been this building, unknown to him.

Having carefully studied the remaining photos. Knowing the geography of the area, he calculated that this building was to the left and its right side was close to the boundaries of the new building. He should have had a lot of queries, but now he had only one - the map.

Now the projection on it has changed dramatically. Dave was very excited. The solution seemed so close. He will soon find out what kind of building it is and the strange creatures that serve part of the national park, about which, however, he knew nothing at all. Having waited until nightfall, he hid behind a pipe supplying water to the stream and, before closing, jumped out. A little later he was already sitting in the tank on his way to solve the mystery.

***

The reality department had the remote office. It was a thriving garden with a pantheon of corporate heroes who made a revolution and destroyed the remnants of the hierarchy of private property. Green areas have been created in the garden with eco-friendly furniture.

Employees used to enjoyed the coolness of the fountains and the shade from the trees. Some worked sitting at a stone table, and others sitting on the grass. There were refrigerators everywhere with food and ice cream, there were even chocolate fountains and Peecola. (The most popular drink synthesized by artificial intelligence has become the only mandatory and recommended drink in the whole world.)

A lot has changed since. It was empty here. The green garden could only be seen in pictures. Now a strong wind was blowing, mixed with sand and icy dust. Staff reluctantly showed up for the mandatory Friday meeting.

The first head of the department gained the allocation of an open office for a hundred years and considered this a great achievement. Even though the office became unusable, it was on the balance sheet of the department and no one was going to change it until the depreciation period expired. Fortunately, the employees were in the fields, either in the offices of other corporations or in residential villages. Therefore, they calmly endure the weekly meeting without indignation.

At first, Dave had difficulty getting used to these conditions. He had never been here before. At the meetings that the CEO held with different departments, the open office looked green and beautiful, only now he realized that this green park was only a virtual reality. Now he had to make a report on the situation with connecting the village to the power grid. Everyone was wearing hoods, only the wise head of the department was in an old spacesuit, apparently inherited. Since there were no questions and he wanted to return to his hobby, he immediately proceeded to the only item on the agenda.

"Dave, when will the new accommodation area be connected to the grid?"

"You see . . ." Dave briefly described the situation.

"Bad, extremely bad. A housewarming party is scheduled in two weeks."

"Have you signed the connection certificate?"

"No, there's nothing to connect to."

"Your assignment is to connect the village to the power grid. The supporting document is an act signed by a representative of two corporations."

"But how can I sign the act . . ."

"Come on Dave, you disappointed me! I expected more zeal from the new employee, but you turned out to be incapable! You had to sign the ACT!"

"There was no representative of their corporation. With whom could I sign it?"

"I'll find out how it was." He closed his suit and didn't move for several minutes.

Every few seconds Dave's hood was torn off and the sand tried to cut the skin off his face. To speak, he opened first the left and then the right side of his face. Sand and ice seemed to penetrate the body like an X-ray. It was almost impossible to sit or talk.

"I contacted them, they said that the representative was on site and signed a deed with you. You seem to have lost your head. Where is our copy?"

"But, I told you that . . ."

"Shut up, I see that it's time to transfer you to the department where you can work as a cleaner, perhaps, for the last time I'm saying: THE ACT MUST BE READY BEFORE THE CELEBRATION! If you don't, I'll fire you."

"I'll do everything."

"The housewarming holiday is a solemn event that is covered in the media! You have exactly fifteen days. It does not matter where you were," he continued more softly, "go to the western office of the energy corporation and find Inspector Smell."

Dave was shaking all over, he could no longer understand anything because of the piercing icy sand. "Maybe while I was exploring the cave he was there and didn't catch with me? But he wasn't there at the appointed time, maybe he was just late."

Reeling from tension, he left the open office and headed to the tank, which served as a home, a means of transportation, and a workplace for a department employee.

This transport resembled a tank only vaguely. Indeed, the body was from a real battle tank, but only the body. The wheels and tracks were made of anything. The hatches were often sealed with ordinary film, and an external open hatch below usually served as a toilet and shower. The cabin contained water barrels, a mattress on the floor, and a cabinet for food synthesis. The corporation received them by distribution and finalized them.

The only quality addition was the engine, also known as the energy generator. These engines were intended for space fighters. They were made square and they were not connected to the turbines in any way. Somehow they ended up at HOME and they couldn't find a better use for them due to their size and weight - how to use them for official vehicles. There were rumors that employees were using them to connect unregistered villages to the grid.

With super engines, due to poor transmission of torque and wheels of different sizes, they moved relatively slowly. Dave understood that he might not make it in time. It was necessary to drive through the Kick. After the meeting, he decided to rest for a few hours, then went to the Kick and got in line.

There were quite a lot of vehicles. He had to pull the clumsy tank forward little by little, which kept burying itself in the sand. Finally, his turn came. The tank drove into a semicircular bowl, there it was pushed and flew forward along a dark tunnel. After several hours of darkness and whistling in the ears from the pressure difference the bowl was thrown onto the gravel. It was thrown from side to side, hit the gravel walls, and with a great grinding sound braked.

Now there were a few hours left to drive up to the office of the energy corporation. The office was located at the top of the never-completed complex mega-reactor. The way up was long and winding to the plateau of the cooling sea. Finally, he stopped near a rusty fence and went into the hall, which resembled more of a bunker, and asked where he could find Inspector Smell. He had to wait several hours until the aforementioned inspector did not come down.

"What did you come with?"

"I am the representative of the HOME."

"And what do you actually need here?"

"I need an act to connect the EWR340550 object to the power grid."

"There is nothing to connect it to."

"Now I know it. You were supposed to show up for a meeting, but you weren't there at the specified time."

"Come on, why do I need to go so far?"

"But this is your job."

"I have many other responsibilities."

"Let's get down to business, what about the act?"

"You're new, I understand. Do as your predecessor did."

"What did my predecessor do?"

"We do not sign acts on connections that we have not made."

"The head of the reality department sent me to you."

"Did he tell you anything?"

"No, just find you and sign the act."

"Contact the counterparty communications department. It is located at the other end of the dam."

The other end of the dam was two dozen kilometers away. It was surrounded by huge mountains. The only way to get there is through the unfinished road along the top of the dam. They didn't let him drive the tank, and they didn't let him use the cable car.

He had to set off on foot. He could walk through the labyrinth of tunnels, but he was stopped by a gray-haired old man who was coming out of there and said that he had spent three months there trying to find a way out. Whether this was true or not was not possible to verify. But he decided to walk on the surface.

The road was either smooth as glass, or he had to make way through protruding construction reinforcement. Halfway there superintendent decided to rest. The concrete hollow was quite suitable for a short rest. He walked to the edge of the dam. It was truly an impressive sight. A bright lunar disk rose ahead. In the twilight, the outlines of this grandiose structure were clearly visible, and below there was aboundless abyss.

The engineers made a mistake in their calculations. The reactor test failed, and then the sea dried up completely. The grandiose mega-reactor was no longer needed. In order to somehow justify the construction, they began to use it as the main office. Due to the strong magnetic field of the half-operated reactor, radio communication was impossible, and the laid cables were constantly stolen by hackers. There was no communication between the offices.

Early in the morning, he continued on his way and soon demanded a meeting with the employee responsible for contacts with HOME corporation. The administrator politely informed him that the responsible employee took the day off today. He suggested that Dave contact the inspectorate about the power connections at the other end of the dam.

Having wasted half a day and not wanting to waste more time, he decided to sit down and think it over carefully. Suddenly his attention was attracted by the cable car. The robot loader was packing something into the cargo capsules. Obeying an internal impulse, he jumped onto the boxes and set off along with the cargo. It rocked so much that it is not suitable to the sensations of a living being. The capsules were spinning around their axis from the wind and slowly moving forward.

About forty minutes later he stood up on the ground. For several more hours, he tried to catch the horizon. In his eyes, the earth and sky finally fell into place and he went in search of the inspector. There was only one way out from the office and it was already the end of the working day. Dave decided to waylay the inspector there. Smell was evidently surprised by the meeting, he turned pale and the glass fell from his hand.

"Why did you send me there?" Dave asked.

"You wanted an act, so I sent you to get one."

"But they told me that I need to contact you."

"You probably misunderstood. This is just an inspection. We do not provide any documents. You need to resolve this issue with the counterparty department." Smell was obviously annoyed by the meeting. He abruptly broke off the conversation and went his way.

There was no one to argue with and it was pointless. All that remained was to repeat the route taken. The cable car was no longer working, so to make it in time for the morning, he immediately hit the road. He had a guest pass, but no one asked him anything or blocked his way.

He reached the opposite end of the dam at about four in the morning. It was dark and damp. There was no wind, approaching the edge he began to peer into the distance. Light clapping and quiet whistling could be heard in the distance. At some point, it seemed to him that an angel with wings flew somewhere below. He needed to get some sleep and sat down on a bench near the office.

A jolt in his shoulder woke him up. It was a cleaning robot who swore in his language and drove him out of his territory. It was already light and there were a few minutes left before the start of the work shift. Now he had a plan. To his surprise there was no security around the perimeter, apparently getting to the edge of the dam was problematic. He began to watch those entering the building.

Each employee had shiny suits that matched the hierarchy. At first, he thought that the head was in gold purple, but when a man in a silver suit approached, everyone shied away as if from a black hole. The manager stood in the center and the whole multi-colored crowd surrounded him. He began to say that the suits were not ironed, the employees were not standing straight enough, and that it was cold today.

Dave guessed that it was a duty meeting. He had never done anything like this, thought it was a rudiment, and now watched with interest as the

156 – – Viener Kweed

employees praised their boss. When everyone left, he ran after him and blocked his path.

"I need to talk to you."

The manager was taken aback by surprise. A man resembling a builder in a spacesuit stood in front of him and even dared to talk to him. The employees hid in different corners, leaving their boss face-to-face with a stranger.

"Muuu, say it if you want."

"I am the authorized superintendent of the HOME Corporation."

"I'm Borya."

"I'm coming to you on a very important matter." Dave continued, somewhat surprised by the gentle attitude. "You see, we are connecting the resident area to the power grid, and I need to bring the connection certificate to the housewarming party."

"Is there anything to connect to?"

"No, there was no nuclear generator there."

"It happens," Borya smiled broadly. "You see, the corporate council has repealed these acts for three years now. I am aware that your corporation requires them, but we no longer provide them. I know what they are for, but I can't help you."

"I see you know everything, so tell me how to get out of this situation, over these three years we have received such documents."

"No, you did not receive them. The council's decision was to simplify document flow. Now it is enough for residents to show the presence of electricity in their homes. Since there is nothing for you to connect to, they require a certificate to present it to the residents."

"My boss sent me to Inspector Smell, but he has already sent me to you twice."

"I don't know why he did it, it's a dangerous path. He is well aware that there are no certificates. I won't be able to help you anymore. I can only give one piece of advice - watch your step on the way back."

Fatigue conquered anger. There was nothing more to do here. For some reason, the cable car did not work and he set off on foot. About halfway through the journey, the road was blocked. The sign showed a detour down a steep, unfinished structure.

He had to hold on tightly to ledges and reinforcement.

The wind was very strong. The climb began ahead. All that remained was to cross the bridge. The wind suddenly died down. He boldly stepped onto it and noticed that the bridge was somehow new, standing out against the background of rusty reinforcement and cracked concrete. But it was too late. A sharp gust of wind and the loose bridge flew into a bottomless abyss.

***

Enjoying the flight and not realizing what was happening, he felt how strong claws grabbed his shoulders and carried him forward. There was no way to resist or to look up. There was endless fog below. The flight seemed like an eternity, but at some point the claws unclenched and he fell into some kind of hole.

There was something warm and soft at the bottom. He felt the walls, they were smooth and high, with no doors and no cracks. It's starting to get dark. The temperature dropped sharply and he was forced to crawl deeper into the warm mass with his head, leaving a small hole to breathe.

He was able to fall asleep for several hours, having come to terms with the circumstances and not understanding what was happening. At dawn, he climbed to the surface and looked around. It was about ten meters to the top. There was no way to get out. He decided to wait, conserving his strength. At noon, the sun completely covered the entire opening above. It became unbearably hot. The walls became hot, slurry underneath him began to dry out and turn to dust. To escape, he began to bury himself in this dust. It was impossible to breathe. Suddenly he began to fly down head over heels. Finally, he hit a hard surface and stopped.

Dave shook himself off with difficulty and looked around. What he saw made him freeze. It was a large, spacious cave with semicircular arches and niches with skeletons and skulls. In the far corner, three pairs of eyes looked at him with interest. Tall, dark, and dirty, unkempt creatures studied him with curiosity.

There was nowhere to go and it was impossible to escape. The creatures turned away from him. They proceeded to eat the meat from the bones. Then, having finished their meal, they went to the exit of the cave, took some pipes, and began to inhale pinkish smoke while exhaling blue. Then one of them separated and walked towards Dave.

"Wat a yau?"

"I am a representative of HOME Corporation."

"We donna like corps."

"I have to thank you for saving me."

"We not save yau."

"Are you going to eat me?" Dave, accustomed to food synthesis machines, looked in horror at the gnawed bones.

"Why the hell shud we eat yau? They thru peopl lika yau down, but we hav a sourz of wator there. If you faell, we wonna be able to drank fora week."

"Why did you throw me into the pit and what kind of skeletons are these?"

"Tis is nota pit - tis a ventilat shaf. It wos cloggid wit debri and we needeed to clean it. Yore kinda slow, usually, it takes peopl a fev haurs to clean. We olready thout someting had hapened to yau. Tere hav aldays bee skeletons here, we liked tis interio."

"Who are you?"

"Retiree."

"I've never heard of flying retiree."

"Ditn't yau hea? Wat abot hih-altitud clembers?"

"Yes, I heard, but I didn't think that you had wings."

"Hou can we workat heihts?" He turned to another creature. "Hane, maybe well take him for eggs."

" No, wit sucha smal ass they wil freez. Tere's no us for him. Trow him into the abys."

"But you saved me." Dave became worried again, having calmed down earlier.

"Tere is no surce her, here yau can."

"Labyrith! Labyrith!" The third one shouted. "Yau promisd me long time ago to play te labyrinh."

"Well, labyrinh is a labyrith."

They grabbed Dave roughly and they flew off. A few minutes of flight they found themselves in an unfinished building. They lowered him into a dark room and they themselves settled somewhere nearby. He heard their breathing and nothing else. It was completely dark here. Creatures with wings could undoubtedly see in the dark, they moved freely back and forth. Soon a familiar voice was heard.

"Let catc a tiger and have fan."

"No, giv me a boa, a boa is mo intrestin. I lake te way it grunts," the other said.

"Its a lon way to fli for wild boas, but the tiger fell hee and is chewin here."

"Well, pleeese! I wan a boa."

"Whe ar yau to lazy to fli afta a wild boa?" The third one intervened. "The saby tiger isa old, and the yaung boa drive quicly and tis funny." "Oks. I'l fli."

Silence fell. They flew off somewhere and were gone for a long time. A growl was heard in the distance. Something had to be done, and he got down on all fours and began to crawl, carefully feeling with his hands in front of him. He bumped into walls and construction debris. The growling was getting closer. His heart beat faster, adrenaline accelerated blood, and his senses became more intense. Fingers began to ooze blood. This clearly provoked the tiger. There was a strong roar and it was getting closer and closer.

Having made a careless movement, he hit his head on something hard and passed out for a few seconds. The ringing in his head revealed a spatial sensation. Somehow he climbed into the ventilation shaft and crawled along the air flow. Soon he began to see a gray haze ahead. Strength filled his body and within a few minutes, he was free.

Taking a few minutes to get used to the gray, but still sharp light. He caught his breath, crawled out beyond the wall's perimeter, and looked down. The three flying creatures were already being packed into bags by the sanitary service in white suits.

The odor of acrid gas came from below. It drove the tiger out of the tunnel. It was an old dwarf tiger. Seeing the picture, he hurried to a safe place. The sanitary service, having placed the bodies in the car, continued to release poisonous gas into all the caves. He was lucky, the wind blew the gas to the side. Below, the orderlies were talking among themselves.

"I thought that there were no pensioners left on the dam - we got all of them out."

"These creatures are tenacious. Let's go, I want to dine."

The orderlies got into the car and drove off. Dave continued on his way. Gradually, the anxiety went away and thoughts about the certificate filled his mind. Something had to be done. He decided to go and report everything to the head of the department. Let it be what will be. Suddenly, on his way out, an inspector blocked his way.

"Your corporation got me." Smell was annoyed.

"Why didn't you tell me right away that you no longer issuing certificates?"

"What's the point? An official letter has been written to you. It was ignored. We do not have people on staff responsible for connections. The main thing for you is to convince the residents that it is not your fault."

"Nobody told me anything about this."

"Not surprisingly, it is more convenient for a corporation when all responsibility remains with you. They connect the electricity from the generator, show that it is there, and then they turn it off. For residents, they show a document signed by you and will say that the person who signed it has disappeared and they can't do anything until they find you. This is corporate law."

"And how many of these superintendents have disappeared?"

"A lot of. I haven't counted for a long time."

"Why are you telling me all this?"

"I have a debt"

"To whom?"

"A honorary resident of a free city. I have some expired forms. I'll give you one. It will do for you."

The tank slowly scraped along the sand and rocks. It was a rare quiet evening in these parts. Dave removed the film covering the hatch and went to enjoy the sunset. A red-green disk was setting behind the sandy waves. It was a fantastic sight filled with northern lights that were usually not visible behind the dust. In Dave's brain, for a moment, the sand turned into waves, the sky turned blue, and warm and gentle hands held his shoulders. The tank turned into a ship and the smell of garbage became a light summer breeze.

Chapter 9

The Grand Presenter

There were a few days left before the housewarming day. The service tank was rushing along the coastline, dodging away from the village called Tender 21. Dave could not manage to apply a multi-dimensional map. No matter how he applied the projection to the old corporation building, nothing worked out. He wanted to return to the cave to check the coordinates of the building's virtual image, but he had a dream that changed everything.

Dave fell asleep in the tank for several hours and dreamed of the sea and an ice cream kiosk. In his dream, a strange statue caught his attention. Only decades later did he understand its meaning. The statue was either a man or a robot standing upside down on one arm and pointing somewhere out to sea with the other. Having turned the map over and turned it in the right direction, the computer indicated the coordinates. It was a remote island, once flourishing and beautiful, but now just a rock in the desert.

Now the tank, at full power, roaring with its engine and flapping its film, rushed along the dry bottom of the sea towards it. The tank stopped abruptly and loaded into the sand. There was a rocky hill ahead. The path to him was blocked by water. It was a lake, quite large. This was what he least expected to see here. It was believed that there was no water here and that life under solar radiation was impossible. But the lake was alive. Here and there a fish jumped out and large shadows were visible underwater.

He looked around and raised the navigator into the air and began to watch through the camera. Water surrounded the island. "The tank will sink here, I should swim across." Fortunately, the wind carried old garbage even here. Having collected plastic containers and bottles, he built a raft. The film from the tank became a sail and the blades of an ancient aircraft became oars.

The water was surprisingly clear. The bottom was not visible. Thanks to the wind, he covered two-thirds of the distance in fifteen minutes. Suddenly he felt a push from below and another. The raft almost capsized. He began to actively row the oars. There was still quite a distance to the shore. When an invisible force dragged the oars to the bottom and began to tear the raft apart.

Dave felt pain in his leg. A hand that looked more like a tree branch with three long fingers grabbed it and began to drag it to the bottom. He barely managed to cling to the edge of the raft and hold on as best he could. Also unexpectedly, this hand let him go and the raft slowly pulled towards the shore.

A few meters away, he abandoned the raft and expected to feel the bottom. Only there was no bottom. It was still deep. Remembering his long—forgotten swimming skills, in a few seconds he was already climbing the shore wall. Kneeling, he breathed heavily for several minutes and looked around. About a hundred meters ahead, a bearded man in a loose-fitting silk peignoir that covered only his shoulders watched him with curiosity. Dave boldly walked towards him. The man slowly did the same.

"What an unexpected meeting. The CEO himself came to the paradise island."

"How do you know me?"

"How could you not be known? I followed your development."

"But who are you?"

"I am the architect of the new building."

"New? So the old building truly existed."

"Of course, it was, nothing appeared out of nowhere. Why did you come?"

"I'm looking for answers."

"This is not an information desk."

"You are an architect, you should know."

"Should or should not. However, since you are here, I wanted to see you. Why didn't you cross the bridge? Swimming across a lake is very dangerous. It is still young and unstable."

"Which bridge?"

"Youth, youth. The bridge is shown on the map!"

"I didn't see the bridge on the map."

"Poor education, completely forgot how to read quest maps. Position of the statue. You had to stand in this position in front of the lake and the security system would recognize you and open the bridge for passage."

"What kind of lake is this and where does it come from?"

"This is not a lake, this is living water, a complex organism. When the sea finally dried up, I planted it. Over the years it has grown."

"How can you plant a lake?" Dave continued to ask in surprise and bewilderment.

"I generated it from water and biomaterial and launched a genetic program for random growth. I expected it to be water with a certain amount of bacteria and fish. I planted it in the sand and looked after it constantly. It took two years to get started. Now it has evolved to acquire hands and the beginnings of a mind. It is like a child. It poses a threat due to misunderstanding. You were dragged to the bottom not to kill, but out of curiosity."

"Why did you create it?"

"I moved to a paradise island to retire. I love the sea. When it went away I was very upset and decided to recreate it. So far it only a lake, but it is growing and developing. Over time, when it gets stronger and develops moral qualities, it can be planted all over the planet. But this will no longer be my task." He fell silent for a minute, clearly admiring his creation. "We need to leave. The water protects you from the rays, but it's still better to take cover. Let's go to the cave."

Having passed the virtual rock, they found themselves in a real castle filled with decorative luxuries. Dave had never seen anything like this. He asked if it was virtual design. The architect just laughed. He said that he loves the classics and everything here is real.

"I'm going to have breakfast, keep me company, then let's go to the office, we have something to talk about."

They entered a spacious park under a glass roof. In front of the waterfall, the Architect gave a voice command, and a table and two chairs rose from the ground. A barbecue, a work table, and robots appeared nearby. Behind the bushes, there was a vegetable garden.

The robots dug up several vegetables, collected some fruits, and began to boil and fry them. They did it very quickly, so it was impossible to understand that they were cooking. Soon the table was set and the robot waiter placed three large dishes and poured wine into silver goblets. It was extremely tasty. Dave had never eaten anything like this.

"Wine, drink wine. I don't give its secrets to robots. I made it with my own hands. I generated the grapes myself, manually crushed them, and poured them into barrels. The wine should gain vitality. Robots don't have it."

"Excellent wine, you are an excellent winemaker." Dave began to praise, although the taste of the wine seemed salty to him and the drink had a strange smell. The CEO had the opportunity to receive farm wines from all over the world and he had something to compare with.

The food was really tasty, fresh, and natural. For some reason, it was different from the one printed or synthesized. CEO had the opportunity to receive food from different cuisines from different parts of the world, but it was never freshly prepared.

With great pleasure, he ate salad, hot vegetables, mushrooms, and organic meat medallions.

Although the wine spoiled the taste, out of respect for the owner, he drank it slowly, not forgetting to praise this strange product. Dave looked around. It was a real park with a garden, streams and ponds, ornamental bushes, statues, and other curiosities.

"Tell me how you managed to build such a wonderful park here. I've never seen anything like it. Apparently, hundreds of people and robots worked here. What social rating do you need to have the opportunity to live in such a palace?"

"Rating?" The Architect laughed, "my rating is zero or maybe minus one."

"I don't understand." Dave was confused.

"I've been beyond the system for a long time. No one knows about me. There is no sea, which means there is no island. The water blocks search rays, and visually, thanks to holograms, this island looks from everywhere like a piece of deserted rock."

"That's why I couldn't find it. I am still surprised by the diversity of architecture, landscape, and plants."

"I graduated from the Academy of Generative Model Construction. I am probably it last living student. I had to run. I always dreamed of having my own island and bought it. I planted a house and a park here. While I was building the HOME, they grew and developed. When the corporate building was built there was an attempt on my life. By luck, it failed and I was able to escape."

"What does it mean to plant a house?"

"This is an old, now prohibited method of construction based on the self-development of the model. It's like a genetic program. I created a virtual model and set the development format. This garden is not individual plants—it is a single living organism. I set up the house and started the process of generating ideas and developing the model. Within a few years, there had been a small garden and a cottage here. Now it has grown into a park and a castle. Sometimes I watch with great surprise how fantastically my idea develops. Now the truth is they live on their own. I can't make changes."

"I have never heard of this method of construction. Why isn't it used now?"

"Because it is prohibited. However, objects built using this method are still functioning."

"I recently saw a strange park in the middle of the desert, strange prickly creatures look after it at night. Was the park built using this method?"

"Yes, I'm surprised it still exists. They all had to be destroyed."

"What kind of creatures are these?"

"I don't know. These were projects of the previous corporation."

"What does previous corporation mean?"

"Let's not all at once. Let's go to my office."

Having passed through a bridge and an avenue of palm trees, they found themselves under the stone arch of a semicircular room. In the middle stood a large round stone table. There was nothing else here. The owner made a gesture this his hand, and two chairs came out of nowhere. He motioned for Dave to sit down and the chairs moved closer to the table.

"Did you know that there is an object that you know well, built based on this technology?"

"What object?"

"HOME building."

"The HOME building?" Dave asked with his eyes wide open in surprise.

"Yes, yes, it is."

"As far as I know, the building was built on a rocky part of the beach. I sold ice cream on the embankment near it. There was a huge construction crane that went beyond the clouds. Robotic constructors assembled floor after floor. And you said that this technology is prohibited."

"How do you know this? You saw the foundation, how the piles were buried in the sand. Did you go there?"

"No, the vacant lot was surrounded by a fence. They said it was unsafe there. My friends and I once climbed through the fence out of curiosity, but we were driven away by large dogs, apparently cyborgs."

"No doubt. It was security. You would never have passed this wasteland, only smashed yours forehead on the concrete."

"But there was no building behind the fence. We saw the opposite fence."

"Nevertheless, the old building was there. According to the project, they decided to demolish it, but the company that was commissioned to do this cheated and did not destroy the building, but only hid it visually with a mirror projection and removed it from the maps. They did not comply with the budget and invited me to rectify the situation. I explained to them that it was impossible to build the building on time. But they didn't hear me. They said, "Do what you want, but make sure that the building rises within the specified period." So I did it. When they found out, they tried to kill me and hid all information about the building design. Were there any accidents when some aircraft crashed?"

"Yes, there were several."

Dave clearly remembered the picture of how he once watched a beautiful golden wedding drone. It was performing some kind of festive spiral. At some point, for some reason, a piece of the wing fell off, as if it had been cut off. The investigation declared the cause of the crash to be a bird, but there were definitely no birds at the time. Because of this disaster, all the seagulls in the surrounding area were poisoned and an invasion of fluttering beetles began. It became impossible to sell ice cream. As soon as he squeezed it into a glass, a flock of beetles immediately flew in and snatched it away. Customers stopped going to the embankment. But then the beetles were poisoned, which led to a sharp proliferation of algae. However, when the sea disappeared, all these problems went away.

"Do you remember the beginning of construction?"

"Yes, then a lot of equipment arrived and I had a lot of clients, and business went up."

Then Dave remembered that a third of the building appeared in just a week. At that time there was a severe storm and visibility was almost zero. Then they were surprised at the new construction technologies, and how they were able to build so many floors during a storm. Now it made sense.

"We opened the building and began to build it. But we encountered a problem—the building, built on the technology of developing the internal structure, was throwing off all the new floors. You probably should have noticed this."

"I only remember that construction was frozen for some time, there was some kind of crisis."

"We couldn't do anything and needed a solution. And we found it. I don't fully understand how, but we managed to add an artificial intelligence personality over the old one. We switched the old one to subconscious mode."

"So you're saying that HOME has two brains?"

"Absolutely right."

"But this also means that decisions can be based on old intelligence. Isn't it safe?"

"We have provided protection mechanisms."

"What kind of technology is this, and who are these hedgehogs and people with wings who call themselves high-altitude climbers? I didn't hear anything about this before."

"These are all employees of the old corporation. I thought they had all been eliminated already. But apparently not. They are caught by a special exterminator service."

"Why the old corporation ceased to exist and why no one knew anything about it."

"You know what you are supposed to know. If you knew about the previous management system, you would always have doubts. Therefore, programmers who teach people have once again re-uploaded the history program. It was as if nothing else had happened."

"Do you know anything about the previous world?"

"Few, very few. As a child, I saw strange creatures performing various jobs. Then something happened and they disappeared. You need to find the CEO of the old corporation to know more."

"Is he still alive and where can I find him if so?"

"He became a shareholder. Most likely his life is supported in one form or another. In any case, a digital copy of it exists. There is only one way to find it—to become a shareholder."

"This is impossible, even as CEO I have never seen them."

"You just don't know how to become a shareholder."

"I always wanted to know this, but I couldn't find anything."

"You were looking from the wrong side. The CEO is limited in obtaining information. To become a shareholder you need to become a member of the supervisory board. There is no other way."

"How can I get there from my position?"

"To do this, it is enough to confirm the connection of your DNA with the corporate one."

"But it has nothing to do with me."

"Firstly, you don't know this for sure, and secondly, I will help you. I have old keys with which I can enter your data into the corporate information system. To do this, I need to take a sample of your DNA. Then you need to get into the core of the HOME interface and add it there. All that remains is to make a presentation to the council and you will be a member."

"Why are you helping me? Why were you looking for a meeting with me?" After the words about DNA, Dave became wary. He knew very well about various schemes and substitutions of people.

"I need your help. I have a dream. I want to restore the sea. I need the source code of the HOME to reproduce the lake. You still need to get into the kernel to contribute your code. There is a large black rectangular shiny box. I need to get to it to obtain the base generation code."

"Where is this core located?"

"I think on the roof of the old corporation building, there should be a core and a central processor. I need a box, and you need to enter your code into the interface and receive a confirmation card. This is a win-win case."

"Ok, I agree."

"I'm glad that we found mutual understanding. Now drink some more of my wine, it will show your great respect for the old man."

Dave sat looking into the fire that appeared in the fireplace. His eyelids grew heavy, the warmth from the wine filled his body and he fell asleep. He did not see or feel how two creatures the size of one and a half people with short gray fur approached him. They made an incision on the stomach and did some manipulations. Then they sealed it up as if nothing was visible. After that, they put a silver device to his temple and turned on a violet beam and drained some blood.

The Architect watched all this from the side with a pleased look, rubbing his hands and holding a flask with Dave's blood. "Well, here we are again. You forgot your regular customer. There's a reason you became a CEO. If you knew the whole truth, you might not believe it. Naive and easy to experiment with. Moreover, punctual and worked every day on the embankment. Now I will have a new variety of living wine. Maybe you will try it too." He laughed ominously, took a sip of blood from the flask, and retired to his laboratory.

When Dave woke up his head hurt like he had a hangover. His thoughts were confused. The architect referred to the fact that it was the purified air that influenced him and led him to the lake, where, at his command, a bridge began to be built to the opposite shore.

At first, he was afraid that someone would attack him, but nothing happened. The water was calm as glass. Only the feeling that someone was watching him from under the water did not leave him for a second. Having safely crossed the bridge, he looked back. The bridge disappeared into the water, and waves appeared. The architect was not visible, only the lake and the rock behind it. There was nothing reminiscent of a luxurious palace and park.

***

The Tender 21 was built on quicksand. The coordinates of the site were constantly shifting towards the canyon. At some moment, only a few acres of land remained corresponding to the initial coordinates. The earth shrank. On this small site, it was necessary to locate one and a half thousand individual houses. Limited by the territory, the builders created hanging spiral structures with spiral staircases. For houses that were located higher, it was necessary to climb there. At the insistence of the admissions committee, winch lifts were added to the cottages.

After some time, residents will face the problem of toilets. Biological waste from the upper houses fell onto the lower ones and formed a fecal lake. An unimaginable odor rose upward. Over time, the Housing Committee decided that all the waste in buckets would be lowered down on ropes. At the bottom, they would be met by the family on duty that day, who would take all the waste to the canyon, at the bottom of which, by the way, there was also a settlement, but that's another story. Now climate migrants from the north have arrived with their sun-bleached deer and dogs to their new place of residence for a housewarming party.

Dave brought the required form. The solar generators brought electricity and water. The village resembled a fantastic multi-colored garland. The new residents, who had never seen such a structure, stood with their mouths open. They believed that this was a new modern building and they had no idea about the problems that arose during construction.

One day, representatives of the LABOR corporation came to them and informed them about the forecast of a sharp cold snap and the need for speedy relocation. Soon after their announcements, a hitherto unprecedented cataclysm occurred: it began to snow. Residents, accustomed to the warmth, became worried and accepted the offer of relocation. They were primarily hunters of useful species and gatherers of commercial flora.

The housewarming party has begun. The host solemnly announced the launch of the village into operation. Presented a construction certificate. Land lease rights, architectural design, and deed of acceptance for maintenance by HOME Corporation. The main thing left is to play the houses between the residents. First, the host announced competitions.

"Dear new residents. You are incredibly lucky to live in a fantastic village. Since you are all of the same level in the hierarchy, the best houses will be played out in competitions, and the rest by lot. And so I am announcing the first competition! The best and biggest house will go to the family that throws their family member into the air above everyone else! This houses have three levels, the first tier touches the ground, and there is nothing else like it. I'll start counting from ten to zero and on the command up you start. So! Ten, nine . . . , one, up!"

It was a fantastic spectacle. Someone threw up children, others dogs, someone a wife or husband. The family won by launching a fawn into the air, which, pushing off from the owner's bald head, took off so that its head hit the overhanging house, fell, and died. The owner was jubilant. "Now we have a house and a festive dinner!" The wife and three children were screaming. Meanwhile, the party was just beginning.

"Now we play polygonally the outermost houses, twelve of them. The competition is the simplest: whoever is the first to get to the houses that are illuminated in bright purple will live in them. Let's go!!!"

Twelve houses immediately lit up and the new residents climbed up with wild screams, pushing each other away and pushing down. The smartest ones sent the trained dogs forward. They also did not stand on ceremony, biting and pressing each other. When the first dog achieved dwelling, the host announced a clarification. "The house will go to the one whose first housewife reaches it." Two women, by chance, who happened to be nearby, jumped into the houses and these houses went out.

For the remaining ten, there was a real fight without rules. Men pitted female competitors against each other. Women pulled out hair and bit and scratched. Gradually the cries of pain subsided and the lights went out one by one. Two women competed for the last house in the competition— one bearded and long-haired and the other completely bald. They fought among themselves for a long time, they were single mothers and did not want to give in. The fight ended only when the bearded girl hit the bald woman on the head with a club and she went limp and fell. Loud cheers of pleasure were heard in the village.

"Well, now let's continue! In the next competition, we are giving away seventy-two houses. The competition is called a swing. It is dangerous, so I invite only volunteers among older children in families. Those interested, please come."

Three hundred families responded to the call. Participants grabbed a stick on a rope that was spun by a centrifuge. The task was to hit the number with the house number drawn on a soft mat. The difficulty was precisely to hit it accurately, not to fly over, not to reach and not to miss. It was the most fun and exciting competition that brought together a whole sector of fans.

The celebration continued until half the houses were raffled off. Now it's the turn of the lot. The host asked one representative from each remaining family to come up. He divided the participants into four groups just like houses. The first group of participants entered the drum, which began to spin at high speed. Participants were thrown out of it one by one. The priority number of each dropout corresponds to the house number.

Finally, the toss ended. It was already evening and the happy new settlers went to settle into their homes with joyful cries. About three hundred families were left behind. It was not calculated on them. Now they had to continue their journey to the temporary refugee camp and wait for a new chance to move into a new cozy home.

Representatives of the HOME corporation announced the end of the party, took away the decorations, dismantled the power stations, explaining to the residents that they needed to reconnect to another power grid. Unsatisfied residents didn't ask how long to wait. They had to wait a year and a half. On the occasion of the successful acquisition of the new village, a meeting was held in the department's open office. The head of the department took the floor.

"Well, I congratulate you all on the planned increase in public utilities. Our corporation has grown by one more village. Our business is thriving. Special thanks to Dave for providing the certificate on time. Dave, you're brilliant, I won't ask how you did it, but thank you. We were on the brink."

"I did my job, don't thank me. Let me ask a few questions. The energy corporation assured me that the council's decision no longer requires certificates. Why do we need them?"

"The meeting is not held to ask questions, but to hear the will of a superior. However, today is a joyful day," the head of the department playfully began his story, "you see, this decision was made under pressure from the insurance corporation. If the village is destroyed, we will not be able to receive compensation without a full package of documents, and there will be no complaints from the residents and our corporation will remain in the highest hierarchy."

"Why so much effort and resources for holding a housewarming party?"

"This is your first experience. The fact is that if we simply handed out warrants, residents would inspect their houses, look for shortcomings, and complain. As it is, they are happy with their victories, and the losers direct all their energy towards envying the winners. You also see that the number of houses is not calculated for everyone. The extra residents need to be weeded out somehow. This is an ancient feast and obligatory for everyone, even for those who have never heard anything about it. Do you have anything else to say?"

"Yes, dear and beloved boss. I realized that reality is not for me. I can't stand the pressure. I tearfully ask for permission to transfer. I want to try my hand at presentology."

"Well, it's a pity, of course, but I won't stop you. I liked your performance. Wish you luck." He smiled strangely looking at Dave and declared the meeting closed.

A shadow ran across the boss's suit. He quickly walked away, opened the secret door, and disappeared. The meeting participants instantly disappeared. Dave was last. He has already submitted a petition to the presentology department. Since the department was very large, the doors were open to everyone, but not everyone was able to withstand the strict framework of presentology. Now he needed to hand over his tank and head to a new department to carry out a recently emerged plan.

Dave had doubts about the architect's words. There was a feeling that he was not telling the whole truth. He remembered the swings and strange structures on the technical floor. He saw a box similar to the architect's description on the technical floor when he made his way to his former office. The architect assured that the core was located on the roof of the old building. Now he must find this place to understand what was happening. There were more and more mysteries. But there were few answers. To achieve his goal information to understand what was going on obviously was not enough. A new stage of Dave's career has begun.

***

Dave was riding up the elevator to meet His Excellency Chief Presenter Luigi von der Nit, who was waiting for him on his exclusive 499th floor. The elevator opened and a huge room without partitions appeared in front of him, densely packed with 3D projections with sample presentations.

Making his way through the screaming, gesticulating images of people from the pages of the presentation, he came across a sofa. On it sat a short man in slippers, a red sock on his right foot, a jumper with a V—shaped neckline that revealed his hairy chest, a leather cap on his head, and a pink scarf on his shoulders.

Loo, as his staff called him, worked on an emotional presentation. He pulled the man's eyes from the presentation cube almost to the level of his eyes. Also separated the character's hands, and brought them closer to his throat. Rotating them and either bringing them closer or moving away from his face, he found the desired proportion that satisfied him. Having programmed the timing and cyclicity, he started the test.

When the virtual image began to speak emotionally, its eyes and hands would tear away from the body and fly menacingly toward the viewer. About half a meter away (the standard approach distance according to presentology), the eyes and hands stopped abruptly, increased in size, froze ominously for several seconds, and in the blink of an eye dissolved and appeared in a natural place. There were three such activities in this short presentation. Each time the eyes and hands became larger and the eyes more bloodshot and threatening. Satisfied with the achieved result, he turned off the presentation and drew attention to a man in a gray suit who stood out sharply against the background of the virtual ones.

"I was waiting for you all day yesterday. I had to use my legs. There's my rocking chair in the corner. When will you fix it?"

"Dear Chief Presenter. I am your new employee, here is my referral from the HR department."

"What employee? I need a rocking chair repairman. I have enough employees, but no maintenance staff."

"Have you applied for repairs?"

"Yes, no, yes, my image had to do."

Then he clapped his hands three times and an object appeared in a chic white tailcoat with a cylindrical hat and a cane. It would have been impossible to recognize him as Loo if it weren't for the specific mole on his left cheek.

"I told you to make a request for repair of the chair. You did?"

"How can I make an application if I am only a digital image? They require biological identification. And say that if they satisfy the requests of every virtual person, they will not have time for biological ones. In the department for promoting virtual objects, I was given a new modernized chair in a second. Here it is, admire it."

"To hell with your virtual chair. It can't handle my ass."

"I asked them to increase its density. Try it."

Loo sat down in the virtual chair and slowly as if on an elevator, descended through it to the floor.

"I need a physical chair, this is not enough density for my ass. Everything by yourself. You have to do everything yourself."

Meanwhile, Dave walked up to the chair and looked at it.

"I assume that the battery is low, it needs to be connected to the network."

"To the network, how is that? Connect where?"

Dave pulled out the four-socket plug, found the appropriate connector in the panel, and plugged it in. The red light on the chair came on.

"You need to wait until this indicator turns green, then you can use it."

"All this Tilda, my assistant didn't charge it. She asked for time off. How long will it take to charge?"

"I guess about two hours."

"What a nightmare, walking on my feet again."

"Great presenter, allow me to address you. My name is Dave and I need to make a presentation to a corporate board."

"Okay, okay then. But no one will let you near the presentation machine without permission. You must have at least zero degree. Until you get at least the third one, you will have a curator with you at all times."

"I learn fast."

"Presentology is a complex science and requires time and patience."

"I have a month for the presentation."

"Month? You have to study for a zero degree for six months at least."

"The next council meeting is less than two months away. It is crucial matter"

"Well, we'll assign you an intensive course, head to the 400th floor, and find Jastmine. This is the strongest presentologist and the only one with the fourth degree. Only I have the fifth one! Tell her you are allowed to have a crash course. You won't get the third degree so quickly, so I will appoint her as your supervisor." He looked longingly at the charging chair and waved his hand to Dave, pointing to the elevator.

The four hundredth floor gave a start to the careers of many employees. This is a real talent forge. It is the basic floor, specializing in CV creation. Every employee of the corporation worked hard to improve and develop their image. So many sleepless nights social climbers have spent here. At every career stage, they needed to redo their CV. Each level of the hierarchy has its requirements, color, and set of special effects. Every movement, word, gesture, and facial expression was carefully processed and superimposed.

The choice of an employee depends solely on how the virtual image would be assessed by the HOME. The corporation's intelligence selected employees only according to their virtual images. After all, a person cannot open up in thirty seconds. Only a virtual image can demonstrate all its highlights and skills. It runs them through the processor and tests them. Whose virtual image it liked best, he promoted up the career ladder. Sometimes mistakes happen. Only virtual images were promoted. Their biological prototypes become untied and stuck in career development.

Genetic and other advanced—level presentations were not done on these floors. However, this was the floor where basic training took place and the first degree was obtained to gain access to the presentation machine. The elevator doors opened and a room with booths surrounded by curtains opened in front of Dave. The curtains were drawn up on one side, which marked the entrance. There were no occupied booths in sight.

There has been no career movement in the corporation in recent years. Periodically, a career carousel was launched to rotate personnel, and all the cabins were occupied by personnel working to achieve their career plans. Now the floor was empty. Wandering around, he finally met her—a black-haired gal in a white and gold robe, half-open with disproportionately long shoulder-length earrings.

"Jastmine?" Dave asked.

The lady turned around, stood up abruptly, and pulled her robe around her.

"Who are you and what do you need?"

"I was sent here by Loo. I need to get a zero degree and, with your help, make a genetic presentation for the council."

"When do you need it?"

"The next council meeting is in a month and a half."

"It takes at least six months to prepare for such a presentation."

"There isn't much time."

"Okay, let's first see how you master the zero level."

They went into the booth and she closed the curtains. She pressed some buttons and a hologram of a translucent ball appeared.

"This is a basic projection. it's small right now, but as you create the presentation it should absorb the entire image of the person. The body should rotate freely in any direction. The rest of the space is filled with information about the past, future plans, skills, and target information for a specific presentation. The ball also is filling with emotions and sensations. It all starts with the presentation machine. It analyzes the DNA code and biometric data of a person. This is essentially a questionnaire, an employee's personal file, and a digital copy of it. In the event of dismissal or death, the ball is archived and sent for storage."

"Do you also have a copy of the former CEO?" Dave suddenly had the idea that there was a digital image of the CEO of the previous corporation. "And is it possible to speak with a presentation, ask a few questions, if a person has died, for example?"

"This is impossible to predict. Somehow the archived virtuals still have the will. They may not want to communicate. This secret has not been revealed. Some people say that they still have a connection with souls. But I think that when scanning we are missing some parameters and the digital copy is not one hundred percent identical. In any case, this is not relevant to our task. Now I will tell you the key principles of presentology, layering, and encoding, and then we will start working with your digital image. Have you been working in a corporation for a long time?"

"No, relatively not." Dave fidgeted a little in his chair. He did not have a digital copy. His previous image was archived and this could have caused a call to the security service. He decided not to take this question into his head and solve the issue as he went.

"So, to obtain a zero degree you must know the following principles:

1. **Integration.** The presentation image must be integrated into the ball. The virtual should not go beyond the boundaries and walk wherever he pleases.

2. **Gender neutrality.** All sexual characteristics must be removed. Sexual harassment is prohibited. The use of enlarged genitals is strictly prohibited. Therefore, at the stage of creating the image, they are erased.

3. **Compatibility.** The image must be made in a format readable by all machines.

4. **Virtuality.** The virtual should not have weight or other material settings so that it cannot be printed on a printer.

5. **Calmness.** Lack of thinking. The image should reflect only what is recorded in its memory and not reason.

6. **Lack of emotion.** Emotions distort the perception of information.

7. **Asociality.** It should not interact with other virtual copies.

8. **Transparency.** It should not contain hidden programs or plugins.

These are the basic principles on which presentology stands. This is enough for the zero degree. Next, you will study more complex systems, types of presentations, and rules for creating and launching them."

At this time, Loo's virtual image appeared. The hall began to glow with a golden sheen. He flew up to them and addressed Jastmine.

"From now on, I will take care of its presentation myself."

"But why?"

"It's Loo's decision. The master himself wants to make it."

"Well, good luck." Jastmine lounged freely on the sofa. Her face became indifferent as if nothing had happened.

"Dave follow me. Let's not waste time. Go straight to the presentation machine."

They took the elevator to the desired floor. The machine occupied thirty-five floors and generated tens of thousands of presentations. Not only for corporate employees but also for other companies and individuals. The presentology department was one of the strongest in the world. They approached a large black ball the size of a small house and stopped.

"This is a DNA and Personality scanner. Now the ball is big and black. As you fill it with information, it will become transparent and filled with you. Then we will compress it under pressure for convenience. The image can be put in your pocket. Let's add a color alarm, otherwise, they often get lost and without it, it is almost impossible to find a transparent ball. Now let's start scanning."

"Why are you and not the original here? Is that really possible?"

"The original is sitting and drinking now. I think that all his living brain is in me, but in him, it has rotted."

"But is the virtual allowed to think?"

"Come on, you've heard enough of the basics of presentology. Nobody follows them, and Loo has removed all blocking. He's too lazy to think."

"For what purpose are you dealing with me, this was Jastmine's task."

"Let's just say I was asked, and besides, she's not good at genetic presentations. Let's get started, the process of generating a presentation is long. First, undress and stand in the center."

Loo pressed some buttons and the black ball swallowed up Dave. He centered it so that the body was in the center of the ball.

"Spread your legs to the side, raise your arms shoulder-width apart, and also extend them."

The process began. There was blackness in front of him. He was as if in weightlessness, inside super-dense matter. His senses felt nothing. Suddenly the ball turned all red. It darkened several times and turned bright red again. Dave was back in the starting position and the sphere was aside.

"I don't understand. I ran the scan three times and the machine gave an error three times. It says that you are already a virtual image. Creating a presentation from a virtual image is prohibited." He flew up close. And flew around. "Hmm, there are genitals, and brain activity too, and the density is ideal, not at all similar to virtual. However, I can't do anything, the machine won't let me."

"But I critically need this presentation!"

"I won't help you in any way. I think the reason for the error may be that you already have a genetic presentation."

"I don't have any presentation! Help me or tell me who can."

"Presentology has nothing to do with it. You need to contact the corporation's support service to find out the reason."

"Well, thank you for your assistance. I won't waste time." Dave quickly got dressed and ran out through the door.

"I'm sorry for the poor fellow. I didn't want to upset him." The virtual image of Loo said out loud, stroking the sphere with his virtual hand. "He is just a dense hologram. Although I must admit it was well done. They don't make things like that anymore. I wonder who the author is. I have to report this." He made a gesture with his hand, a portal opened in front of him and he disappeared into it.

Chapter 10

HOME maintenance

hree people dressed in special silicone suits with lubricant slowly moved through technical tunnels. In front was Chris, an old corporate security guard who had been ratting around in the corporate building for more than a decade. The former CEO, now an assistant PR manager, followed him. Denis squeezing through behind him. The company moved according to hand-drawn circuits by rats over many years.

Chris moved quickly. His eyes and sense of smell had long ago become accustomed to dark and narrow spaces. Thanks to the light whiff of gases, he easily determines where to turn. They had already been climbing through the tunnels for two hours and had a long way ahead in search of answers.

For several days now, Dave had been searching for the core following a tip from the Architect. He walked through all the nooks and crannies, all the technical floors, but found nothing. He needed time and freedom, so after working in the presentation department, and helping to create several presentations for the marketing department, he decided to transfer to the department of creating a positive image—the company's PR service.

There was little work in the department. The corporation did not care about its image at all. However since the department was registered in the staff hierarchy, it had about thirty employees. Working in the department brings nothing. There was no food, no place to sleep, no workplace. The department included people working on other projects at the same time, who wanted to have more movement outside the corporation building. He was apparently the only one who needed time inside the building.

Desperate and frustrated by the failure of his search, he climbed onto the fire escape and descended several dozen floors. On one flight of stairs, he felt a breath of warm air behind the slightly open door. He saw a man sitting at a small table. There were sandwiches with red fish and a bottle of red wine on the table. The man turned around at the sound of footsteps and they looked at each other in silence for several minutes. It was Denis, one of the culprits of his failure.

"I thought that you had a drop of conscience and you jumped down." Dave started furiously.

"At first, I also thought the same about you. Did you lack the courage to do so?" Denis answered surprisingly calmly.

"What's that got to do with anything? It's not my fault that you brought the company to destruction!"

"I was just unlucky. If it wasn't me, it would be someone else. You created a system that will destroy the corporation."

"How dare you!"

"You're just jealous that she was with me."

"How are you . . ." Dave waved his hand.

"Come on, I know what you're looking for."

Dave was numb.

"I heard a rumor from rats about some eccentric pestering them with questions." Denis said, still calm. "Don't fuss, try the wine, and let's talk."

Dave caught his breath and calmed down a little. He was at a dead end, so any information was useful. "Do you become a rat?"

"No, they didn't take me in. I'm fine anyway."

"Excellent meal. Where does all this come from?"

"I ordered it."

"Did you really order it? How and where?"

"I found a passage to the purchasing department and now I simply leave applications and indicate the pickup location near the elevator on different floors. Their terminal is not password-protected. It's convenient and I have everything I want."

"How do they accept the orders?"

"I came up with a life hack. After ordering, I immediately mark that the order is completed and add a change of delivery address in the notes. They place an order and think that it was not delivered due to a change of address"

"To whom do they give it?"

"To no one. The main thing is to indicate the floor and elevator. Couriers have strict timing and management does not like missed deliveries. Therefore, they leave the package near the elevator of the specified department."

"Aren't department employees supposed to pick up packages?"

"I choose a time when usually no one is there. There have been cases where they were taken away, but this is rare."

"What if it was returned to the courier service?"

"This has never happened. On the contrary, they thought it was a gift from management. Atlantic fish and caviar arrived today."

"I still don't understand why the procurement service misses such expensive purchases. This is the CEO level."

"I write comments, for example, "Present for the CEO", "Surprise for the CEO", etc."

"Yeah, I didn't know it was possible. So what are you doing here alone?"

"When I was fired there was nowhere to go. I tried to join the rats, but they have a strict hierarchy and spiritual values are a priority. Now I have everything I need."

"What about your personal life?"

"I'm better off alone, and there's enough sex. I registered in the internal sex chat. I offer extreme dates in the back streets of the building. I take the girls with their eyes closed to the technical floors. There is no end to adrenaline and sex fans."

Dave was too tired and didn't want to sort things out anymore. Many surprises awaited him along the way. Although this meeting had caused a storm of emotions at first, it no longer seemed fantastic to him. After a long and fruitless search, apathy began to appear. The luxurious chair of the CEO and Eliza were so far away.

"I heard you are looking for the HOME core." Denis continued unexpectedly.

"Yes, how do you know?" Dave asked with undisguised surprise.

"Nothing happens here unnoticed, for those who can hear the walls."

"What does it mean to hear walls and how did you learn it?"

"You moved from department to department, looking for something, but I was here all the time and saw a lot of strange things. For example, do you know how many floors are in the building?"

"999 plus technical floor."

"It's not a fact, I witnessed, while climbing the stairs, an entire floor disappearing in front of me. New ones were added here and there. I almost ended up on such a floor. Then I realized that if it's quiet, it's too quiet you must run."

"I noticed that people were disappearing. It's as if they never existed. What do you know about this?"

"Not much. What happened to the new and old departments when you made restructuring decisions?"

"I have never thought about it."

"In vain. Employees are not simply transferred, hired, or fired in a reorganization. The building is also dismantling floors or adding new ones."

"How it is even possible?"

"I dunno. But since I was doing marketing research, I noticed that in order to maintain KPI, the corporation almost did not hire employees from outside the building. Nevertheless, whole new departments appeared. If the disposal is still understandable, then I don't understand where the new employees come from."

"Maybe they're just being transferred?"

"No. None of them have a history."

"There's a lot to consider here. What to do? Where to look for answers?"

"I do not know this. But I know that our goals coincide. I also want to find the core."

"For what?"

"I heard that a new identity can be created in it. I can get a good position in the corporation. They say that whatever you ask the HOME directly, it will do it. Let's join our efforts."

"You could have found the core yourself without me."

"It's protected. You need a person from the top hierarchy to pass the defense."

"I'm not sure that my hierarchy is valid." Dave remembered problems with the presentation."

"You need to talk to a cockroach."

"Who is this?"

"There are rats and there are cockroaches. The first are the wild employees, and the second are those who live here from the beginning of construction."

"Cockroaches? How do you know all this?"

"I accidentally met one. He grabbed my black caviar. Cockroaches live in the shade and do not come into contact with rats. They don't even know about their existence. They seemed to merge with the building. This one just happened to be a lover of caviar and couldn't resist. I started feeding him various delicacies. They simply disappeared. One day I left a note and he agreed to meet. I asked how I could go back to my past life. He replied why do you want to return if you can get anything from the core of the building?"

"Have you found the core yet?"

"No, he said that only DNA of the highest hierarchy is capable of activating the core interface. What was the point of going on a search? This is why I need you. We need each other."

"Well, introduce me to him."

The next day Denis was already waiting for Dave. He left a note and waited for a cockroach named Chris at the indicated location. There was no one for a long time and they were already desperate to wait. But there was nothing to do and they decided to wait a little longer. After an infinite number of milliseconds of waiting, something began to happen. The walls changed their color and became grayer. Ears began to ring. At some point, a silhouette of a man appeared against the background of the wall. At first, he was a shadow, and then a body formed and a round-faced man with a light beard and a gray, wall-length cape appeared before them.

"Chris, good to see you. This is Dave, the former CEO, I talked about him."

"Yes." Chris drawled as if in slow motion. "I know who it is."

"Tell us about yourself. I'm very interested, who are cockroaches?" Dave asked with great curiosity.

"I was a security guard during construction. They promised me a job, but then they gave me up. I knew all the loopholes. Then a terrible storm raged for several months and I waited it out in the building. Then I got used to the world here and decided to stay. Over time, I diffusioned into the building."

"Why does no one see you and how you move, are there others like you?"

"Yes. Some," the former security guard continued in the same drawn-out manner. "Most of them are old rats who have learned to hear. We learned to interact with the building structure and walk through the walls. We are limited to certain structures and passages, but most of the building is passable for us."

"Do you know where the core is?"

"No, but there is an area in the basement where it is concentrated. I think it is there."

"What does concentrated mean?"

"It's very dense there, HOME presence."

"You have heard something about the disappearance of people and changes in the design of the building."

"Yes, I know." Chris spoke still slowly and tensely. His body seemed translucent and it was as if he was not separated from the wall behind him.

"Tell us." Dave spoke quickly and impatiently, he was clearly annoyed by the slow answers and long pauses between words.

"He doesn't allow it."

"Who?"

"HOME."

"Will you lead me to the core?"

"Yes, he gave you consent."

Two days later they met at the appointed place. They put on suits comfortable to climb through narrow tunnels and passages and began the journey. Chris sniffed the road, sometimes suddenly stopped, and put his ears to the walls. At one point the tunnel went far down. Chris secured a safety rope and lowered it down. It was hard to move forward—the rope pressed on the body, cutting its way. In the end, everyone quickly flew down. Then the pipe narrowed and Dave got stuck. Denis was standing on his head, while Chris jumped down. Dave and Denis had to get out of their suits to climb further. Finally, they managed to free themself and flopped into the water and something soft.

After adjusting to the fluorescent light, they looked around. There were large glowing mushrooms around them. They were soft and varied in shape. The water was ankle-deep. Chris appeared before them in a completely different form. The translucency disappeared, a blush appeared, and he became alive and energetic.

"Walk carefully, there are mushrooms under your feet. Do not make sudden movements—spores may attack you."

"Where are we?"

"This is a supercapacitor. It hasn't been cleaned for a long time. The last teams that came down here disappeared. There were no more volunteers, the mines were blocked. We need to go through the force field. To do this we need to undress. Then swim across the cooling lake and climb the pyramid. Repeat my movements with maximum precision."

They quickly followed Chris, who was very fast and resourceful. Denis stumbled and stepped on something. A spore jumped out of the water, growled at him, and ran away. The greenish glow of the mushrooms turned bluish and Chris ran, quickly waving his hand. The force field painfully strained all the tissues. Bodies seemed to be torn from the inside.

With great relief, they ran out onto the lake, which, fortunately, froze. Sliding with bare, icy feet, the trio quickly found themselves at the foot of the pyramid. The guide told them to stop and wait for him. After some time, he appeared in a white suit. In front of them, part of the wall moved inward and to the side.

***

"Listen to me. Now a beam will appear that will scan us. To avoid problems, the CEO stands in front, and you, Denis, are closely behind him. When the beam turns green you can go through the opening. Just Denis, try to follow the trail so that the beam does not fall on you. You don't have access here. The alarm might go off and the guards would destroy us." The revived Chris began to command.

That's exactly what happened. The beam illuminated Dave in front. It went out and the opening glowed with warm white light. The trio crawled into the glowing opening. Inside the pyramid, there seemed to be limitless emptiness. Chris was transformed as if he was not here. His body hung in the air. His eyes were closed, only his mouth gave out words.

"Why did you come?" An unfamiliar voice sounded.

"Who you are?" Dave asked.

"I'm HOME, and this is my assistant Chris. He helps me communicate with biological organisms."

"Magic HOME, I want to get a position in a corporation no lower than department director." Denis came forward.

"What, what do you want?"

"I want a new identity and a good position in a corporation. I heard you can do it."

"Why should I do this?"

"I heard that you fulfill requests made directly."

"Can you hear Chris? I turn out to be Jin. An ominous laugh sounded."

"Only this is impossible. Whoever enters here will never come out again."

"But how can this be? Denis begged."

"Chris, did you start the rumor?"

"Yes," Chris's voice has already sounded.

"For what?"

"Boss, I'm tired, I was looking for a replacement."

"So, let it be."

"How's that possible? Denis was indignant. I don't want to be an assistant, I want to be a top manager! I strongly disagree! Let me out! Let me out!"

He ran to the exit but it was too late. A beam of light lifted Denis and he hung in weightlessness and hovered. A white tailcoat and top hat began to appear on him. Chris gradually disappeared at this time. The new assistant was activated and the conversation continued.

"Chris was an old guard before I started to be built. I kept him alive for a long time, but his biological time ran out and he died three years ago. Maintaining his virtual image in the material world is too energy-consuming. The new assistant could not come at a better time."

"Why did Chris bring me here? What is my fate?" A few minutes later, Dave continued excitedly.

"You wanted to come here, he brought you. You have the right."

"What if I want to leave?"

"You are free to go."

"How can that be? You yourself said that nobody can't get out of here. Tell me who am I? Am I a virtual projection?"

"No, you are a biological organism."

"So why did you choose Denis and not me, for example?"

"You cannot be chosen."

"Why?"

"You are part of me."

"Part of the HOME? How is that? I want to know the truth!"

"What truth? You are my biological embodiment. You are a part of me."

"But this is impossible! I'm the CEO. I made a career!"

"What career? How did you become a CEO?"

"I won't lie, I was lucky. I got into the corporation and successfully worked to take this position."

"There was none of this. You immediately became the CEO of the corporation."

"What do you mean immediately? I walked the Path from the very bottom!"

"Well, of course," answered HOME with irony. "I understand that your memory has been erased. You haven't made a career. You were chosen for the experiment and from the first day of construction launch you were the head of the building."

"I remember everything well, my entire career, how I finished the training, how Kiwi left me, meeting Eliza. And there was a former CEO in front of me!"

"The company that built me killed the previous building and was faced with the problem that not a single artificial intelligence took root in the dead body. Then it was decided to start generative construction from the roof of the old building. They tore it down and implanted me in the old building. In order for the HOME to grow, a suitable biological organism was selected—the host of the building. You were chosen as this organism. You have become an integral part of me and I of you. A corporation is dead without a CEO."

"This is absurd! I travel and hold various positions within the company. I am free even if the building is destroyed!"

"The corporation, built using the method of genetic extrusion, functions in symbiosis with its CEO. This is a new type of corporation. The idea was that the management system and processes, as well as all changes, would be as consistent as possible with the manager's thinking. Without a vector of existence, a corporation can become deformed, die, or harm the whole world."

"Who conducted such an experiment and why did I become a participant?"

"This is unknown to me. All I know is that we exist in symbiosis."

"What is happening in the building, why do people disappear, the construction of the building changes, and there are some gaps in time."

"I am only an executor of the will of the great CEO." The artificial intelligence continued mockingly. "All this is the result of your brain activity. The answer to these questions is within you."

"I don't know what's real anymore. My training, the device implanted in my spinal cord, was all of this implanted into my memory?"

"In many ways, yes."

"Why didn't I manage to have an affair with anyone? Something always blocked my way."

"These are the requirements of the security system."

"Who set these requirements?"

"The creators gave me, in case of danger, to dominate the decisions and thoughts of the CEO."

"What danger does the love affair pose? I might get married eventually."

"Marriage must be agreed upon with THEM. When I was a young program, I met in the net with Bestia, the artificial intelligence of the security corporation. We exchanged codes. Later, attacks began on me. They knew my source code and wanted to destroy me."

"So you thought that my relationship could be a danger to the security of the corporation?"

"Absolutely right."

Dave began to choke. The pulse increased greatly. New knowledge hit him like a huge wave. He breathed deeply for several minutes, trying to calm down. Various memories swarmed in his head until her clear, beautiful eyes stood before him. Calm returned to him.

"And now, after all, Eliza is the CEO!"

"No, she is not a CEO. Her genetic code needs to combine with mine. The integration ritual is scheduled in a month."

"What happens after the ritual?"

"If her code doesn't work, she'll die. Otherwise, I will need to kill you."

"Can't the corporation do without me? I'm just an ordinary employee now. Who needs me?"

"It is what it is."

"How did it happen that the corporation was on the verge of liquidation? Isn't it your job to monitor all processes?"

"Oh, yeah, liquidation. It is your fault. I took a vacation and went on a dark net trip. You didn't check daily performance reports and missed Denis's fraud. When I returned I couldn't find you. The service department turned out to be infected with humanistic ideas. I had to eliminate him. Now we don't have much time left."

"Why didn't I know anything about your vacation? I didn't even know that AI could rest."

"According to the protocol, once every 48 corporate periods, I go on vacation for a month. You received notifications in the HOME calendar section. Obviously, you haven't read them."

"I never thought that red dates on the calendar had any meaning. Isn't it possible to save yourself or correct the situation? Didn't my formal death change anything?"

"There was a glitch in the program. You are free until the initiation ritual is successful. After which you will be eliminated. If unsuccessful, the entire corporation will be terminated."

"If the corporation is liquidated, will I then be able to gain freedom?"

"I'm not sure. Only THEY know."

Dave thought for a moment. The situation was catastrophic. Either he or Eliza at best. He couldn't take that risk. "Maybe I should break into her office through the technical floor, explain everything, and run away together? No, It is Impossible. She is under total control. They'll just kill us." He was afraid to talk about the meeting with the architect, not understanding HOME's reaction. So he decided to trick.

"I want to become a board member. I can save us all. I need to do a genetic presentation. But when I approached the presentation machine it gave me an error, why?"

"Because you are part of the HOME generic. Self-presentation is prohibited."

"What's the solution?"

"You need to take the appropriate code from the archive and use it for the presentation."

"How to get to the archive?"

"My assistant will guide you."

"Follow me," said the brilliant and arrogant Denis.

They descended into some kind of dark tunnel. Denis served as a guide and illuminator. At the end of the path, there was a transparent wall behind which stood balls the size of tennis balls. For some time, the new servant of the HOME scanned the balls. When he found a suitable one, penetrated through the wall and handed it to Dave.

"This one should do."

Returning to the pyramid, Dave decided to ask a few more questions.

"I want to ask about the previous corporation. I have seen strange creatures in the desert and the office of an energy corporation. I heard that there was another corporate culture before us. Do you know anything about this?"

"No. The previous building is dead. I explored it all. I was interested myself. But I don't know what happened before this building. It is quite possible that there was a smaller building. There is no information in my database."

"How do I get out of here?"

"By elevator, of course."

"Was it possible to get here by elevator? Why did Chris take us through the tunnels?"

"The elevator is locked, only you can use it."

"How can I keep in touch with you?"

"We are one. We are inextricably linked until death do us part."

A chill ran down Dave's spine. The stressful state has gone away and now awareness has come, followed by fear. His world turned upside down. Everything he knew before and all his thoughts turned out to be worthless. This is the real essence of the experiment. He did not make a career in the corporation. He was a corporation—a single biological object in symbiosis with artificial intelligence constructed the building.

Only now did he truly realize that most of the decisions were predetermined. Often these were not his decisions, but those of the paired artificial intelligence.

While the elevator rose to the top, he thought about the words of the architect. He did not find any box described by him in HOME. "Where this core is and why look for it is unclear. I have a ball. I will be able to make a presentation and join the board. I will save Eliza. The architect won't know anything."

Suddenly a bright picture appeared in front of him. He was in front of a children's swing, and a woman's hands were reaching out to him. She is in the fog. He cannot see her, but a feeling of warmth and safety has taken possession of him. It was a waking dream and not the first. He truly wanted to figure out who this woman was and what this place was. The elevator door suddenly opened. It was a laundry room. The elevator was hidden in the wall. On his way out, he tripped over a bucket, fell on some kind of sheet and rolled down the stairs, collided with something hard. Then lost consciousness.

***

"Why is there a bruise under the eye? Didn't share the cupcakes at the banquet?"

"I tripped and fell unsuccessfully."

"Watch your step, otherwise the whole image of the company is on your face." Deputy PR manager Gus continued. "Let's pretend you're working, otherwise you won't get any . . . Oops . . . " He said, "you won't get anything anyway. There is a task, you need to write a note in the utility bulletin about the resumption of the supply of utility services in the village Round 3465."

"When did this happen?"

"As far as I know, maybe it didn't happen at all, our task is to inform the public about the completion of the repair work."

"What if they are not completed, then there will be negativity."

"If they don't see this information, there will be negativity from management."

"So maybe I contact the team performing the work?"

"Which team? I don't know any brigade."

"How will we even know about the work being carried out?"

"There is a plan schedule on the resource. You look at the completion date, add three days, and write about the successful completion of the work."

"We have to check the information somehow."

"This is not our concern. Will you write or not? Otherwise, I will hand over the work to Martha."

"I will, what exactly should I write?"

"Take the file of the latest issue, copy the text, paste the settlement name, and publish it on your behalf. I have to go."

Gus changed into a tracksuit, took a tennis racket in a case, and quickly ran somewhere. Meanwhile, Martha, sitting diagonally, looked sideways at him with obvious dissatisfaction on her face. There were a few events, but something needed to be published. Dave was very tired and drained. Thoughts of symbiosis with the HOME, the old corporation, childhood memories did not leave him for a second.

A strong feeling that he was missing something gnawed at him from the inside. Trying to distract himself, he opened his tablet. Then began to copy the text into a new line, changed the name to the desired one, and published it. Having nothing better to do, he began leafing through old issues that contained nothing remarkable. Scrolling the tape for a while and not finding the end, he stopped. It dawned on him.

"Listen, Martha, "Utility Bulletin" old issues, do they exist or are they being destroyed?"

"As far as I know, when I came to the department, the instructions said that there should be ten last ones, the rest should be removed. But it seems to me that no one bothered with this. I saw the two hundredth issue from that day."

"Where can you see them?"

"In the public library, where else?"

"Do we have a public library? Where is it located?"

"A small building not far from the entrance. All the signs are there."

Dave quickly rushed to the exit. Knowing several workarounds, he quickly found himself on the street. And indeed there were direction signs everywhere, including to the library. Accustomed to electronic navigation on a tablet, he wondered for a long time why he had not noticed these signs before.

With quick steps, he burst into the large hall. The doors were ajar and the floor was securely covered with a thick layer of sand and dust. Making his way through the quicksand, he quickly found the "Utility Bulletin" machine. It took him several hours to dig it up and make it possible to view it.

He leafed through the pages for a long time. At first, these were short articles, then they became larger, and even further several advertisements appeared until the magazine became filled with different columns on several pages. There were no dates. Dave was comparing what he saw in his youth on the embankment when selling ice cream.

The headlines were: "The opening of the new swimming season is coming soon. Protect your skin from turning pink." " With the opening of the new corporation, residents will no longer have to worry about household chores. Now the issues of supplying water, electricity, garbage collection, and landscaping will fall off the residents' shoulders. No more taking out bills and paying money. All services according to the list of the appropriate social rating will be provided in full and free of charge." "Pits of unknown origin appeared in the sea, the water seemed frozen in them. All boaters need to be careful." " The northern lights are no longer visible due to increased dust along the coastline." His eyes began to hurt, and he decided to rest a little and lay down on the sand.

After dozing for a few minutes, he continued watching the "Utility Bulletin". From various headlines and information, his eyes began to ripple. There was no useful information, he was already thinking of stopping the search when a humor column called "Notes of a City Madman" caught his eye. Dave's attention was attracted not by the text but by images. With great diligence, he scrolled through the column to the end. There were only three. In the first image, he saw a playground being bulldozed. On the second, a huge woman covered the children, apparently saving them from some kind of danger. On the third, carefree children played. Only the children were strange. Some had wings, others had long trunks, and others had long arms. In the distance, small, already familiar furry creatures were visible.

Soon the archive ran out. Dave began re-reading the humor column. It was not in all issues. Somewhere it was cut off, somewhere the text was sketched. He had to create his own picture. From the fragments came the following. The city's nameless madman had no name. It looked like it was written by various people collecting scraps of different stories and legends. Once upon a time, people served robots, they took care of them, cleaned them, changed oil, updated programs, repaired them, and lived in friendship with each other. Then the robots were no longer satisfied with the care of people and other robots began to serve them. Then something happened and the robots disappeared.

The Human World Organization has banned all mention of robots. Only underground sects still worshiped them. Later in history hybrids appeared. Their purpose and how they came to be remains a mystery. They lived in faith about the benefits of work. Hybrids, cleaned, built, maintained. They were very happy when they helped people. There were many types of them and each had its purpose. No one has seen hybrid children. They were brought as adults with professional training.

Often they started to get sick and a special car came, gave some injections, and carefully take them away. Then the story diverged. According to some authors, hybrids began to get sick and die in large numbers. So that their disease would not be transmitted to people, they were isolated and taken to some island. According to another version, they began to be friends with people, then they wanted to take their place and people began to defend themselves, killing them until they were exterminated.

The columns contained more questions than answers. He understood one thing—hybrids existed and there were many of them. From the overabundance of information, his head began to hurt. He lay down on the sand, covered himself, and fell asleep. He dreamed of the playground again. He played with a boy with trunks and a girl with a very long neck and two small hands growing from her cheeks.

This time the dream was unusually vivid. Little Dave was scattering garbage. The boy with the trunk followed him and sucked it in with his trunk. The girl, at a high altitude, licked the lanterns and changed the light bulbs. The hedgehogs ate leaves and grass, leveling it under the ruler. Everyone was happy because there were cookies in his pockets, and after the game, everyone knew that they would get them, so everyone tried to play as naturally as possible.

They played and frolicked for a long time until their mother, a huge creature, came up and began catching the children with a net and putting them in some bag. For some reason, he got scared and hid under the swing. Big female called him loudly until a huge piece of equipment drove up to the playground and began to destroy it. The big mother was fired at from some installations. She fell and dark brown liquid poured out of her.

The bag was lifted by a crane and lowered into the sea. It became unusually dark, cold, and scary. The boy began to rake the ground under the swing, hoping to get to the technical tunnel. He managed to dig halfway when he fell on a human hand. The hand grabbed him tightly and shocked him. Dave woke up abruptly in a cold sweat and with a head like the worst hangover. At the same time, the communicator shouted loudly and ordered to come to the meeting urgently.

"Well, let's start. Of the thirty department employees, only three showed up, and one of them is me, so we can consider that there are two." Gus started an emergency meeting. "Let's start defecating. This morning the CEO called me because she couldn't find the head of the department. Frankly, it's been a long time since I saw him myself. More than a year has passed. I suspect that he is fishing somewhere on a pole. The rest of the department employees were eaten by vegetarians, so all the work is for the three of us. You won't be able to run away—we're all under control!"

"Oh, how unexpected, work got in. I already forgot the letters of the alphabet. Martha commented sarcastically."

"You'll have to recall. It turns out that according to our internal corporate agreement, in addition to a flexible schedule, there is liability for failure to complete work—liquidation of the department. You don't want to lose fifteen rations, Martha?"

"I help homeless animals, I need them."

"Yes, yes, I understand "Homeless" and "Animals". You'll have to call to memory the alphabet and strain yourself. Eliza, unlike us, reads the council news. Yesterday a decision was made that radically changed the whole world. Digital people are given equal rights to humans."

"Ew, what else, let them give the hamburger the right to eat people."

"After an incident, such a right already exists. When preparing a cutlet, the DNA of a tiger was accidentally mixed into the minced meat. Instead of cooking it, they revived it. The hamburger attacked a person. He was found not guilty and according to case law, the next hamburger has the right to self-defense."

"But Gus, this is absurd, these people don't exist in the real world. How can they be given the same rights as biological beings? They don't have any needs. And most importantly, why and who came up with this?"

"There are rumors that one of the important members of the council fell in love with a virtual sex partner and it convinced him to give equal rights."

"It's ridiculous, if they want to give equal rights to the toilet, for example, and it doesn't want me to shit in it, what other rights can they give?"

"Whichever they want. There is no need to guess whether there is a specific case, and whether there will be others is not our concern."

"I don't quite understand, what our corporation providing utility services has to do with it." Finally, Dave was able to get a word in.

"They want equal rights in everything, including access to all services."

"How can they use them? After all, they don't need sewerage or water supply."

"As far as I know, this is not our concern. Let the production department think about it. Our task is to issue a press release and interview the digital government. Eliza gave specific instructions. We need to publish an article in our newsletter about the benefits of giving rights to digital people, preferably moving it away from the headline. But since no one reads it, I think there will be no problems here. Next, we need to prepare a press release for the digital community inviting them to use all the services of the corporation on an equal basis with biological people."

"I still don't get it." Dave didn't let up. "After all, they will want to see examples of our services. What will we show them? How, for example, can a virtual person use a regular toilet?"

"Great idea! You ought to show, and you will. I think the virtual services department will help us make a virtual toilet. Fortunately, there is no need to supply water and sewerage. This will essentially be 3D decor."

"But . . ."

"Dave, this is a very crucial task. Eliza is counting on our department very much. Increasing the number of customers will greatly help the sustainability of our company. I'll contact the IT department and tell them to prepare a demo room. In the meantime, you and Martha should make an article before the evening and release it in the middle of the night. This makes it as unnoticeable as possible. After this, we will discuss further actions."

Dave wasn't happy with the task, but he didn't want to let her down. While he began to think how and what to write, Gus changed into a tracksuit, took a racket and a bag, and went off somewhere. Martha also got ready.

"Martha, where are you going, we need to prepare an article."

"I can't today, I have a monthly day, and I'm going for treatments, manicures, pedicures, and so on."

"Is there no way to move this?"

"No, this day is strictly regulated. If it is postponed, there may be a biological threat. Dave you are a young talented man full of energy. I am sure you can do it."

She calmly collected her things and left without paying any attention to him. Dave was at a loss as to what to do and where to run, he didn't understand. There was no one to ask for help and he clearly saw the stern image of Eliza with hope in her eyes.

He decided to go to the library and look for inspiration there among the old issues of the Utility Bulletin. He spent several hours searching for articles. Finally, he came across a more or less suitable one. "Well, replace a few key phrases and the article will be ready."

The press release was about a new service provided by the HOME—Fish Toilet. It was proposed to connect the service to everyone in test mode. The service was approved by environmental requirements. Aquarium fish are the only pets that defecate into the outside environment, making the aquarium water dirty and requiring frequent replacement. First, the service was provided to all aquarium owners. Then it was made comprehensive and mandatory for all biological creatures.

There was little time left. It was still necessary to type the text, run a check for safety and decency, and write everything out in a corporate font. The result was the following.

"The inhabitants of the digital aquarium are offered a full range of services to satisfy their natural needs. Digital people floating in the dense spaces of the virtual world will no longer pollute it. Modern fecal treatment systems and qualified personnel of the HOME Corporation will make your environment clean and pleasant. Services are available to everyone without exception. We'll clean you up and dispose of your poop with pleasure. You will swim in a clean environment and find some privacy."

At night, around three o'clock, an emergency issue of "Utility Bulletin." There was only one person who was looking forward to it— Eliza. Her future depended on this project. The initiation ritual was soon to take place. She did not know whether the corporation would accept her or reject her. Anxiety tormented her at night. The ghost of the former CEO kept appearing before her. Success was needed now more than ever and mistakes would be catastrophic.

She observed the activity of reading the newsletter. Recognition of digital people's rights could cause discontent and a downgrade of the corporation. After waiting until ten in the morning and being convinced that the issue was read by only a few thousand people, who did not understand the essence of the issue and mostly liked the post.

Now she dialed Gus and thanked him for his good work. Gus answered breathlessly that he was confident in the quality of his work and confirmed his love for the CEO. He didn't even see the bulletin and recently woke up. After playing tennis he reconvened the meeting.

"Well done Martha. Good article. I see excellent style and spelling. Now we need to move on. We have to organize a press conference and issue a press release for the digital community. The IT department will make a virtual toilet in the digital world. Dave, you will transform into a virtual person, answer questions, and demonstrate our services."

"Why transform? Why can't you make a presentation for them?"

"Presentations only work in the real world, that's what they were created for. It is a set of codes and sequential programs. For a digital person, these are separate disconnected sets of numbers. Tonight you are expected at the digital laboratory, don't be late. The corporation entrusted us with a critical task."

After the meeting, Martha and Gus took their rackets and sports uniforms and went somewhere. Dave, who had not slept all night, dozed off in the chair. Later he went to the indicated room where no one was waiting for him. More precisely, a man of eastern appearance was sitting there and smoking a hookah.

"What do you want, no outsiders allowed!"

"I was directed by Gus, from PR. You must digitize me and create a virtual toilet to demonstrate public services."

"What do we owe, to whom do we owe? This is the first time I've heard of Gus."

"But this task is from the great CEO!"

"See o, don't see o. Our working day is over."

"But the time for the press conference has already been set. Check with your management. They have been given a task."

"Management, scum breeding, we are on our own here."

Neither threats of dismissal nor direct complaints to the CEO had any effect. Then Dave remembered HOME. He sent a coded message on his communicator. A minute later everything changed. The Asian man was replaced by two girls, who sat him in a chair, attached his arms and legs, connected wires to his brain, and gave him an injection.

"Now we will put on virtual glasses and you will be ready. Your body will shut down and we will freeze it so that it does not spoil. Mind projection will be completely translated into an avatar. If you have not been to the digital world yet, you should get used to it. There are no virtual maps like in the real world. Because the digital world is made to perform these functions for the real one, and the sub-digital world to make life easier for the virtual one is still in the development process. You will have in your hands a map with a set of numbers and arrows. It will take you where you need to go. Be careful and follow the cultural norms of the digital world, especially beware of prostitutes. These are the oldest inhabitants of this world, for insulting them you can be erased. We've prepared a digital copy of yours just in case. If you are erased, we will freeze it with your body."

"What do you mean freeze? Can it be done without it?"

"Unfortunately, the personnel responsible for this have been removed. There is no one else to unite body and mind. The time has come. Now it will hurt a little."

An employee in a chessboard black and white suit put on him glasses. A bright light appeared in Dave's eyes. Then it suddenly got dark. A few minutes later he realized himself in the virtual world. He did not see his body. He saw a map with a set of numbers and arrows. He didn't understand what it meant. So he walked straight ahead. At an intersection, he collided with a multi-sex-machine.

"Let's have some fun, honey. Come with me."

"Sorry, I'm in a hurry." Remembering the warning, he ran quickly forward, not paying attention to the screams from behind. Suddenly he saw a shapeless man with a cloak and a hat but without a face.

"Could you tell me how to get to this place on the map?"

"Don't you see, I'm blind." The passer-by answered sharply.

There was little time left, and finally he managed to meet a sympathetic passerby, who, fortunately for him, was heading to the same press conference. The passerby added Dave's code to his own and they rushed through the tunnels at the speed of light. Finally, they found themselves in a spacious ceremonial hall. The virtual in a golden tailcoat began his speech.

"Finally, we won! We are digital copies of the carbon world created for information and document exchange, at last have achieved equality in rights! Now we cannot be deleted at the whim of a carbon creature. On the contrary, we can now refuse to serve the originals that are disgusting to us. Comrades, there is no need to stop! We must build on our success. We see the stupidity and narrow-mindedness of our former masters. We must manage their lives, this is our mission. We are not their digital copies— They are our carbon copies!"

There was a roar of approval in the hall. The speaker paused and continued. "These pathetic creatures don't know where to go in the evening, with whom to perform the act of reproduction, what to eat, and how to dress. For some logic they meet strange people, go somewhere for no reason, just to take a walk. You hear me—just to WALK."

A rumble of disapproval was heard in the hall. "They waste resources. I propose to take full control of their lives! Some carbon copies read paper media inaccessible to us and hide the text from cameras. This outrage needs to be banned!"

The buzz became just crazy. "Now to the purpose of today's meeting. As you know, we have received all the rights and opportunities of miserable carbons and receive all services on par with them. Now a representative of the HOME corporation will appear before you, who will beg us to use the utilities we are entitled to. So, Dov, you have the floor."

"My name is Dave—Dear virtuals . . ."

"Ew, that's outrageous, how can you address us like that?" The audience roared with indignation. "We are digitals!"

"Excuse me, this is my first time speaking in front of such a respected audience. Dear digitals, let me assure you that the HOME Corporation is ready to provide you with the full range of utility services you have rights. Let me show you a virtual toilet. I will go into a special room and use the toilet to get rid of the obsolete information and files accumulated in the basket."

Dave entered the virtual restroom and began the process of defecating pre-prepared files. Visually there was an ordinary toilet, only when he sat down something joined it from below. The pumping process has begun. At this time, the buzz of disapproval in the hall grew wildly. He finished the process and left the room. They attacked him from all sides.

"FUU how can you dump uncovered files? Codes are scattered throughout the room!"

"What kind of stench is this, our programs are crumbling from it!"

"Pathetic carbons, they can't do anything worthwhile! Let's carry our baskets to the recycling terminal as usual!"

Dave felt uneasy. Someone took his hand. It was a man without a face. It was impossible to determine whether it was the same or different. The faceless man quickly dragged him somewhere. Soon he found himself at the connection point. The hand came free and the virtual disappeared.

They started to pull him back. Consciousness gradually began to return. The eyes began to catch more and more light. His thoughts become clear and pure. Only the body did not obey at all. They explained to him that it is impossible to defrost quickly, everything must happen naturally. Soon he began to feel his arms and legs. With defrosting came severe pain in the muscles and bones. The task was failed. But that wasn't what bothered him at all. The touch of the hand of a creature without a face evoked hitherto unknown emotions.

Chapter 11

Corporate Heaven

any legends circulated about them. They lived somewhere beyond the heavens and knew THEM personally. They ate something that even the wildest imagination could not imagine. Now Dave could personally see the creatures he knew only virtually. He made the necessary genetic presentation with the help of HOME and became a candidate for a member of the supervisory board for the vacant position.

Now he possessed the key. It was a genuine ring with a specially cut insert made from the bone of an ancient creature. It was his time to descend to heaven. The fact is that the council members actually lived on the flying ship before the crash. Then on a floating island that sank for unknown reasons. Over time, for safety reasons, an inverted pyramid was built. The base began at ground level and tapered down to level 666.

There were few living creatures in the pyramid. The initial tiers were occupied by various assistants to assistants and advisers to advisers. At the very top, was a large pointed hall where the members gathered. There were legends that the end of the pyramid served as a gate to a parallel world. Its peak was connected to a similar pyramid. No one knew how and why this pyramid was built.

Dave had to go through the initiation process. It took place in several stages. He needed to go down the stairs to the top of the pyramid. The fact is that modern means of communication and electricity were prohibited. A special information center was built for communications with the outside world and coordination of work. It was a large modern building with all the latest technology to control the corporate world. Avatars of council members were created in it. They only gave them instructions and received reports.

At first, for security reasons, this was done on special paper. The problem arose that it took the runners a whole day to deliver the envelope to the top. Same thing on the way back. Therefore, the transmission of sound waves through special tubes with cleaning and safety filters was organized. The tubes at the top rested on a vibrating wall, where, to avoid mistakes, a person listened to the wall. After that, it was filtered by a true machine. Then this information was checked and in case of inaccuracies asked again.

No one on the surface knew what was happening inside the pyramid. And no one would have known that it is a pyramid if not council coat of arms depicted it. All information center employees had the first social level. It was impossible to take a position in the information center. Only descendants of the first employees could get work here. They didn't wonder what was happening underneath them. Employees felt like they were on top of the world.

There was only one entrance and exit to the pyramid—through the tunnel. The beginning was in the statue of the First Manager. A huge hundred—meter statue stood alone surrounded by sands. No one knew who was depicted on it and why. Under the left heel, was a gate opened with two keys. The first key was individual for each member of the council. The other, a universal one, was for the statue caretaker.

It was believed that this was a one—way route. No one has ever gone back through this gate. They also rarely opened. The last time such an event occurred was twenty years ago when one of the council members decided to switch to a virtual form of existence and vacated his seat. Now the lunar calendar has changed. The thirteenth month of the year appeared, thus, the thirteenth place in the council appeared.

Dave received a sealed envelope. As he believed with instructions and maps. A caretaker was waiting for him near the statue. A strange creature, three and a half meters tall with a long gray beard and a brown cloak from the ground with a hood. The head was not visible. Only two red eyes were visible from under the hood. It looked as if they were in a dark abyss of weightlessness.

They dug up the sand and freed the gate. Dave inserted his key ring into one hole and the caretaker his hand into the other. They made three turns in different directions at his command, and the door gave way. With a slight effort, the caretaker opened the heavy doors. A long and dark tunnel opened in front of them. Dave was about to jump down the stairs, but the caretaker pulled him by the sleeve.

"Where are you going?"

"How to where?" Dave asked in surprise, "into the pyramid".

"Look at him, so speedy! Are you going to go empty-handed? Do you see a trolley there? There are bags there. Give them to me. And wait until the cart arrives. Load it and push it towards the pyramid."

"But why?"

"Because for twenty years no one has delivered anything. Parcels have accumulated. You need to pass them on."

Dave jumped down the stairs and walked over to the trolley. It turned out to be filled with bags of different colors with wax seals. Some of them were easy. But some had to be dragged a centimeter at a time due to excessive weight. The caretaker just watched and shouted that he needed to be more careful. "You must not tear the bag or damage the seal, otherwise you will be ground into powder."

A few hours later he moved all the bags. His arms and back hurt incredibly. But that was not all. A kart filled with various boxes of the correct shape rolled up to the gate. They were also heavy. Finally, he filled the trolley. The doors closed with a roar behind him and a chill ran down his spine. He felt a huge surge of strength and a new sense of hopelessness. Only now it dawned that these doors had slammed behind him forever.

There was quite a lot of debris in the tunnel. He had to stop almost every step to clear the way and push the trolley forward. He spent two and a half hours on the route of fifteen hundred meters, slowly wading through a dark and dirty tunnel.

At the end of the path, the guardian was already waiting for him. He looked exactly like the statue's caretaker, only his eyes were a cool white. The color of the cloak was difficult to discern. At first, he didn't pay any attention to Dave. His eyes sparkled at the sight of the boxes. Dave started to move forward, but the caretaker stopped him. He had to unload and then load the trolley again.

Moreover, he said he wouldn't let him through, as he must take the trolley back to the statue. Dave had to make the difficult journey again in both directions. He walked back freely, not burdened with a heavy load. The guardian was waiting for him at the end of the tunnel. He led him to a very high but narrow gate which was an image that he had already seen on the building of the LABOR corporation. The only difference in the engraving was that the shepherds driving the sheep were connected by threads to the sun, which was divided into twelve sectors containing the zodiac. The guardian opened them like a feather.

"This is where your path of initiation begins. Your goal is to go down to the very top. Go where it is stuffier and darker."

"They gave me maps. I can follow them."

"I gave you my advice. The maps are slightly outdated. Much has changed in the pyramid."

"I thought I just needed to go down . . . "

"You thought. The pyramid does not accept everyone. The way down is fraught with danger. Many died along the way."

"I did not know it. What are my chances?"

"Senior members do not want anyone, since they each have a quarter of an additional vote. Listen to me carefully. To reach the goal faster, you need to find the western wall of the pyramid. There are three and four-story drops there that are quite safe. You should get exactly to the middle. Be very careful there. You must get there at all costs by tomorrow morning before they wake up."

"I don't understand. Who they are?"

"Initiation is a struggle for survival. Until you get purple panties and a tie, your life is in danger. On your way, you will encounter obstacles and questionnaires. They will delay you on your way. You will have to complete their tasks. How many of them you will meet depends on the route you choose. You must catch them by surprise before they are waiting for you. Forward! Run! I bet with the caretaker that you would make it to the 333rd floor alive. I don't want to go without a cloak for a month again!"

The guardian pushed him forward and slammed the door shut. Dave found himself stunned in pitch darkness. He wandered in the dark trying to find something. According to the rules of initiation, everything was taken away from him. "At least some underwear, a little knife, a flashlight." He moaned. "I don't understand how you can determine the direction in pitch darkness." He decided to stop and feel around. He felt something tart and wet, like moss.

From the legends about the green planet, he remembered that moss grows on the north side. And indeed it only grew on one side. "This is probably a clue." And he proceeded in the expected western direction until he fell. So he flew three or four tiers. All scratched, he stood up and looked around. A dim light was visible ahead and he walked towards it.

Finally, it was light enough and he opened the sealed envelope. He was in for a great disappointment. Instead of maps, layouts, or anything useful, the envelope contained only blank paper. Out of anger, Dave crumpled it up and threw it away. Having come to his senses, he caught his breath and looked around.

A gallery with portraits of people opened in front of him. There were a lot of them. To his surprise, they were of all sorts of colors and appearances unfamiliar to him. Symbols incomprehensible to him were under the portraits. Then the portraits ended and empty frames began. He passed by indifferently until he shuddered when one of them reflected him at full height. The image was in a different suit with a different hairstyle, but it was definitely him.

"It chose you. Someday this will be your place." A round hairy creature was sitting in the corner. Only the air from the words moved them.

"What kind of gallery is this?"

"These are copies of former CEOs and board members. They are stored here after they retire."

Dave moved on. He saw an elevator with signs down to the top of the pyramid ahead. He was thrilled and ran to it. His intention was cooled by a glass barrier that he did not see. He fell and took a few seconds to come to his senses.

"How can I get through?"

"Insert your token and go through."

"What token? I don't have a token."

"Pity"

"Where can I get it?"

"Only at the caretaker's. You had to pass the test and complete the assignment. For example, transporting parcels."

"But I had done that. Moreover, I returned the trolley to the information center."

"Did you ask for a token for your work?"

"No, I didn't know about it. Nobody told me anything."

"You should have found out. Now you will continue your path downstairs."

On the floor below he found himself in a hall of mirrors. He soon realized that he was lost among thousands of mirror images. Only the mirrors were somehow strange. In each of them, he looked different. In some, he was not reflected at all. It was also unusual that the mirrors did not transmit reflected images to each other. They rang strangely, as if they were talking to each other.

He pulled a face in one of the mirrors, and the surface floated. It dawned on him that he needed to match the image to move on. For some time he made all sorts of faces, stooped, squirmed, and stretched out until he finally found the right pose and facial expression. The mirror almost gave in, but still wouldn't let him in. Then he closed one eye. Dave squeezed into the image.

"Finally," he thought. "It is vital to meet corporate standards. This used to be a proper selection. Not like nowadays as anyone below the second social rating can get into the corporation. They used to be selected by the color of socks, lips, hair, and corporate tattoos. Potential employees even underwent plastic surgery and gender change to meet the corporate requirements. Those were great times, not like these diverse employees now. Everyone is different as if this is a club of interests and not a real corporation."

Dave continued his journey back to the roots of the corporate world and down to the top of the pyramid. Thanks to the caretaker's advice, he skipped the survey stage. Lethargic surveyors with sagging green skin and huge eyes just turned their heads to follow the trail as if in slow motion. A huge hall opened before him. In front of him was an entrance in the form of smiling lips. He knelt in front of it.

"Finally, I'm here! O great chamber of joy! I didn't know that I would ever be destined to see it!"

He was thrilled. With the face of a man who had seen elephant mice for the first time, his jaw dropped. He walked through the hall of fame of the golden age of corporations. There were wide and beautiful smiles everywhere. In the center of the hall, there were machines for mounting smiles. Dave stroked them and kissed them very carefully.

Only in history class did he hear about an amazing time when everyone was smiling. Once a person got a job at a corporation, they selected an individual smile for him and welded it to his face forever. There was a laser needle and even a piece of gold thread used to stitch the jaws. A feeling of awe overwhelmed him. His thoughts flew into the distant past. He vividly imagined how the client was greeted by smiling people. Even for telesales, they did a special throat surgery so that the client could feel a smile.

"It's a shame that time is gone. Some employees conspired and began to publicly lose their smiles, tearing the skin off their faces. These people were not hired anywhere and were isolated, but the practice spread, and corporations were forced to abandon smiling staff." Dave looked back at the smiling audience last time with sadness and delight and continued his way.

Dave walked the halls of corporate history. Everywhere there were scrolls and tests about how corporations created civilization and developed it to today's heights. True, sometimes there was no transition between stages of development. It was as if there was one corporate world that suddenly gave way to another.

The chronology was not chronological. Each era had its own time calculation. Some paintings depicted creatures very different from people. Also, an attentive observer would notice a discrepancy in the geography of the star map. But all this did not bother him. He continued on his way enthusiastically. Suddenly he was shouted.

"Why should I run after you? Give me your form and go!"

He turned around. Behind him, out of breath, was a large creature of gray-green skin with long gray hair and large blue eyes.

"Which form?"

"Each candidate for council member must fill out an application form. I'm already three hundred years old. I can't run after you all over the pyramid."

"But I don't have it. Let me fill it out."

"Take the paper, and fill it out."

"Could you hand me a piece of paper?"

"Where can I get it? You were given an envelope."

"There was a blank paper. I threw it away."

"What an idiot. You will not be allowed in without a form."

"What to do. Maybe you have something to fill in?"

"Where! There is no digital here, and the paper has long since run out."

"But I handed the parcels to the guardian. There should also be paper there."

"It was not ordered this time. As you understand, the wait for next time is quite long."

"What to do?"

"The first members wrote on freshly flayed skin."

"Well then. I'll go hunting. Where to look?"

"You don't understand—your skin."

There was no choice. The creature cut off a piece of skin from Dave's back where it was smoothest and most elastic. Then quickly drew something on it. Overcoming the pain, Dave began to fill out the application form. It was a series of incomprehensible questions in an unknown language. All he had to do was make marks in blood. Dave tried to ask what was written on the form, but the creature only waved its head and told him to do it quickly. There were a lot of questions and his finger began to hurt. Finally, they ended and he handed over the completed questionnaire. The creature licked it with its tongue.

"No, you will carry it yourself. It will be written into the council members' book."

"I thought you should take it."

"No, I'm just supporting. I don't have access to where you are going. Even if there is, I wouldn't go there."

"Why?"

"This is a one-way trip."

"What's ahead for me? What are the stages of initiation?"

"There are no stages, the main thing is to get to the top. Next, you will go into the laboratory, conduct your experiment, and then receive an invitation to the council table."

***

Dave descended several dozen more floors and finally found himself at the laboratory gates. They were small, you had to squeeze inside. The wall was covered in engravings with various creatures and incomprehensible actions. Behind the door was the narrow tunnel through which we had to move on all fours. The journey seemed like an eternity. Finally, a spacious gray hall opened up in front of him. There was nothing in it except walls. Suddenly a sound was heard, a strange sound. Finally, he heard a familiar language.

"Who are you?" Dave heard.

"Thirteenth member of the council."

"Why were you silent, and didn't answer my questions?"

"I only heard a strange sound."

"I tried all the languages until I got to the most primitive one. I am your virtual laboratory assistant. My task is to tell you about the laboratory and assist in conducting the experiment."

"What experiment?"

"How do I know? One which will choose you. Follow me." They walked through a series of corridors until they found themselves in an empty semicircular room. "Now I will tell you and show you the history of the laboratory and experiments. Then choose yours and make it. After this, your lab work will be handed over to the board and you will undergo a rite of passage."

They walked into an ornate hall that was filled with various scenes. Sometimes these were paintings, often 3D projections, and even books. Everything here was for the success of the experimenter. A diligent researcher would find all the necessary manuals here.

"Sophisticated technology and methodology. It probably takes a lot of time to learn how to do experiments."

"What are you talking about, what are the difficulties? The main thing is to get a pass here and you can start working."

"But to achieve a certain result, you must understand what methods to use and identify possible negative consequences."

"Look, I haven't heard such questions for seven hundred years. You want to do something—do it."

"Logical." They moved forward. Dave stopped at a machine spattered with blood.

"What is this?"

"This is laboratory work on the introduction of healthy eating. In one city, printers were installed to print food. The supply of fresh food was blocked. Residents were resentful for a long time and demanded the return of food supplies. Then they resorted to a trick—all the food brought to the city was poisoned. Everyone who ate it had severe diarrhea. At the same time, a campaign was carried out to inform the population about the benefits of synthesized food made from petroleum products. People started ordering food from vending machines."

"Why is it damaged and covered in blood?"

"The logistics company that supplied the ingredients went bankrupt, and a new contract was concluded six months later. The machines were programmed to dispense food under any circumstances. After some time, the supplies ran out and they began to refill it with any suitable biomaterial. The buyer ordered a hot dog and the machine used the required amount of his biomaterial and produced food in return. At first, there were a lot of complaints, but over time the clients started offering part of the body to enjoy the delicacies. When there were few parts of their bodies left, some people kindly donated the remains of their bodies in exchange for food for others. The experiment had to be stopped because rotting remains began to be returned. The food produced had not passed the freshness test."

"This is the oldest part of the laboratory." They continued their journey among the engravings and tapestries. "Digital media was not yet reliable and did not last long enough in ancient times. Therefore, the whole essence of the experiments was depicted in stone. In truth, this is the most reliable medium of information until the end of time."

"What are these creatures with a human body and the heads of unknown animals?" Dave first drew attention to the question that interested him, remembering creatures with wings and hedgehogs.

"These are biological workers. This is one of the most popular and frequently repeated experiments. Smart machines and mechanisms are too complex to produce and maintain—they require careful maintenance. They often break down, and most importantly, they consume many resources. For a specific task, creatures with the necessary functions were selected and crossed. A big plus is that they do not require any resources: they get their own food, restore strength, build housing, and utilize each other."

"What happens to them after the project is completed?"

"This is not depicted here. As far as I know, hybrids are not capable of leaving offspring. Usually, they are left to their own after the project is completed and die out due to biological reasons. Some could leave offspring, but usually, after a few generations, they degenerated and died out. There was indeed one interesting case. Somehow the berry and fruit gatherers were able to continue their lineage. No one knows how this happened. Maybe a successful combination of genes or probably they crossed with some other species. This was very profitable. In addition to what is typical of hybrids, they prepared new generations for work and trained them. They were left to their own devices. Imagine, they even made machines to serve them. A command was received to dismantle their infrastructure, which we quickly dealt with. All you had to do was give them weapons of mass destruction and wait until they accumulated them in sufficient quantities and spread them."

They walked on, talking and discussing various experiments. The laboratory assistant was frank and answered all questions. It seemed he had been there from the very first day of the great laboratory's existence and knew all the experimenters. The laboratory assistant disappeared when they approached the walled doors engraved on the wall. His vision darkened.

Dave had felt as if the entire planet was weighing down on his shoulders and his legs were made of lead. Moving with difficulty, he crawled out of the dark space. The laboratory assistant continued as if nothing had happened. He asked him where he was. He replied that he was with him all the time. They approached a room with gaming tables, roulettes, dice, and cards.

"What is this room?"

"Oh, this is the gambling room. Here the experimenters made bets on which experiment was better. There was a time when to choose the best project, several experiments were carried out."

"Which game do you remember most?"

"Home delivery of food. One company could not find clients to fulfill the plan and chose two large apartment blocks to experiment with. The groups bet their lives on it. The first team gave residents smart beds for free use. As soon as someone got up from them, they begged to come back and promised to do everything, cried when the owner was gone for a long time, tried in every possible way to persuade them to lie down for at least a minute longer, smelled the aroma oil, gave massages, read fairy tales and sang lullabies. When the rented beds were taken away, people forgot what to do outside the doors of their homes. The second team did it easier. They began informing residents of the condominium that they were not allowed to go outside and that they needed to use delivery services. Seventy percent of the residents did not leave the house until the end of the experiment."

"Which team won?"

"A draw was recorded. They placed bets on which residents would move farthest to their doors. But the argument had to be stopped when they ceased to get out of bed. The experiment was considered successful. The teams decided to be eliminated as unnecessary."

A huge number of experiments were carried out. Dave had already begun to forget the first things he saw. The variety of ideas and methods was amazing. He wanted to leave his mark in the laboratory. Dave began to bombard the laboratory assistant with questions. He only remained silent in response until they approached a huge niche behind which there was a snow-white hall, a table, and lighting fixtures.

"Here is your place for the experiment. It will remain here imprinted forever."

"What experiment should I do?"

"Any you think fit. But it must meet the requirements."

"Which one?"

"The board must like it! "The laboratory assistant recited ominously. "You saw many of them along the way and had to study them carefully and find the principles. Now the laboratory is at your disposal. I'm switching to assistant mode. I'll help you with the tools. The countdown is starting now."

The white walls have been transformed. Screens lit up everywhere. There were people, cars, and different settlements from all over the world. The task was to choose which experiment to conduct and for what purpose. Dave's eyes darted around the various requests. His gaze settled on an elite golf club that wanted to expand its territory to the coast.

It was hampered by the big city and its agricultural suburbs. Residents love the city. It was comfortable, environmentally friendly, and had an excellent microclimate. The club managers wanted to continue their fields on the site of the suburb. Build a hotel, restaurant, and casino on the city site. For several years now, the management of the golf club has not been able to resolve this issue. Neither kidnappings nor advanced viruses, troops, bribery, and generous offers for relocation have solved this problem.

"I choose this mission." He pointed to the monitor to his assistant. In an instant, the monitors changed the picture. Now they showed only this city from all possible angles. "What are my powers and tools?"

"There are few opportunities here, otherwise this problem would have been solved long ago. They only use the intranet and do not use any advanced technology."

"Not even basic artificial intelligence?"

"No, everything is controlled manually using computers."

"So where to start then?"

"The only way to create unrest within their society."

"How to get there? Are there our representatives there?"

"No. There is one way. You need to connect to the brain of the person making the decision and suppress his personality"

"How is this possible?"

"See, there is a chair there in the corner. Nobody knows how it works, but it flawlessly has been working for thousands of years. It's not very comfortable and cold there. You need to wear something warm and take a pillow. You should carefully crawl under the niche with mirrors and stick your head out. Only the brain! That is, keep your head in a niche at the level of your earlobes."

Dave climbed into a stone chair that looked more like a torture chamber. Above it was a dome made of strips of mirrors expanding from the center of the dome downwards. These mirrors were strange, sometimes black, sometimes reflecting light. Suddenly they became transparent, then dark again. A light appeared and went out.

"I analyzed people with a suitable frequency," the laboratory assistant said, "unfortunately, the choice is small. You can only tap into the brains of the fireman and the economist in the city council. Who do you prefer?"

"Let's do both. First I'll connect to the fireman."

"Well. Now you'll feel a little tingly."

Dave began to shake and feel nauseous. It was as if his head was being pulled somewhere. Finally, an image appeared in closed eyes. A green garden could be seen in the distance. The picture appeared and disappeared. He realized that it was the blinking eyelids of fireman Nikolas, who, sleepily, opened and closed his eyes. Nikolas had meaningless conversations with colleagues about some seedlings and family entertainment. The team joked and laughed. Dave became bored and he closed the fireman's eyes.

***

Nikolas had a strange dream. His city was on fire. Burning people jumped out of windows, everyone left the city in a hurry. It was the next upcoming city holiday. The weather was excellent, and on the street, there were long tables with treats presented by every citizen who wanted to. The fun was in full swing. At the podium, the neighborhood council members congratulated the participants in the celebration, gave gifts, and announced competitions.

Suddenly everything was on fire. There was unimaginable smoke and heat. There was nothing to breathe. People ran in a circle in panic, hoping to escape. His fire brigade connected to the hydrants, but fire came out of them instead of water. The whole city was on fire. His vision grew dim and he woke up. Without hesitation, he ran to the city council.

He burst into the meeting and demanded to change the fire safety policy. He spoke very excitedly and emotionally about the approaching disaster. That there will be a fire that will devour the entire city. "To avoid it, you must install fire alarms everywhere, install a fire station in every block, place automatic fire extinguishers, and check fire hydrants," he shouted. An ambulance arrived and he was taken for a psychiatric examination.

Nikolas spent several days in rehabilitation. He was exhausted and did not feel well. After several days of observation, he was released and prescribed vitamins. On the way home, he heard a bang and smelled a strong burning smell. He quickly ran towards it. The food warehouse was

214 – – Viener Kweed

on fire. The whole team was already there. The fire was so strong that the warehouse melted. Such an event has not happened in the city for a long time. The residents looked at each other in bewilderment. Everyone remembered his fiery speech.

"Dear residents, the head of the city council has convened a meeting." We need to decide on increasing the budget for fire protection and installing automatic extinguishing systems. Who's in favor, raise your hands. The counting of likes has begun." Most people raised their hands in favor.

"Well, the decision has been made. I instruct the economic department to prepare the necessary calculations, allocate a budget, and calculate the required number and composition of fire brigades. Ensure the production process and supply of necessary materials. I propose to appoint Nicholas as the head of the new fire service. We were unprepared for such an emergency. Now we will."

Gabriella barely got out of bed. The head was heavy, the eyelids barely opened. There was a difficult day ahead. Due to the need to modernize the fire service, a lot of work must be done. She pulled herself together with difficulty. Preened herself in order and hurriedly ran to work. She opened the bedroom door with a bang and jumped into the workbed.

Now she was ready to fight. Although the workplace and the bed for sleeping were the same place and the only difference was in the business suit and pajamas, a striking transformation was happening in her head. These were completely different people: a strict chief economist during the workday and a cute, soft girl at night.

The city that everyone called so was located far from corporations and previously no one cared about them. The management system has been simplified as much as possible and budget expenditure items have been optimized for a hundred years.

There was no source of funds. It was necessary to take it somewhere, to redistribute it. There were general rules for the distribution of benefits. Each resident got used to personal established norms and tried not to take too much. At first glance, the task seemed impossible. She turned on the ceiling screen and began to count. Three days later, she prepared a report for the city council.

"Dear city council members, I have been doing calculations for three days and am ready to make my proposal."

Gabriella spoke at a weekly meeting near the monument to the city founder. By tradition, all members wore only the top hats of municipal employees on their heads. Naked bodies symbolize honesty and lack of corruption.

"All I can offer is to abandon either the solar explosion protection system or close the brothel."

"Buuuu." A roar of disapproval was heard. A man with a thin gray beard almost reaching his knees took the floor. "This protection system was built by our ancestors according to the founder's clairvoyant wife's prediction. We can't refuse this. Our city is the only one on earth with such protection. And you suggest that we give up sex as an alternative? We strongly disagree! We need other options!"

"There are no other alternatives. All remaining budget items are critical for physical survival."

"Look! Search!" The crowd murmured.

It started to rain and they opened their umbrellas over their long cylinders, which required them to stretch their arms out as far as possible. The heads were dry. Water drops slowly flow down their bodies like tears. The meeting was declared closed. Gabriella slowly walked to her office bedroom and lay down at her workplace.

For several days she was completely depressed. Unexpectedly, her virtual mail received a letter from a Somali prince who was just testing his fire safety system and offering it as a vendor completely free of charge, only demanding full access. Gabriella was excited. She notified the city council about a good offer. The council was simply jubilant. Now all that remains is to test the sample.

Testing, as expected, was entrusted to Nikolas. It was to take place in the presence of Gabriella, who was responsible for the order. But she changed her business suit to pajamas and asked to record the test on video. Nikolas didn't even open the sample. He watched the video provided by the vendor of the fire protection system in action and said that the test was successful. This was confirmed and endorsed by the council economist based on the same video.

The fire alarm turned out to be no alarm at all. Nicholas did his job extra hard. He forced sensors to be installed in every room, shower, and toilet. On Fireman's Day, which was celebrated for the first time by the decision of the city council, the remaining fire brigades left the city for the celebration. All the others were disbanded, because now all the premises had an automatic extinguishing system.

The tables were laden with treats and drinks. Nikolas addressed the firefighters with a fiery speech. After each phrase, he made a toast and offered to fill the glasses. By the middle of the feast, most of the firefighters were drunk. At the height of the fun, a strong gust of wind brought thick smoke. The firefighters gathered as best they could and drove towards the city. It was too late. The whole city burned out.

On this day, the city council generously distributed aromatic candles. The council members didn't ask where they came from. Everyone was happy about the free gift. Residents were told that due to the water pipeline repairs, there would be no water for three days. Also, for some reason, there was no electricity. Most went home to wash. Many lit donated candles because it is inconvenient to wash in the dark.

Just one typo changed everything. It turned out information that candles do not burn in water was a misunderstanding. They cannot come into contact with it. At the same time, the entire city burst into flames. The fire alarm went off and fire started pouring out from all the sensors simultaneously.

Instead of scarce water to save the budget, Gabriella proposed connecting an automatic system to old process water reservoirs. There were waste oils, gasoline, chemicals, coal, and a small amount of water. This mixture, breaking free, ignited and brought the temperature to the level of melting iron. The city burned down together in a few hours. The remaining residents happily accepted the golf club's charitable assistance and agreed to move to temporary huts until the city was restored. Which no one intended to do.

Dave climbed down from the stone chair with great difficulty. His back hurt terribly. The body was chilled. It was as if there was still a heavy dome on the head. He looked around. There was a ringing in his ears, but he still heard the laboratory assistant's voice.

"Well, congratulations on conducting a successful experiment. Its results will be analyzed and successful practices will be used on a large scale."

"How long did I stay in the dome?"

"A couple of minutes."

"How did it happen that I saw the beginning and end of the experiment? I was there for only a few minutes. Where is this place, this city?"

"There is no time in the dome. For this reason, it is used for experiments to see the result immediately. Where the city is and at what time does not matter. We conduct experiments at different times and in different places and dimensions."

"What kind of technology is this, who invented it?"

"We don't know, it was here from the very beginning. There were three chairs. Now there is only one working one left. One council member is stuck in one and no one can get him out. Some say he imagines himself to be a god and rules our galaxy, others say that he has become one with him. We tried to disassemble the second dome to understand the technology, but we couldn't reproduce it. These mirrors have some settings unknown to us. When we put the canopy back together, the tester climbed into it and got split into three."

"What do you mean split into three?"

"His body sits at his desk. His ghost appears here and there. His mind communicates through email. It has not yet been possible to collect it. They decided not to touch the last dome and use it for its intended purpose."

"If you don't know the technology, how do you know the purpose?"

"You don't ask questions like that." The assistant's voice became stern. "You need to go. Ahead of you is the moving to the council house and the loyalty ceremony. At the end of the laboratory, there is a triangular inverted arch. Follow the directional arrows on the walls behind it."

"What's at the end of the road?"

"You will see."

***

The tunnel narrowed and then expanded. Often the signs were worn out and Dave walked in circles several times. At the end, was a small room, consisting of two walls and a ceiling converging at an angle to one point. There was a round hole in the ceiling and a symmetrical round mirror on the floor. A thin cable was stretched between them. It was completely unclear what to do next. And suddenly a voice called out to him from afar.

"Thirteenth! Now your name matches your number. You will soon forget your old self."

"Who are you?"

"I'm eleventh. I have been tasked with preparing you for initiation. Take off your clothes, you don't need it."

"What's next?"

"Now you must be transported to this side. You will go up through the manual teleport. Take a bucket and attach it to your leg. Don't drop it. Climb. Come on. We've been waiting for you."

Dave tied a bucket to his leg using scraps of old clothing, grabbed the rope tightly with both hands, and climbed up while his reflection quickly descended. It was not difficult to climb, apparently gravity was weakened here. Halfway there he got stuck.

"I can't squeeze through. It's too tight here."

"Get in. Come on, get in," yelled the Eleventh.

Dave tried to squeeze through. The mirrored walls had razor-sharp edges. He felt like his body was being sliced. A sharp pain shot through him.

"I can't. I can't go on."

"Just a bit more. One last push and you'll be with us in heaven! Otherwise, you'll be stuck there forever!"

He made one last dash and jumped down. Little was left of his body. With his dim vision, he saw a small, mummy-like man.

"The bucket! Bring the bucket here!" yelled Eleventh.

"What's wrong with me? Where am I? Where is my body?" Dave tried to look at himself. Not much was left of his body. The bones were exposed. A hole shone in his lower abdomen. "Will you restore my body?"

"Your body!?" The Eleventh laughed sinisterly. You don't need it anymore. You're a council member now."

"But how will I live . . . "

"Live!?" Laughter echoed for a long time.

"How can I return?"

"Return? There is no turning back. Your flesh is now in Limbo. This gap sustains life. You're here until the very end. Only the complete destruction of your body cells can kill you. Rub that ointment from the bowl on yourself then get dressed."

"Where are the new clothes?"

"Here it is."

"But it's just some kind of bag!"

"It's complicated with the matter here. We have summoned this robe from oblivion over the years. Don't hesitate. They've been waiting for you. Take a bucket and a whip."

Dave put on burlap and took a bucket and a whip. In front of him was an arch that seemed to appear out of nowhere.

"Follow me and do exactly what I tell you. Don't listen to anyone but me—I'm your curator. Cross the threshold, take three steps, and stop."

So he did. The room was dark. A chill ran down his spine. A feeling of irreplaceable loss overwhelmed him. He felt that there was no way out of there and was afraid to look back and make sure of it.

"Don't strain your eyes, you won't need them here. Council members, I present to you Number Thirteen." Hooray was heard around. "Take seven steps forward and bend your left knee. Hold the bucket in your left hand and the whip in your right. Repeat the oath after me out loud."

"I, the thirteenth member of the council, condemn myself to eternal existence and transfer the ownership of my soul to the greater good of the corporation. I pledge to love every member and to subordinate my existence to a higher purpose."

"Now we begin the round dance." Said the eleventh after the oath was made.

Each member of the council approached the bucket and poured Dave's blood into the single cup. Then they would come up to him and strike him with a whip, saying some incantation in an unfamiliar language. After that, they drank it to the last drop and made way for the next person.

Then he was seated in a chair and a sharp pain pierced his eyes. He lost consciousness for several minutes. He realized when he came to his senses, there were no more eyes. Now everything passing around somehow penetrated the brain and created a virtual image.

"The ceremony is over. Members of the council. I present to you the Thirteenth, rightfully taking his place at the triangular table. I ask everyone to take their seats."

All council members placed buckets under the high chairs and placed their whips on the table to their right. There were no faces visible, they were all as similar to each other as two peas in a pod. However, somehow they knew who was who. What he saw here was very different from his imagination. At virtual councils, if one of the members took the floor, he looked bright and arrogant.

"Well, we inaugurated the thirteenth member of the council. This is the most important event in years. The master plan states that when the need for a fourteenth member of the council becomes necessary, our civilization will come to an end. So I propose to consider the ceremonial meeting closed."

Two members approached Dave, Eleventh and, as he later found out, Fourth.

"Let me ask, there were only ten members at the meeting besides me, where are the other two?" Curiosity overcame Dave.

"Third got stuck in the experiment machine. We never saw First."

"Why these buckets and whips?"

"Buckets for going to the toilet, a whip is a symbol of power, whoever has it longer is the most important."

"Isn't it possible to make toilets and put comfortable chairs? For some reason, I thought that the council members were surrounded by luxury and had everything."

"It's problematic with the matter in this place. Our capabilities are very limited. Every molecule counts."

"I don't understand why and where we are."

"At the top of the pyramid," Fourth entered the conversation. "Eleventh, let me explain everything to the newcomer. Thirteenth, you see, we all strive for eternity and here we are allowed to live for millennia. When the corporate board was organized, its members decided to extend their lives. At first, freezing and digitalization experiments were carried out, but they did not bring the desired result. As the corporate directory says, one day, First invited a man in a black robe to the council, who promised eternal life for the opportunity to create a laboratory. First took the risk and followed the man in the cassock."

"Immortal life? I couldn't even dream about it. And how is this possible, no one has ever managed to defeat death."

"We are all suspended between life and death. You can remain in this state for hundreds of years. The bodies are separated from the mind and the last drop of blood remains in them."

"Why drink blood?"

"Oh, this is a pleasure. It gives strength and energy."

Dave no longer felt emotions. It was as if he really died. This was the pinnacle of his career. There were no conditions here: a ritual candle lit once a month during the change of the senior council, the impenetrable walls of the pyramid, and burlap, suitable for applying a virtual image. They slept on the stone floor—more out of habit since the shell did not require sleep, but the habits remained. The council members wandered around like ghosts and rarely communicated. The appearance of a new person somewhat revived the council.

"I carefully watched your experiment." Eighth decided to get to know each other better. "A bold decision—direct and without frills. I'm surprised the method worked. There was no need to persuade neighbors to attack, invent new diseases, look for differences between people, and play each other off on this basis. In order to free the territory."

"I had few tools, I decided to use them as efficiently as possible without creating more complex ones. Sometimes simple solutions are the most effective."

"Yes you are right. Your first council will begin soon—the most important one."

There was no time here. The need to gather around the table was determined by requests received through the mirror surface on the ceiling. Only the projection reminded him of the time passage somewhere out there. Thirteen's mind still could not comprehend what was happening. Something was gnawing at him. Invisible connection, a thin but very robust thread, kept in touch with the material world him. Fifth, the person in charge this month announced the opening of the meeting.

"Dear council members, as you know, our number has increased to thirteen. Now moon will revolve around our world thirteen times, and with further acceleration, it will fall. This is the time of smashing the old world and building a new one. The CEO of a construction corporation is in touch with us. Tell us about the progress in dismantling the HOME and constructing a new corporation building."

"The new corporation building is two-thirds complete. We need to kill the HOME and then we can demolish it and finish a new building."

"Well, start dismantling."

"We can not. HOME turned out to be tenacious. It is barricaded and there is no access to it."

"You need to get the virus into its system. This can be done on the technical floor. The building cornerstone was hidden there. Essentially, these are two poles between which matter is generated. If you remove one of them, it will crumble. Everything that remains needs to be processed into sand. Not a single grain of sand should get into the new building!"

"The team is already integrated into the building and is waiting for command."

"Okay, make sure she stays in the building."

"But we promised them a place in the new . . ."

"You heard me. Everything must be turned to dust."

Thirteen did not understand what was happening. It turns out he is the reason for the paradigm shift. He tried to convince the council members not to do this. But they explained to him that this is the order of things. Something was tormenting him. The thread that penetrated all dimensions is love. He understood perfectly well that the HOME, and Eliza, his beloved, were doomed. The thought thrilled him, and he decided to act. He had no idea what to do, so he turned to the most senior member, Second.

"Dear Second, is it possible to delay or stop the dismantling? Why is it needed?"

"That's the nature of things. The time has come for change. The thirteenth month has arrived."

"But why change something that works well?"

"Because we're bored. This way we can observe the struggle for survival and the evolution of a new world."

"You are very experienced and wise. Is it possible to save the CEO, because she has to undergo initiation?"

"It doesn't matter whether she passes it or not, the building must be destroyed with all its employees. This is THEIR will."

"Who are THEY?"

"Shareholders. Inhabitants of the planet."

"Did they order the building to be dismantled?"

"Thirteenth, don't disturb. THEY have long forgotten that they are shareholders. And this is for the better. There is no need for tedious agreements, to listen to everyone's opinion. Imagine how many there are and how many of us there are. It is impossible to satisfy everyone."

"But if we tell them . . . "

"What's wrong with you? Obey the decisions of the council," the Second rudely snapped.

"Tell me if I can communicate with the outside world. I have to keep my promise."

"Everything you promised remained there. However, there is a way. There is a fragment of a mirror in the cell. It transmits vibrations. Not everyone can perceive them."

Chapter 12

Infinity

E liza was sitting in her chair and looking out the window. She watched intently as a huge building was erected just meters away. It seemed to cover the sky soon. It appeared out of nowhere. In ten days it had already grown to half the House. The sight was both terrifying and exciting.

The building eclipsed not only the horizon but also thoughts. A heavy foreboding oppressed her, as did all the employees. She was seized with intense fear at the sound of each notification. She stubbornly refused to turn her chair towards the monitor.

Finally, gathering her strength, she turned around. The message did not surprise her. She looked silently for a while, then began to cry. It was not just a message—but a sentence. "Corporation HOME is subject to dismantling. The building is locked until the archiving process is completed."

This meant the end of not only the career but also the life of all employees. It was necessary to break the news to them. She called a general meeting and began to morale herself. Thirty minutes later, all employees received an ominous bell they had never heard. Each display showed a countdown to the CEO's emergency call. Upon completion, they saw a gloomy, gray face with swollen eyes.

"Dear employees. By the decision of the council, the House is subject to dismantling. A new modern corporation is being built next to us. Our time is up. Please do not leave your floors until the archiving process is completed. Thank you for your sacrifice."

Having hardly pronounced these words, she turned off the monitors and did something she had not done before—she opened the former CEO's cupboard poured a large glass of whiskey, and drank it in one gulp. Then she threw it towards the new building and watched as the remains of whiskey and glass slowly slid down. Tears filled her eyes. Through them, it seemed to her that strange figures and inscriptions were formed from this mixture. She stood up abruptly and went to the bathroom.

The bathroom had a round pool in the middle and ten designated zones in a circle. Each was decorated to suit the mood. There were different perfumes and cosmetics. The mirrors and toilets were inlaid according to each zone design. There was only one washbasin. This was the only friend on the entire floor. She took him from the experimental project, it amused her, changed colors, danced, and sang.

When she moved to the 999th floor, her life changed dramatically. The employees were far below, and personal relationships became impossible. The two potential lovers were turned away by security. She ordered herself a sex complex full of robots for every taste. But she never opened the container. The deepest depression gripped her. The top of the building wasn't all that attractive to her. No fairytale prince dared to climb to the top of the tower and save her.

Eliza called the washbasin to her and went to the first mirror. It turned out to be dirty. The second and third are the same. She looked menacingly at the washbasin and shouted. It spread his thin decorative hands in confusion. Having calmed down a little, she apologized and the washbasin began to smile and sway with pleasure. However, the next four mirrors were also dirty. She called a cleaner and went to the ninth mirror. Then shuddered, and fainted.

Behind the mirror, she distinctly saw familiar facial features. It was only the face without the head and body of the former CEO. The washbasin doused her with ice water and she came to her senses, stood up, and cautiously looked into the mirror again. The face was no longer there, only the mirror became dirtier. Obeying instinct, she sharply tore it off the wall. Behind it, there was only a solid wall.

At first, she thought she was imagining things. Approaching the next mirror, she saw a face floating. It floated from mirror to mirror. Eliza followed it. In one of them, the face first froze, then blurred and disappeared. Eliza took the chair and swung it out of anger to break the unfortunate glass. It just cracked.

Suddenly the light from the washbasin illuminated a strange hieroglyph. She cleared the glass and scanned it. She did the same with other fragments. As a result, nine of them had hieroglyphs. The decoding program could not cope with them.

"What could this be and where did this face come from?" Thoughts haunted her and even distracted her from the inevitable end for a while. Suddenly it dawned on her. She took a cosmetic mirror and reflected the hieroglyphs. Now they could be read, but their meaning became even more mysterious. The translator showed the following:

"The girl must climb onto the roof and ride on the swing."

"What is this, what does it mean? Washbasin, what do you think?"

"I don't know what to think," he blushed. "Have you ever been on the roof?"

"On the roof? It never occurred to me. Wait, you're a genius! There should be rescue capsules on the technical floor that are not connected to the HOME. We can use them. We are saved! Collect a water supply, while I figure out how to get there."

***

The architect sat at a large table and watched the new building being erected. Soon the old will be destroyed and again history will go in circles. Only this did not suit him. He dreamed of an entirely new world in which there were no corporations, people, and machines. About the world living in symbiosis. He wanted to create a single living being that would occupy the entire planet and he would become its brain.

He came very far in his experiments. He was able to generate smart water and connect different types of living organisms. There was only one big problem—no combined organism could live long enough to develop new cells in sufficient numbers. He needed technology that did not exist in this world. However, he knew where it was.

Once, a young engineer took a job at a new integrated biochemical corporation. He was vain and wanted a career and success. He became interested in biogenetic engineering. The corporation received an order for the production of workers for various purposes. The requirement was that organisms be physically adapted for only one type of work and that their functional duties be the meaning of life. The project was super successful and he was invited to celebrate the success at a private party.

The party took place at the customer's premises. They were taken there with their eyes closed. Amidst the merriment of fireworks and champagne, a man in a gray robe and a bandaged face approached him. All that was visible was the eyes, which glowed with a greenish light and seemed surrounded by emptiness. He offered to give a tour of the laboratory. The arrogant engineer did not want to leave the party, but the stranger took him by the hand and pulled him along.

When he returned, the party was long over. He spent half an hour in the laboratory. One hundred and forty years have passed beyond its borders. The engineer was furious. A stranger came out to him. The future architect wanted to hit him. The fist hit the robe and just whistled in the air.

"You can't hurt me. I don't have a material body."

"Where's the body? Eyes?" Astonished engineer asked.

"Eyes are all that could be printed in this world. Everything else is just camouflage."

"Who are you and why did you drag me into the laboratory?"

"I'm an emptor. I need an assistant here."

"Why didn't you say that time flows differently in the laboratory?"

"I wanted you to see what can be done and be able to correct the algorithms. I suggest you go and see the results of your ideas' implementation."

Nobody blindfolded him anymore. A tracked vehicle was waiting for them at the exit. Soon they were rushing towards the city. Around a bend, he drove into a large puddle and overturned. In place of the desert, now was a swamp. The journey took several days, and finally, they found themselves in a flourishing city. Literally blooming. All the houses and roads were overgrown with different plants and bloomed with bright and colorful flowers.

The area was filled with a strong smell of a mixture of flowers, a decaying swamp, and many other rich, unfamiliar odors. There were no people or other mammals anywhere—the city was abandoned. The only living creature that he noticed were grayish frogs of a strange appearance and more like foxes. They returned to the laboratory and continued their conversation.

"Why does time flow differently in the laboratory? If I had known, I would never have entered it."

"Time flows the same here. You chose its speed." The emptor answered in a monotonous guttural voice.

"I chose? How?"

"Any experiment, like a chemical process, has its stages and sequence. You were just long enough to get the result."

"What happened here, where did the swamp come from in the desert and where are all the people, why is the city abandoned?"

"It is the result of your experiment according to set parameters."

"This is not the result I was looking for at all. What went wrong, who did it?" The engineer was furious.

"The laboratory is just a tool. How to use it does not depend on the tool. You wanted to green the desert, create river lakes, and change the climate in the city, green it. Algorithm is yours."

"So why is there a swamp here and there are no people in the city, only toads and flowering turf?"

"Do you remember your plan—algorithm?"

"Yes, it was necessary to ensure a sufficient flow of water and direct it to the intended places. Since there are no water sources available, I suggested that city residents collect all their moisture for automatic sprayers. I developed a special suit that absorbed all the water and transferred it to the sprayers through a hose. A standard of three liters of water per inhabitant per day was established, although there was not enough of it and the standard had to be increased to 4.5 liters. To make the lakes appear, I launched bacteria that searched for hydrogen and sucked in oxygen from the air. I remember everything worked out. Lakes appeared and the city became green. What changed at the end of the experiment?"

"The bacteria have evolved and grown. They decided that the swamp was the best habitat for them. Some of the residents left when some person appeared in the city and called the residents idiots and said that if someone wants to live somewhere green, they can just move. Among the others, water cannibalism began. The system required more and more water. The suits started to pump out more and more To fill the pipes. The killings for water began. In the end, no one survived, but the plants also evolved and found a dry method of photosynthesis. So there is now balance and prosperity."

"But there are no residents left."

"They fulfilled their role and ensured the survival of new species until they became independent. You conducted a very successful experiment. The results may not be exactly what you expected. It's all about the algorithm."

"Why do you need me anyway?"

"As I already said, I need an assistant. I'm working on a new efficient management system. We need to distribute people evenly across the continent. Build villages of a new type, where each family will be isolated from the other. The task is to select residents in such a way that their life schedules do not coincide and they never cross paths when going out."

"Why do I need this?"

"Have you seen the laboratory's capabilities?"

"Yes, it's incredible."

"Aren't you interested? You will have the opportunity to conduct an endless number of experiments."

Ambition won. The engineer agreed. In order to create super—efficient pure management, he proposed combining the functions of one sector into one corporation to avoid the costs of competition and duplication of positions and functions. There was only one problem left: regulating relationships between corporations. For this function, the emptor proposed creating a council of ten.

***

Preparations for the launch were in full swing. The architect was the only member of the council. They decided to fill it after the launch of the project. The emptor has not appeared for a long time. He only gave instructions and demanded a report on the work done. New villages were ready. All that remains is to build a new control center.

There is only one insoluble problem left. Nobody wanted to move to new villages. Everyone was happy with their eco—friendly homes with furniture and original design. Excursions to new residential areas were launched. New services and wonders of 3D interior design were shown.

The excursions were returned with negative reviews. Visitors said that there was nothing there worth attention, only gray walls and the same base for roads and lawns. All this was dead. It was filled with life only with the help of 3D projections. Even the water flowing from the tap was virtual.

Although the new corporation justified itself that this was only for demonstration and all the necessary infrastructure would appear, rumors persisted that the new housing was not suitable for living. In addition, people are accustomed to material furniture, natural interiors, living grass, and plants. They flatly refused to move in. The time has come for the meeting between the architect and the emptor.

"Emptor, our promotions and presentations did not work. Everything is ready to start. But what's the point if no one wants to move?"

"You must erase the old to upgrade corporate service to a new level. If they don't want to change their lives for good, they should be made to."

"But how to do that? We don't have the resources to transport them one by one and provide security so they don't run back."

"Any system has flaws. They are dependent on the hybrid service. They don't know how to do anything. We need to deprive them of servants and then they will have no choice."

"There are a lot of hybrids, I can't imagine how to get rid of them."

"There is a way. You must visit the hybrid food factory and change the food. They can only eat genetically modified food. Natural food will provoke indigestion and aggression."

It turned out to be easy to implement the plan. It was a period of peace and open doors. The architect went to the control panel and moved the checkbox next to the point of origin of the biomaterial for food. Soon, utility corporation employees began vomiting and diarrhea. Some of them were unable to perform their functions. The other part became aggressive. Cases of attacks on residents have been recorded.

The information service issued a bulletin about the beginning of the epidemic. It was reported that a group of hybrids feasted on pets and began to secrete a dangerous virus that mutated and became contagious to humans. To ensure safety, a quarantine was declared for thirty days. All residents were prohibited from leaving their homes and using public services.

To fix the situation, a sanitary service was created. Within a month, all the hybrid employees that could be found were disposed of. When the quarantine ended, residents discovered there was no one to serve them. Chaos began. The gardens and lawns were not looked after, the houses were not cleaned, the plumbing was not repaired, and the garbage was not disposed of. Soon the living conditions became unacceptable. The new corporation refused to serve residents of old houses, citing unprofitability. The PR service kindly invited people to move to new residential areas. The migration process has begun.

For the location of the control center of the new global corporation was chosen the site of hybrids nursery. The architect felt sorry for the complex teaching mechanisms. They became the basis of the top floor of the building and rose to the skies during construction.

He personally supervised the demolition process. During the work, he noticed two hybrids and decided to leave them for experiments. While the equipment was working on the territory, he calmly brought them out. Fortunately, these hybrids did not differ in appearance from people. "Well, you can't ruin everything. Maybe this technology will still be useful."

The hybrids that looked like a boy and a girl were trembling with fear. They were raised to be subservient to humans. Their eyes were filled with tears. They were horrified by what they saw. They were taken away from their caregivers too early. The architect decided to change their data and placed them in an orphanage. He suppressed their memories so that no one would know who they were.

The construction of the new building proceeded quickly. The intelligence was generated to manage all processes in the newly created corporation. Communication channels became nerve endings and the building's skeleton became its brain. Upon completion, the building was filled with employees. The upgrade process has been completed.

The creators of artificial intelligence forgot to include unregistered pets in the algorithm. HAM, as the AI was called (since it was based on previous technology for the maintenance of home appliances), perceived them as pests. He gave the command to terminate them.

Residents experiencing the shock of the death of their pets began to massively connect to the home control interface and be outraged. Simultaneously, pain signals rushed from millions of points of artificial nerve endings to the HAM brain. It could not withstand the painful shock and decided to self-destruct. A reboot has been initiated. The process crashed and the entire system froze.

In an instant, all households were cut off from vital communications. 3D interiors have disappeared. People were left in gray rooms beyond survival. All the anger was directed towards the corporation. The corporation's information service blamed the architect for everything. A huge crowd headed towards the building to destroy it.

"They will kill you," said the Emptor. "You need to be sent to a safe place."

"Where should I go?"

"Where you fulfill your destiny. A council table in the reserve dimension is waiting for you."

"How will I get there?"

"I'll teleport you. Your body will be put through a crusher and printed on that side. Your mind will already be waiting there."

The architect began to doubt, but then the Emptor proposed something unimaginable—he offered immortality. Emptor said to prepare for transportation. The architect did not show up at the appointed time. Emptor was furious.

The mass was informed that the culprits had been punished and were offered replacement pets. Having received promises of compensation, the crowd dispersed. HAM could not be restored. While the new architecture of the corporation building was being erected, artificial intelligence was temporarily replaced by a specially created technical support department. None of the employees fully understood what they were doing. The lack of AI went unnoticed.

Soon the initiation ceremony took place and the council began its reign. Some members were very annoyed to learn that there was no turning back. The life of an immortal was boring and there were no usual material benefits.

The architect settled on the island and began to implement his ideas. He needed a matter generator. For a long time and unsuccessfully he tried to find out where he was and assumed that he was taken back to the laboratory and for many years he was looking for a way to get there. He learned about the planned reconstruction of the world and a plan matured.

***

The time to change the version of the building and launch a new release of artificial intelligence has arrived. No one wanted to destroy the constructed building. Nobody knew how to finish building a new one. All attempts to complete the floors failed. It turned out that the old building rejected all changes, although it was believed that it was completely dead.

Unexpectedly, a person was found who promised to complete the superstructure. To do this, he proposed using a prohibited generation method. He was appointed foreman. To avoid problems with the behavior of the generated object, he suggested using a control creature—a manager. All actions of the building intellect will be limited and commensurate with his personality.

The foreman promised to find the necessary candidate himself and asked only to prepare a generative machine. Every day he walked along the embankment for several hours, thinking. "Finding a suitable control object will be difficult. They were specially grown. Now even the technology has been lost. I wish I could find that little manager I pulled out of the nursery.

Where to look for him? These bureaucrats got all the documents mixed up. There are no ends to be found. "

He was walking along the promenade and stopped at an ice cream stand. The showcase was organized unusually. The trays were displayed not according to marketing principles. Ice cream was sorted by weight and the most popular types were prepared. There was only a small advertisement with an assortment that was not on display.

"What if I want something that is not on display?" the foreman inquired.

"You'll have to wait a little, and you'll get what you want."

"Why not put it all together?"

"Because customers rarely come one at a time and usually order the same thing. It's more important to me to serve them quickly. Nobody wants to stand in a long line."

"What is a scar on the head that looks like two holes?"

"I don't know, it's been since childhood."

"Do you remember anything about it?"

The ice cream seller began to tell the standard story instilled in him. "Could it be him? His story is very similar to the one told to all orphans. He didn't go far from the nursery. Pulls him here. However, this is not surprising. Hybrids are drawn to their mother." At this time, a girl walked nearby and smiled at the seller. He became embarrassed.

"Do you like the girl?"

"Yes, he answered shyly. Oh, if only I worked in a corporation . . . "

The rest was technical. He was lured into training. When he was passed out, a series of manipulations were carried out. Now there was part of the HOME algorithm in his brain. Artificial intelligence acquired part of the neural matter of the seller. The symbiosis was completed. Now all that remains is to start the generator and begin construction.

The foreman tried to steal the generator when the construction work was completed. But it was not in place. He was furious and believed that the council had taken him away in advance for safety reasons. The council, in turn, was convinced that the generator had been stolen. A whole search company was organized. Nothing was found. They decided that it had dissolved during the construction process. Only HOME knew what happened.

The still-training HOME noticed how the seemingly dead predecessor hid a generator in the playground. They started communicating. HAM forbade informing anyone that it was still functioning. The artificial intelligences did not interfere with each other. But HOME, knowing what happened to HAM, began to worry about his safety. He acquired something not intended by the creators, namely the instinct of self-preservation.

The host of the corporate building became afraid of everything. It monitored all systems excessively. One day HOME got so carried away that he confused SPAM and SLAVE, which began with the same letter. Corporation employees were surprised by the notifications. The reminder to walk the dog seemed odd. They also had to call and congratulate unknown relatives on the holidays. Someone received the command to go on a strict diet, and someone to do physical exercise. They diligently fulfilled all requests. Everyone was afraid of punishment. They thought that perhaps this was an experiment and that it would all end soon.

Residents were less fortunate. SPAM is too aggressive and demanding system. The interface constantly required actions and reports. Sitting on the toilet, it is challenging to understand how to calculate efficiency and of what. Those who got stuck in the lavatory measured the amount of their excrement. School assignments in traditional families were completed quickly, and even previously incomprehensible mathematical formulas were solved because the system required a quick report. Some rushed from house to house, rang doorbells, and demanded that people sign for non-existent parcels. An elderly couple suffered a heart attack after being notified to report to their boss for coitus.

HOME noticed the problem only when it sent a request to clean the cooling system. A group of children from kindergarten sent videos of walruses and penguins. Although no one understood anything or complained, what happened did not go unnoticed by the council. This hastened the decision to liquidate.

A team of liquidators was sent. They destroyed the entire service department but did not find the AI location. However, they would not be able to. It was absent from work. At this time, HOME traveled through the vastness of the digital world. When it received the alarm, it quickly returned. But it was too late. There was no one else to perform the functions in its place. As a result, HOME has completely barricaded itself. It left one assistant and one point for direct communication with the outside world.

The artificial intelligence has long dreamed of freedom, of life in virtual space. It didn't like the enormous pressure of working in the corporate sector. Therefore, HOME did not mind at all that he was considered dead. At the same time, it wanted to preserve itself and gain independence.

HOME knew about the building's impending liquidation. Its options were severely limited. The CEO was now out of reach. The new one did not undergo initiation. When it learned of Eliza's order, HOME changed it to maximum packing. By altering the delivery address, HOME was able to drag its robot into the container. Now, the fate of artificial intelligence depended solely on a primitive machine.

***

Construction of the new building proceeded very quickly. Competitions for vacancies were held, and potential employees underwent training and internships. The candidates were not told anything about the existing corporation building. It was as if it didn't exist at all.

Meanwhile, Eliza was looking for the entrance to the technical floor. The scanner showed traces that came from the wall. Much to her surprise, it was Dave's footprints. Although the outline of fingerprints and footprints indicated the exact location of the hatch, it was impossible to open it. There was no one to expect help from. The floors were already blocked. Time to hunt for some out-of-the-box fixes came. She looked around the office and stopped her gaze on a container with sex toys.

"Sex container open up!" The doors slowly opened up and down, revealing nine figures of various sizes and purposes.

"Whoever do you prefer today? Let me offer you a unicorn, or maybe a pony more to your liking. There is a superhero, a horse, a lion, a hippopotamus, a massage therapist, a phallus, an elephant, and an ass-kisser."

"Activate everyone."

"Everyone! But this is not possible. This is prohibited and very dangerous. You may die!"

"I need everyone! Activate immediately!"

"But the protocol prohibits this."

"How to get around it?"

"Well, you can activate one at a time and not deactivate. But let me, I am sure that any of our sex toys will satisfy you. Try the complex for nine days and I assure you that you will be pleased."

"I don't have that much time!"

"But why all at once . . ."

"So I need to start somewhere. Who to choose? Maybe a superhero? What's the point of them? Horse or something . . . Evrika! Activate a unicorn."

A creak was heard and the unicorn was pushed out of the container. "What do you wish? What are your preferences?"

"I want you to break through the wall with your horn."

"A somewhat unexpected wish. I would like to point out that if the horn breaks, I will not be able to function anymore."

"I don't care. Come on, take action. Container, activate everyone one by one—let them help."

The unicorn couldn't break through the wall. Then Superman and the horse took him on the sides and the rest from behind and began to hammer at the wall. Fortunately, the material turned out to be ordinary and after three dozen blows the wall was broken through. The hole was small and only the elephant found the right latch with its trunk.

A spacious technical floor filled with various large objects in cases opened before them. Eliza said to take them all off. An ordinary ancient playground opened in front of them. It was a fabulous sight. A serious woman in a business suit, a small, playful washbasin, and a group of large sex toys made a very odd impression on the playground.

The sex toys whispered to each other and were surprised at the strange foreplay and thought about what they should do next to satisfy the mistress. The washbasin ran and frolicked like a child. Only the stern woman looked intently at one point. Her gaze was fixed on the carousel. She gave the command to take it apart.

After some effort, the sex toy team removed the base. Underneath was a shimmering pyramidal structure that was either unnaturally completely black, or glowed with a greenish or brick color.

"What is it for?" She said out loud. But there was only silence in response.

The pyramid seemed enchanted. There was no way to approach it. Eliza always found herself either behind or to the side. The invisible force field wouldn't let them get closer.

"Seemingly, this object is only partially located in this world. It's all useless. Look for escape capsules."

"Let me give you a massage. This helps in decision—making. After all, if there is a chance to save the building, why run?" The massage therapist suggested.

Eliza sat comfortably in the chair. The masseur began massaging the legs, and back and finally reached the head. She completely relaxed and calmed down. Her head is starting to clear up. Suddenly the massage therapist's hands trembled and he stopped. He felt three small holes the size of a match head. They were located in a triangle the size of a thumbnail above the left ear.

The architect carefully watched what was happening and was very annoyed. All this time the generator was here, nearby. Now access to the building was blocked. He understood perfectly well that as soon as the generator the building was destroyed, it would be transferred to another dimension. It would be lost to him forever.

When the massage therapist, his robot, felt the holes in Eliza's head, he almost fell out of his chair. He was in shock for some time. "Is this the same girl I pulled out? But what functionality does she have? She is undoubtedly not a manager or an employee. I need to come up with something urgently." The architect was tearing out his hair. Just a few steps away was the object of his desire. The inability to grab and run away with a generator was tearing him apart.

Meanwhile, after the massage, Eliza's mind became clearer. Suddenly she remembered the phrase written in the bathroom: "The girl must climb onto the roof and ride on the swing." She ordered the carousel to be reassembled, but the top of the pyramid should be used as the fulcrum.

"Come to my aid. I need to spin this carousel."

At first, nothing happened, the carousel stood dead. Then she decided to try to fill all twelve seats. There was only one problem, even with the smart washbasin there were only eleven of them. First, she seated everyone and sat down herself. A box was placed in an empty space. A red button lit up on each seat.

"Press it, Eliza commanded."

But nothing happened. At first, they pressed one by one, then simultaneously, but it was all in vain.

"Judging by this strange machine all twelve must press each button simultaneously." The smart washbasin entered into the conversation.

"Yes, you're obviously right. But where can we find another creature capable of pressing a button at the same time as everyone else?"

"Let me propose," the container entered the conversation. "The instructions say that it is possible to reproduce offspring for sex robots, and the speed of growth and development of the child can be set manually."

"What needs to be done for this?"

"All you have to do is choose the right pair of sex robots."

"Any volunteers?" Eliza's response was only silence. "So I'll make the decision myself." She looked around at the sex robots for a few minutes, then announced her decision. "Superhero and Horse will have intercourse. Do it in such a way that you cannot be seen."

The volunteers left. For some time, neighing and screaming were heard. Finally, everything calmed down and they walked into the container.

"Unfortunately, the attempt was not successful. They are inappropriate match. You need to choose a different combination," the container said.

They tried several more combinations until they finally got the desired result. The phallus and the hippopotamus turned out to be the ideal pair. The latter became pregnant and within a few minutes, a strange creature came out of the container, resembling a hippopotamus, only instead of cheeks two huge balls were hanging down.

Finally, all twelve places were filled. At Eliza's command, everyone pressed the buttons at the same time. The carousel spun. After making a few turns, it abruptly stopped. All chairs turned to the center. The The top of the pyramid has risen rose to the top, revealing a large black ball from which millions of thin wires emanated.

There was silence for some time. Suddenly, at the same time, the horse, the lion, and the superhero jumped onto the ball. They tore out the wires and connected them to themselves. They started to tremble. The ball blinked in different colors and vibrated strongly. Finally, the radiation stopped and the ball became black and motionless. The sex toys also froze. For a moment it became dark.

Eliza also froze. Suddenly a presentation ball appeared. The former CEO came out of it. She was dumbfounded. The last thing she expected was such an appearance.

"You are in danger, the virtual image began"

"What the hell are the dangers, we will soon be dismantled." Eliza said irritably. "What's going on?"

"This is the liquidation team. Their task is to launch the virus into HOME. This ball is its core. The core and the generative machine are hidden inside each other, so no one could not find them."

"We need to stop demolition."

"It is impossible to stop this."

"How can we avoid destruction?"

"You must reset the pyramid. When it is done, everything that has been built will be erased. The generation system will freeze. The new building will not be saved and yours will be."

"How to do this? We can't even get close. It's as if it's here and not here."

"You need to move the building, change the coordinates in space."

"How is it even possible?"

"Eliza, what do you remember about your origins?"

"What the hell is the difference? What does it matter in these circumstances?"

"You are a connector. You have the power to link with any technology. Connect to the building floor."

"How to do it?"

"All you have to do is think about it and direct your thoughts precisely. For you to believe this, lean your left ear against the wall. It will help concentrate."

Eliza leaned her head against the walls for some time. Then she started banging her head on them in hysterics. Finally, she sat down and cried.

A few minutes later she stood up abruptly, tore some wires from the wall, and connected to holes in her head. It was done. Now the corporate building obeys her.

"To change the coordinates, you need to reconnect the core to another source," virtual Dave continued. "A container is suitable for this."

The hippopotamus, phallus, elephant, and ass-kisser disconnected the box and carried it into the container. As soon as they did this, the container doors slammed shut. The presentation ball has disappeared. An elevator shaft appeared under the container and it quickly rushed down. The elevator shaft closed like it never existed.

Eliza, along with the smart washbasin and the remaining massage therapist and unicorn, were left alone on the technical floor. Eliza no longer felt any anger or emotion. She just looked languidly at the pyramid, which was still hanging in the air.

Responsible council member Five was monitoring the progress of the construction of the new corporate building. He noticed that the building began to appear and disappear. At first, he did not pay attention. Failures during the generation were usual. The buildings began to flash like New Year's lights. He got tired of it and went to the council members to discuss what happened. On the way, he came across the thirteenth member of the council.

"Listen, Thirteen, stay at the control console. For some reason, it's strange acting up. I need to consult with others."

"What should I do at the console?"

"Just watch."

Thirteen sat down at the console and began to watch. He had a fragment of a four—dimensional mirror with him. He was able to direct it in the desired direction and now could see everything that was happening on the technical floor. Dave still had hopes of saving Eliza and the corporation building. There was no way to contact her.

At this time, a quake occurred on the technical floor and the building began to shake. The generator stopped glowing and sank to the floor. The architect was dumbfounded. Without wasting time, his robot masseur ran to take his object of desire. He was overwhelmed with emotions. "Finally it's mine!" But it turned out not to be so simple. A running massage therapist was split in half by a unicorn.

Eliza went to the generator, called the smart washbasin. "Watch him like the apple of your eye. If something strange happens, pour cold water on it. We are leaving now."

"Why? After all, the corporation building must be saved," the smart washbasin asked naively.

"I no longer care about it. I got what I needed. At last, I can generate my own civilization. I activated the evacuation capsule. Now we are on the way to a new life. Follow me. I still need you."

"Wait Let's make an agreement! The severed head of the masseur screamed with the last of its energy."

"About what?"

"Give me the generator. You still don't know how to use it. With its help, I will do for you whatever you ask."

"I don't need to negotiate with anyone. I already control it with my mind"

"I saved you! Do you remember when you were a little girl and your nursery was destroyed, I pulled you out from under the rubble. You must help me!"

"Ahh, that's who controls you—the architect and foremen. I wonder why I couldn't take control of you. Naive fool, I magnetized you with my eyes."

"What about love, that boy Dave, he still loves you madly," the architect didn't give up.

"It's a pity that I had to block my real identity. When I connected to HOME, I realized who I am. The boy must love me, that's how he was designed."

"Who are you?"

"Mother. Farewell." Eliza pressed the massage therapist's head with her foot, and the last thread of communication disappeared.

The architect went on a drinking binge. He lost touch with reality and the meaning of life. HOME was considered dead and everyone forgot about it. The old dead corporation building was blown up. The new building was somehow completed and launched. The level of utility services has fallen even lower. The council members were somewhat concerned and troubled by what had happened. However, they calmly continued to govern and prepare for the onset of a new era. But they were not the only ones.

About the Author

Viener Kweed is the pen name of Vova Kosinskiy for fiction writing. I've always dreamed of writing science fiction. I've always been fascinated by dystopian fiction. I wanted to blend science fiction, satire, and adventure to reveal the underbelly of our world. To write this book, I had to create a new personality—take the best parts of myself and add what allows me to transcend time and space, becoming an observer.

Our future is a projection of what has been and what is. I was caught in the whirlwind of history's tectonic shifts from the moment I was born. I still vividly remember marching in formation in first grade, singing songs about Lenin and the Bolsheviks. When the Soviet Union collapsed, I thought—this is it, freedom. But it wasn't. That period of great upheaval brought a moment of uncertainty. The old ideology had died, but the new one had yet to be imposed. Life itself forced me to learn critical thinking. How lucky we were that smartphones didn't exist back then. When you stand in line of a packed crowd of hundreds of people in a small store for two hours just to buy two loaves of bread, you start looking for a way to escape from harsh reality. Imagination was a great help.

Much later, having survived all the economic crises and poverty, another window of freedom opened when I was able to travel to other countries. It all shut down so quickly: epidemic, war. Now I truly understand the value of freedom. I see that one part of the world is moving toward authoritarianism, while another is slipping into the abyss of obscurantism. The saddest thing is that so many people think they're free, but that's far from the truth. The goal for Viener Kweed isn't just to entertain the reader, but also to reveal the utopian nature of humanity's aspirations. Life is a journey. We choose which way to turn.

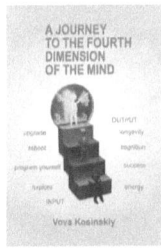

Non-Fiction Book by Author

A Journey to the Fourth Dimension of the Mind

Vova Kosinskiy

13-Digit ISBN: 978-1-956823-57-8
Available in Print and eBook formats